SECOND CHANCE . . .

"Ross, you don't understand. I'm not the same girl you married fifteen years ago. I'm not passive, dependent Ginny who basked in your reflected glory. I have my own glory now and I like it. I can take care of myself, financially and emotionally. I'm marrying Dan because I want him, not because I can't function without him."

"But you don't love him," Ross persisted. "Ginny, I'm not asking you to go back to the past. I know that can't be done. I'm not asking you to give up anything you've worked so hard for. But you're making a decision right now that will affect the rest of your life. You're throwing away all those years we spent together, all of the experiences we shared."

"It's over, Carlson," Dan interrupted firmly. "You're too late. You threw her away once, and she's not coming back to you now you've changed your mind."

"I don't need you to tell me what I threw away," Ross responded angrily. "Ginny means a hell of a lot more to me than she could ever mean to you! You're not capable of any kind of real commitment. You want Ginny now because you've grown bored with the usual women in your life. But you'll grow bored with her, too, eventually because you're like all actors —you're a child who never grew up, who doesn't understand mature emotions."

"I wasn't the one who childishly turned to another woman, practically a child herself, from what I hear. I haven't hurt Ginny. You have."

Dan's words, cold and true, cut through Ginny's heart like a knife. He hadn't hurt her as Ross had. He could never do that because she could never care about him as she had cared about Ross. As the two men in her life fought over her, she felt strangely removed.

Turning back to Ginny, Ross pleaded, his usual arrogance thrown aside, "Give me another chance." He stood there anxiously, his expression tense but determined, looking irresistibly handsome and compelling, as he solemnly implored, "Give *us* another chance."

Other Pinnacle Books by Pamela Wallace:

The Fires of Beltane
Caresse
Malibu Colony

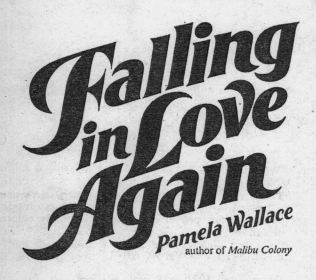

Falling in Love Again

Pamela Wallace

author of *Malibu Colony*

PINNACLE BOOKS   NEW YORK

FALLING IN LOVE AGAIN

An original Pinnacle Books edition, published for the first time anywhere.

First printing, April 1981

ISBN: 0-523-41055-7

Cover illustration by Norm Eastman

Printed in the United States of America

PINNACLE BOOKS, INC.
1430 Broadway
New York, New York 10018

To old friends, Judy, Karen, and Vickie

Falling in Love Again

1.

It was a lovely autumn day in Malibu. The chaparral-covered mountains were still summer-brown, and the leaves on the towering sycamores were turning russet. Ginny Carlson stood in her sunroom, putting the finishing touches on a painting. The sunny, cheerful, plant-filled room was her exclusive retreat—her easel dominated one corner, and her straw hat was flung carelessly over the back of a white wicker chair.

Among her friends, Ginny was generally considered to be the one who had everything—Ross, her handsome husband, who was a brilliant filmmaker; Betsy, her attractive well-adjusted daughter; and a beautifully decorated house on the beach at Malibu. Her life was interesting, comfortable, and secure, filled with all the glamor and excitement that most people only read about. She met fascinating, successful people at Hollywood parties, shopped at exclusive stores in Beverly Hills, and traveled extensively with Ross when he was filming on location.

If there was something missing, if at odd moments she found herself crying for no reason at all, that was something Ginny preferred not to think about. She was the one, out of everyone she knew, who was *supposed* to be perfectly happy. For one thing, she wasn't divorced, as were all her close friends.

Why, then, did she feel that nagging sense of unhappiness, that tiny pinprick of doubt where there should have been contentment? Unbidden, a word flashed through her thoughts—*romance.* Her marriage was successful, her life comfortable, but there was no romance. Gone was the skip of her heart when she looked at Ross, the joy of first love, that overwhelming happiness and excitement that made her glow with the wonder of it all.

She still remembered what it felt like those first few months with Ross. As she walked down the street she positively beamed with pleasure. People turned to stare at her, not because she was beautiful, but because her face, her walk, her whole being was suffused with a joy that was communicated to everyone around her.

"All the world loves a lover." *Unfortunately, I'm not a lover*, she thought pensively, laying down her brush and palette. *I'm a wife and I can't expect romance anymore, just contentment.*

But she wasn't content.

As she stood there, Ginny's gaze was caught by her reflection in the small wicker-framed mirror nearby. At thirty-three she was hardly middle-aged, yet she was disturbingly aware that she was no longer young. There were tiny lines at the corners of her haunting, gold-flecked green eyes and around the corners of her full, generous mouth. With a short, upturned nose and round chin, it was a perennially youthful, baby face that didn't begin to grow up and reflect the character underneath until she was past thirty. She had the kind of look men love—pretty without being intimidatingly beautiful, sweetly feminine yet with an intriguing hint of fire in those shimmering green eyes.

People still described her as a "cute girl." Only in her most pensive moments, when she was concentrating intently on a painting in progress or listening with boundless sympathy to a troubled friend, was the other Ginny apparent. This person wasn't a girl but a fully mature woman of surprising strength and wisdom. It was no accident that in her circle of friends she was the one everyone turned to for advice and support during the bad times. She offered not only compassion but common-sense advice filled with unerring insight.

Sighing in frustration as she looked at the painting that wasn't going well, Ginny decided to quit for the day. Walking out onto the broad redwood deck that faced the ocean, she flopped down on a chaise longue and breathed in the cool salt air. It all felt so good—the tiny, rough grains of sand beneath her bare feet, the comfortable chair, the cool breeze. Malibu was having one of its brilliant fall sunsets, with the sky a painter's canvas of blood red, deep orange, and golden yellow. In the distance where the bay curved was Santa Monica, and beyond it, Los Angeles. In the city was smog and traffic and noise. But in Malibu there were gently lapping waves and soaring gulls.

Everything was at peace in her lovely, well-ordered world—except for that nagging doubt that flared at odd moments.

Suddenly Ginny heard the front door open and close, and a moment later Ross's voice filled the house.

"Ginny, I'm back!"

He had been gone for several days scouting locations for his new movie, and Ginny was glad that he was finally home. The house had seemed unbearably quiet and empty without him.

When Ginny went in to greet him, she was surprised to find him looking tired and withdrawn. Beginning a movie always excited him, yet now he seemed curiously subdued.

"Hi, honey." Ross was tall and Ginny had to stretch up on her tiptoes to kiss him dutifully. At forty-two, Ross was still handsome, with sun-streaked blond hair and clear, intense blue eyes. Rather serious and introspective, he was most appealing when he flashed a rare boyish grin that lit his face and made his eyes sparkle.

"How did it go?" Ginny asked.

"Not bad," he replied wearily, carrying his suitcase into their bedroom.

"Let me unpack that in the morning. You look exhausted," Ginny insisted, following him.

"Thanks. I'd like to have some dinner and turn in early, I think."

For a brief moment Ginny watched him, wondering why her initial excitement at his return had faded so quickly. Then she went into the kitchen and began preparing dinner.

* * *

Ginny brushed her teeth and scrubbed her face, then slipped on a warm flannel nightgown. It was a cold night. Hurriedly she crawled beneath the blankets, where Ross lay waiting for her. He had been so quiet and preoccupied all evening that she hadn't expected him to be in a mood for lovemaking. So she was surprised when he reached over and pulled her toward him expectantly. Instinctively she pulled back, as she seemed to do all the time lately. Then she relented, her body relaxing in his arms. But as she went through the motions of pleasing him, a part of her remained remote and uninvolved. She knew Ross too well by now to enjoy the delicious anticipation of surprise. And as his hands travelled the curves they knew so intimately, she found no pleasure in his touch.

Afterwards, when he rolled over and went to sleep, she lay there for a long time, feeling achingly empty.

The next morning Ginny unpacked Ross's suitcase. She heard him in the next room, talking to the producer of the movie about the locations he had found. Ginny had put away nearly everything when she found a small paperback book in a pile of papers and folders. It was a romantic novel of the kind that Ross would never read, and when Ginny opened it casually she found the name *Lisa Lawrence* written in smooth, elegant strokes inside.

Ginny simply stood there, staring at the book for a long time. The room seemed suddenly still and quiet, and Ginny was acutely aware of every sensa-

5

tion—the smooth feel of the book in her hands, the rapid beating of her heart. There was an explanation, of course. There *had* to be. Ross had never been unfaithful. She had always been certain he wouldn't subject her to that painful humiliation, that utter betrayal of their love. When someone they knew had an extramarital affair, she and Ross discussed it as if it was a disease that they were somehow immune to.

But here was this book, clearly the property of a woman named Lisa Lawrence. And it was in Ross's suitcase.

Feeling sick inside, Ginny walked into the living room where Ross was talking on the phone. He started to smile at her, then saw the book in her hand. The smile disappeared, and for the first time in their marriage Ginny saw a look of shame cross her husband's face. In that instant she knew the truth. And she wanted to die.

He hung up quickly, then, without speaking, poured each of them a drink. Though it was early afternoon, and Ginny rarely drank, she was grateful for the mild jolt of the liquor. It stopped the feeling of nausea and faintness that was coming over her. After another long sip, she said softly, "You were with someone." Somehow she couldn't bring herself to be specific, to say, "You slept with another woman," or "You've had an affair." Saying those words would make it even more real than it already was.

"Yes." His voice was firm, clear, but his blue eyes were pained. *He look*s, Ginny thought, *like someone who has made an embarrassing mistake and is* *trying desperately to hide it so that no one will notice.*

She said quietly, "Please don't make me ask all of the questions. Just tell me what happened."

Ross responded slowly, "You have a lot of dignity, Ginny. It's one of the things I've always admired about you." Then he continued matter-of-factly, "Her name is Lisa Lawrence, she's an actress, twenty-two years old. I met her a month ago."

They're always younger, Ginny thought angrily. *That's one of the most insulting things about it all.*

Ross continued haltingly, "At first I thought it was just a fling; you know, mid-life crisis stuff. Everyone does it."

Not everyone, Ginny thought stubbornly. *Somewhere in the world there must be a husband who hasn't been unfaithful.*

"But it's serious. I care about her, and . . . and I'm sorry I've hurt you, but . . ." He finished lamely, "I'm sorry."

For some reason Ginny remembered something her father had told her when she was a little girl. She had done something bad—she couldn't remember what now—but instead of simply spanking her as usual, he sat her down and lectured her for a long time. At the end, he said sternly, "Sometimes we do or say things that are so serious, they can never be taken back again. The damage is too great to ever be repaired. So think carefully before you do something. Because if you're wrong, just saying you're sorry may not make it all well again."

That was exactly how she felt right now. It didn't

matter how much Ross apologized; it would never begin to heal the hurt she felt.

Reluctantly, she forced herself to face what Ross was saying. "How serious is it? Do you want a divorce?"

His eyes widened in surprise, and his shocked tone confirmed that he hadn't thought that far ahead. "I didn't mean that, exactly. I just . . . that is, I can't honestly say it was a one-night stand that meant nothing and will never happen again."

"I see. You intend to go on seeing her, and I can either accept it or not."

Ross was completely taken aback. Whatever he had expected, it wasn't this. For the first time, their roles were reversed. Ginny, who was normally soft and pliant, was being tough, insistent, while he struggled stupidly to explain himself, to justify his actions.

"For God's sake, Ginny, give me more credit than that! What do you think I am, anyway?"

It was a thoughtless question, under the circumstances. Ginny responded bluntly, "I think you're a bastard. I gave you love and loyalty for fourteen years. I gladly played second fiddle, always accepting your claim that your career was more important than anything I might pursue. I *trusted* you."

Ross, stung by the bitter truth of her words, reacted defensively. "Look, don't make me out to be some kind of monster. It's not like things have been all that perfect lately, as you well know. You've certainly made it clear that you don't want me sexually. How do you think *I've* felt, always being the one to initiate our lovemaking, sensing your lack of passion?"

Ginny blushed, embarrassed and disturbed by this sudden discussion of a problem that she had tried hard not to think about. Profoundly shaken, she said furiously, "Don't try to somehow make it all seem my fault! *I'm* not the one who did anything wrong, *you* did. You can't make me take the blame for your actions. You're trying to twist things, but the fact is you lied to me and you cheated on me!" Coldly, with an awful finality, she finished, "Get out. Pack what you need right now, and *get out!*"

"Gladly! Whatever we had together died a long time ago. At least Lisa knows how to be a woman."

Reeling from the pain that his harsh words inflicted on her, Ginny responded viciously, "Lisa must not require much in the way of a man then, because you haven't been able to satisfy me for a long time."

Saying nothing, his blue eyes cold with barely suppressed fury, Ross turned away from her and went into their bedroom. Thirty seconds later he came out again, carrying one small suitcase.

"I'll call you," he said tightly.

And a moment later he was gone.

Ginny remained rooted to the same spot in the middle of the living room where she had stood stiffly during the whole fight. It was as if moving would break a delicate spell. Finally she collapsed on the sofa, sighing deeply.

The air was charged with the electricity of their verbal assault on each other. There was an almost

9

tangible sense of bitterness, recriminations, conscious attempts to wound as deeply as possible. *Why didn't I say what I was really feeling? I made myself ignore the love I feel for Ross, holding back the thoughts and feelings that were really important. Instead of saying, "I'm hurt, I'm frightened, I don't want to lose you," I was so hostile. Somehow I couldn't let myself be open, vulnerable. I was just consumed by anger. It was easier to say, "I don't love you," than to admit, "I love you, and you have the power to hurt me deeply."*

Ginny was stunned by the force of the hostility that had suddenly been unleashed between her and Ross. It was as if it had always existed and had only been waiting patiently for an excuse to surface. *Perhaps men and women do hate each other, deep inside*, she thought sadly, *because they're so afraid of being hurt by each other.*

That night Ginny sat curled up in a comfortable overstuffed chair in the living room, watching the dying embers in the fireplace. She was alone in the house, and it was utterly still and quiet. Betsy had called earlier to ask if she could spend the night with a friend, and Ginny, trying to sound happy and normal, had gladly said yes. She couldn't face her daughter yet.

The tears that had come earlier were dry now. All that was left was a feeling of emptiness and shame and terrible loss.

How could I have been so cruel? Ginny wondered. *I wanted to hurt Ross and I did, terribly. I instinctively chose his most vulnerable spot, his*

*sense of masculinity, and wounded him as deeply as
I could. What a bitch I was . . . what a cold,
heartless bitch. I've never done anything so mean in
my whole life. But I've never been hurt so much in
my whole life, either.*

She looked back to the time when she and Ross
were first married. They were deeply in love and
everything seemed so right, so good. The future was
filled with limitless possibilities, and they were both
certain that nothing but good things would happen
to them. She was tortured now by confusion and
doubt—how did they lose that precious love? Why?

Their relationship certainly began in a rocky way.
Ginny remembered it vividly. UCLA in 1966. In-
dian summer weather though it was November. Students stretched out on the grass, sleeping, talking,
studying. Ginny was eighteen, a freshman, still excited and surprised by university life—the different
kinds of people, the liberal attitudes, the unaccus-
tomed freedom. These new sensations produced a
rush of both pleasurable and frightening feelings in
Ginny, who came from a sheltered, conservative
background.

And then she met Ross Carlson. A graduate student in the film school, he was older, experienced,
just enough of a rebel to be intriguing. And he was
handsome, a young California golden god. He had
majored in journalism because he was passionately
interested in politics and world affairs, but he
switched to film because it allowed him to fulfill his
creative streak. He talked to Ginny about politics,
social issues, philosophical questions. He was bril-

11

liant, idealistic, uncompromising, and didn't believe in marriage.

Ginny fell totally, deliriously in love with him immediately.

When he took her to his one-room apartment near campus, she knew perfectly well what was expected. Awkwardly, but with a natural passion, she hesitated for only the briefest moment before eagerly making love to him on an Indian-print bedspread on a mattress on the floor.

He was surprised to discover that, in this era of free love, Ginny was a virgin. He felt guilty somehow, but it didn't bother Ginny at all. From the first moment he looked at her, his blue eyes arrogant, his disheveled flaxen hair shining in the sunlight, she knew that she would gladly give him all she had to offer. For the soul-stirring pleasure of his arms, his smile, his electrifying touch, she would turn her back on everything she had ever believed.

But Ross wasn't used to girls as naive as Ginny, and, she learned later, the responsibility of having taken her from innocence to knowledge weighed heavily on him. He didn't call her again.

She was miserable. And then six weeks later, she found she was pregnant. Her friend Martie said simply, "So it *is* true—it only takes one time." Then, over Ginny's stubborn protests, she told Ross.

Coming to Ginny immediately, he surprised her by asking her to marry him.

"But you don't believe in marriage," Ginny said defiantly.

"Imminent fatherhood is effectively revising my

value system," he responded wryly, his usually firmly set mouth softening into a smile.

"You don't love me!" she protested.

His ice-blue eyes surveyed her critically, intently, as a shadow passed over his face. "I've thought of nothing but you for six weeks. It doesn't make any sense. I've had every girl I've wanted since I was eighteen, and you're the first I couldn't walk away from. There's something about you—it isn't just that you're pretty and have a great body. I've known prettier girls, though I've got to admit none had a sexier body."

Ginny blushed, remembering the excitement he couldn't conceal when he saw her naked . . .

"Do you know D. H. Lawrence?"

Ginny nodded. "I've read a couple of his books."

Ross took her hand. "Lawrence wrote about the difference between a man and a woman. He said the man is the pillar of fire and the woman, the pillar of cloud . . ."

He continued soberly. "There's this aura about you of peace and sanity. Like the rest of the world flows around you, not quite touching you." His voice softened, and for a moment he seemed like a lost little boy desperately in need of reassurance. "You're the calm center in my life, the safe harbor. With you beside me, I think I could handle anything."

He stopped, and the silence was electric, charged with a sense of expectancy. *From this moment on,* Ginny thought soberly, *my life will never again be the same.*

He took her in his arms and finished huskily, "Maybe you *do* love me more than I love you. But I suspect that I need you more than you'll *ever* need me . . ."

They were married two weeks later.

A plane passed overhead, and with a jolt Ginny came back to the present.

One thing Ross had said was true—things had been bad between them for a long time, but neither wanted to face it. Ginny simply tried to ignore her growing sense of dissatisfaction, her desire for romance instead of boring predictability. Ross went looking elsewhere for an answer to the emptiness both were feeling. He found it in the arms of another woman.

Ginny didn't want to think about Lisa Lawrence, but she couldn't avoid it. A thousand painful questions flooded her mind—was the younger woman prettier, sexier, better in bed? When did they first make love? Had they been sleeping together for the whole month Ross said they knew each other? How often had he lied to Ginny, telling her he was working when actually he was with Lisa?

The questions, each like a dagger through her heart, seemed to fill Ginny's tortured mind until she knew she would start crying again if she didn't do something. And then she realized that she didn't want to be alone any longer. Picking up the telephone, she dialed Martie's number shakily.

Martie Bass, a tiny dynamo, barely five feet tall with wildly curly red hair, was Ginny's oldest friend, the first of their group of friends to go through what she flippantly called "the Big D." Ginny had known her from childhood on up through high school and college. Not once, in all their eager, curious conversations about marriage, had they ever considered divorce until that Christmas Eve when Ed walked out, insisting coldly that he wanted to spend Christmas with the woman he really loved.

"Hello," Martie answered, her voice excited and expectant.

"Martie . . ." Ginny could hear the sigh of disappointment on the other end of the line, and she knew that Martie must have been waiting to hear from her lover. "I'm sorry to bother you . . ."

"Ginny? God, you sound awful. What's wrong?"

Ginny wanted to say, "Never mind, I'm sorry I bothered you, I know you're busy." Instead she burst into tears and sobbed, "Oh, Martie, Ross has left. It's all over and I'm so miserable."

Martie made the forty-five-minute drive from her Hollywood Hills house to Ginny's in half an hour. Throughout their entire relationship, Ginny had been the strong one, the one who had always been there to get Martie out of trouble, to comfort her when one of her numerous romances went sour. Now her friend needed her in a way that completely took her by surprise. Never in a million years would she have thought Ross and Ginny would break up. Martie had always liked Ross a great deal and thought Ginny was lucky to find him. He was one of the few completely honest men she had ever met.

Though Ginny hadn't said so, somehow Martie suspected that another woman was involved. She'd worked in Hollywood long enough to know how rampant infidelity was. Young actresses slept around hoping to get a part. Slightly older ones slept around hoping to get a husband, even someone else's. It had always amazed Martie that Ross had avoided taking advantage of the constant opportunities this long.

As she drove into Ginny's driveway, Martie hoped that the problem was simply a meaningless one-night stand. If that was the case, she might be able to persuade Ginny to take Ross back. After all, sex didn't mean anything.

But a few minutes later, after listening to Ginny pour out the whole story, Martie realized it wasn't going to be that simple.

"But, Gin, this happens all the time. It's a game *everyone* plays. It's nothing to end a marriage over."

"It's never happened to *me* before," Ginny replied stubbornly, "And as far as I'm concerned, it's no game."

"I'm sure this Lisa person is simply your average struggling actress, out for what she can get, hoping Ross can help her career. I've seen the way some of these girls operate, and, believe me, a man would have to be a saint or a eunuch to resist. It only proves that Ross is human."

"You don't understand, Martie. Every time I think about him being with her, doing the things we do together, it hurts like hell."

"I *do* understand," Martie said softly, and for the first time Ginny remembered that she had been through the same experience.

"I'm sorry. I forgot about Ed."

"Hey, it's okay. I realize now that it doesn't matter. Sex is sex. It's nothing more, there's no mystical, spiritual meaning to it. You do it when you feel like it, and don't expect anything afterwards."

Ginny didn't believe Martie's brave, defiant words, convinced, as always, that Martie was simply trying to hide the pain inside.

"I don't agree," she responded firmly. "Sex should be love, and love . . . should last forever."

"You're a romantic, Ginny," Martie said, shaking her head. "But it's not a romantic world any more." Then, "Why don't you call Ross tomorrow? If you two talk to each other . . ."

"It's not that simple. It isn't just that Ross had an affair. It's everything that's been happening between us lately. We just don't seem to love each other any more. I think we both need something we can no longer give. Life is too short to settle for convenience and comfort. You should be able to have *excitement*."

"But we're talking about marriage, not affairs. Look, Ginny, I used to think I could have it all, too, if only I worked hard enough. I tried to combine a career *and* a marriage."

"I always suspected that Ed wasn't the kind of man who could share his wife, even with a career."

"Well, you were right. But I was as deliriously in love with him as you were with Ross, and I was convinced that everything would work out. When he left me for that stupid little cocktail waitress I wouldn't believe it. I couldn't accept that our love had deteriorated in direct proportion to my rise as a successful agent."

Looking at Ginny sadly, Martie finished curtly,

17

"So now I find it hard to believe romance can survive in marriage."

Ginny hesitated. Finally she responded thoughtfully, "I don't know, obviously it didn't last in mine. Maybe marriage isn't a singular state any more. Perhaps now marriages are stages in our lives, different partners for different periods. I guess no one stays married forever . . . no one lives happily ever after . . ."

2.

Ross drove around aimlessly until late in the evening. He had no idea where to go or what to do. For the first time in fourteen years, he couldn't simply go home. After stopping at several bars, he realized he was on the verge of getting drunk. Knowing he might very well end up getting arrested for drunken driving, he finally made a decision. A few minutes later he was knocking on Lisa's door.

"Ross!"

The last person in the world Lisa had expected to see when she opened the door was Ross. After all, they had just parted that morning, and she knew he was going back to his home and family. A pragmatist, she had no illusions about her relationship with him. He was a married man who had no intention of leaving his wife. That was fine with her, since she wanted no more from him than he was able to give. Ambitious and talented, she was much more concerned with her career than with a casual romance.

Ross stared at her wordlessly for a long moment, unsure what to say. As always, he was struck by her youth and freshness. She had a natural vivacity that had not yet been tempered by experience, and it was

19

that quality that had first attracted him. Though she was extremely pretty, with long platinum hair and a voluptuous figure, those things really didn't matter to him. In his profession he saw too many women who had beauty but no substance. What was special about Lisa was the way she made him feel—as if he were young again and there were still things to be curious and excited about.

It was a feeling he hadn't known with Ginny in a long time. And it was strong enough to compel him to betray her.

"My wife found out about us," he began clumsily, hating the stupid, cheap sound of the words. "We're separating."

Lisa didn't know whether to be happy or worried. It would be nice to see more of Ross, but on the other hand he might expect some kind of commitment from her now.

"I see," she finally responded noncommittally. Then, "Come on in. You look like you need a good night's sleep. We'll talk about it in the morning."

By the following week, Ross was living with Lisa in her apartment in Beverly Hills, and Ginny had initiated divorce proceedings against him. He refused to hire a lawyer of his own. He simply told Ginny's lawyer to draw up an agreement that would give Ginny everything, and he would sign it. The lawyer, who specialized in divorce, was stunned. He decided that Ross was either incredibly stupid or still in love with his wife. He was even more surprised, however, when Ginny refused to accept alimony. He simply couldn't understand her stubborn insistence that she wanted to be self-supporting.

Telling Betsy was the hardest part. At first, Ginny lied, telling her that Ross was still away on his trip. Then, after she and Ross decided on the divorce, she told her daughter the truth.

Ross came back to the beach house that day for the first time since the argument. He was convinced that it was important that he and Ginny tell Betsy together, to avoid any misunderstanding on her part. He loved his daughter in the doting, special way fathers love their little girls, and it bothered him terribly to know he was going to hurt her.

Betsy, tall and slim and still coltish in her movements, grinned broadly when she saw her father. But when she saw the awkward, pained look on her mother's face, she grew worried. Something was wrong. She had sensed it all week, watching her mother act unnaturally cheerful, suspecting that there was something bothering her.

Betsy was extremely close to her mother, whom she adored. But when Ginny calmly told Betsy that she and Ross were getting a divorce, Betsy exploded in shocked outrage at her.

"What do you mean, 'divorce!' What happened?"

Neither Ginny nor Ross wanted to broach the subject of Lisa, so Ginny said simply, "Your father and I, for reasons that have nothing to do with you, have decided to divorce. Though we still care about each other, we just don't love each other any more."

Ross added, "It happens sometimes in marriage, Betsy. People . . . change. But your mother and I both love you very much. That hasn't changed."

Betsy felt that her whole world, once so secure and dependable, was falling apart. Despite the fact that most of her friends had divorced parents, she never thought it would happen to her. *Her* parents were different. They loved each other.

Sullenly, with the obstinacy of the young, she insisted, "I don't understand. How can you just suddenly not love each other any more?"

Ginny glanced at Ross, then quickly looked away. *It wasn't sudden*, she thought sadly. *It began a long time ago and neither of us did anything to stop it.*

"Neither your mother nor I wanted this to happen, Betsy," Ross explained patiently. "Aside from everything else, we would never want to hurt you. Believe me, we've both thought about how difficult this will be for you, and we intend to do everything we can to make things continue to go as smoothly as possible."

"I suppose you'll be one of those weekend fathers," Betsy responded bitterly. "I'll have to sleep on the couch in your tiny little apartment somewhere, and we'll go to movies a lot because you won't know what else to do with me."

"That's enough, Betsy," Ginny said firmly but not unkindly. Though Betsy's anger was understandable, it wouldn't be good for any of them if it went unchecked. When Betsy turned to look furiously at her mother, Ginny was struck, as always, by the feeling that she was looking at a softer, more feminine version of Ross. Betsy had her father's piercing blue eyes and firmly set chin. Ginny knew that in her peer group Betsy was the leader, the one who bossed everyone else, because she was exceptionally bright and more than a little dictatorial.

"You're talking about *my* life, too, you know," Betsy insisted. "It's all going to be different now." Looking at her mother, she continued, "I bet you'll have to sell the house because you won't be able to afford it."

Ginny knew now what was really worrying Betsy. She didn't know what the hell was going to happen to *her* in all of this upheaval. Would her father still see her, still love her? Would she lose the only home she had ever known? *It must be absolutely terrifying for her. Suddenly, without any notice, her whole life is being changed. It's like we're pulling the rug out from under her feet. Well, I can certainly empathize with that feeling.*

"I won't be selling the house," Ginny replied, with a certainty that surprised all of them. Ross looked doubtful; though the mortgage was paid, the upkeep and taxes were substantial. He didn't see how Ginny, who had never worked at a job outside the home, could support all of this. But Betsy looked immensely relieved and grateful at this reassurance in the midst of chaos. Watching her, Ginny knew that she had said the right thing. Whatever happened, she must maintain this place for Betsy. That, at least, must not be taken away from her.

"But . . . how can you afford it?" Betsy asked hesitantly, suddenly realizing, as Ross had done, that her mother was not in a position to support the house.

"My paintings," Ginny answered quickly, without thinking. The words surprised her as much as her husband and daughter. She really hadn't thought about this at all. Since her marriage she hadn't earned a penny of her own. She had absolutely no idea if anyone would be willing to pay for the paintings she had always given away to friends and relatives. The more she thought about it, the more her confidence wavered. There were, after all, a lot of serious artists who were starving while she was just a housewife who dabbled in art.

"Ginny, you'd better think about this," Ross began slowly. "I was meaning to tell you. I saw Eric Langley yesterday, and he said he had a Girl Friday job open at his agency. He'd be happy to take you on."

Ginny was furious at Ross's obvious lack of confidence in her. He was so sure that she couldn't support herself that he had gone looking for a job for her. And a "Girl Friday" post, at that. She knew exactly what it meant—typing, filing, doing menial chores for a poverty wage. That was bearable if you were an eager twenty-one-year-old looking for a way to break into show business. But Ginny was a mature woman with a house to maintain and a daughter to support. For financial reasons, and for her own self-respect, she needed more than that.

"*Many* people have told me I could sell my paintings if I tried," Ginny insisted, a new, steely note of determination in her voice. "And that's exactly what I intend to do."

Ross was taken aback. This defiance and determination was a side of Ginny he had never seen before. From the first moment he learned she was pregnant fourteen years earlier, he had assumed re-

sponsibility for her. Now she was assuming responsibility for herself. And though he knew she was
only doing what was necessary and right, he felt a
pang of anger and regret.

"Suit yourself," he said curtly, sounding more
cynical than he intended.

"I will."

Betsy looked at her parents confusedly. Suddenly
they were so different, so coldly proper with each
other, no longer easy-going and affectionate. She
couldn't believe this was happening, not to *her* family. Though she knew very little about romantic
love, she knew that her parents had been very good
for each other for as long as she could remember. It
didn't make sense that they would change so drastically. Grasping desperately for whatever reassurance she could find, she decided in that moment
that this was all somehow a terrible mistake. They
hadn't stopped loving each other *really*, they were
simply having problems, as everyone did sometimes.
Soon, she told herself, they would realize this and
get back together. It was only a matter of time.

When Ross left a few minutes later, Ginny
walked with him to the door, as if he were a guest.
But instead of leaving immediately, he stopped and
turned to her.

"If you change your mind about that job with
Eric . . ."

"I won't," she responded with more confidence
than she actually felt.

"I didn't mean to insult you, Ginny. It's a decent
job and Eric's a good guy to work for, unlike most

of the people you'll run into. I just . . . I was just trying to help."

His expression was open, unguarded, concerned. For a moment Ginny wavered. Taking this job would be the easy way out of her dilemma. There would be no risk of rejection. And suddenly she felt that old desire to please Ross. *I still love him. God, help me, I still love him, and it hurts so much. It's not nearly as simple as I thought it was going to be when I told myself I didn't love him any more.*

She looked up at him—he was so much taller than she was. She had always looked up to him in every way, as someone who was more experienced than she, more talented, stronger. But now she was on her own. She mustn't forget that. She couldn't look to him to take care of her any longer. Now she must take care of herself. Perhaps, she realized, at thirty-three it was about time for her to learn how to do that.

"No, thanks, Ross. I appreciate the offer, though. I mean that."

"Okay. Well . . . I'll be seeing you. Take care, Ginny."

"You, too." She had to stop herself from adding, "honey."

He left. And in that moment Ginny knew it was really over.

3.

"Do you think they take it *all* off?"

"Sure. They call themselves male strippers, don't they? And strippers, by definition, *strip*."

"I'll bet they don't. I'll bet they wear little sequined jockstraps."

"God, Gin, what a killjoy!"

Taking another bite out of the apple she was munching on, Ginny responded, "Martie, I'm not a killjoy. You know how conservative Joan is. And you want to take her to see male strippers? Are you sure she wants to do this?"

"Of course. Come on, Gin, it's New Year's Eve! We've got to celebrate somehow. Kate's going, too. She's alone, as usual."

"What about you? Wouldn't you rather be with Michael?"

"He's with his wife," Martie explained curtly.

She was in love with a married man, a brilliant young director who was a client at her agency. For the first time since her bitter and devastating divorce, she was involved in a relationship that was more than just a fling. She was growing increasingly dependent on Michael, despite the fact that he told her

27

bluntly he would never leave his wife. Ginny was so upset over her friend being involved in what was clearly a destructive relationship that she could barely discuss it with her. They invariably ended up arguing angrily.

Martie continued, "It'll be the first time the old gang's gotten together in ages. I know you're depressed about the divorce, but brooding at home will just make it worse."

Sighing, Ginny agreed reluctantly, "Well, okay. What time?"

"Seven. We'll meet you there. Be prepared to be wildly abandoned and let your basic middle-aged lust take over. After all, we're supposed to be in the sexiest period of our lives."

Ginny hung up and leaned back in the wicker chair in the sunroom. Even in this quiet, special place, the outside world intruded. She couldn't help thinking that all she and her friends talked about nowadays was divorce. Of the four of them— Ginny, Martie, Kate and Joan—three had already gone through divorces. In three months, when Ginny's divorce became final, it would be unanimous.

Looking through the window at the gently rolling ocean, Ginny thought pensively, *this isn't the way I expected life to be* . . .

She had meant it when she promised to love and honor, to forsake all others. And she believed that Ross had meant it, too. It simply hadn't occurred to either of them that human beings are complex creatures whose needs change, or that love is not a static feeling, but a growing, changing state that can die as easily as it is born . . .

* * *

Arriving late at the club, Ginny found her friends already seated around a small table at the very edge of the dance floor—Kate McGraw, a tall, slim brunette with ice-blue eyes and a flawless complexion, who had made enough money as a top model to retire early; Joan Hoffer, a pretty, dimpled blonde with changeable hazel eyes; and Martie.

"Leave it to you to get as close to the action as possible," Ginny commented wryly to Martie.

"Hey, I'm not gonna miss a single bump or grind," Martie responded, grinning wickedly. "Actually, I did it for Kate. I wanted her to see what she's been missing."

"I *know* what I've been missing," Kate answered levelly, "and it ain't much."

Remote and defensive with strangers, Kate was sympathetic and generous with her close friends. Her carefully maintained aura of cool reserve masked a fragile vulnerability and a nature that was too giving for her own good. As a little girl she had taken in every stray dog in the neighborhood. As a young woman she had taken in every man who seemed to need something from her. Finally, after a disastrous ten-year marriage to a wealthy producer who was a world-class bastard, she had given up on men entirely. For three years now she had politely but firmly turned down all dates. Lacking the defenses necessary to protect herself from being hurt, she simply opted out of the game totally.

At first her friends tried to change her mind, but she was stubborn, and now only Martie, equally

29

stubborn, commented on Kate's self-imposed celibacy.

"I don't know, you might find a real cutie here tonight," Martie continued.

"If anyone gets lucky tonight, Martie, it will probably be you. I swear, you have some kind of radar that zeroes in on the nearest available man."

"That's the truth!" Joan commented enthusiastically.

Everyone laughed, including Martie, who consciously fostered her reputation as a swinger. Only Ginny, who knew her better than the others did, understood that beneath the free and easy sexuality lay a desperate loneliness and profound self-doubt. Those things had propelled her into the destructive relationship with her married lover.

"Ginny, you look fantastic," Martie said admiringly.

Kate added, "She's right. You look better than ever. You've lost a lot of weight, haven't you?"

"Fifteen pounds," Ginny said proudly.

"Well, don't lose any more. Right now, you've got that fragile, gamine look. A few more pounds and you'll be downright skinny."

Ginny knew that she looked good, and it never ceased to surprise her when she looked in a mirror. The weight she had tried so hard to lose for several years seemed to melt off effortlessly now because she had no appetite. And now that her face was thin instead of full, her brilliant green eyes, always her best feature, stood out even more. Piercing, provocative, they were intensely alluring, with a veiled hint of unfulfilled desire. Her hair was longer because she didn't want to spend the money to have it cut, and that made her look even younger. With an immensely appealing vulnerability, she caught the eye of every man in the club.

Suddenly the lights dimmed and the opening bars of *A Chorus Line* blasted out from a hidden stereo. Six young men, all dressed in white top hats, black tuxedo jackets, and jockstraps, came slowly out onto the dance floor, doing the chorus line's high kick. The younger women in the audience squealed, then screamed as the music switched over to "The Stripper" and the dancers did an exaggerated bump and grind.

"All right!" Martie yelled enthusiastically as Joan grinned a little self-consciously and Kate looked supremely amused.

"I *told* you," Ginny said to Martie, pointing to the sequined jockstraps.

Grimacing, Martie shouted over the noise, "Oh, well, it's always a good idea to leave a little something to the imagination."

The dancers then performed individually to different songs. One did a take-off of Gene Kelly to "Singin' in the Rain," twirling an umbrella and flashing open his raincoat to reveal a bare chest and hairy legs. Another danced to disco music, performing so well that he had the audience clapping and moving to the pounding rhythm. And finally a dancer covered with balloons passed out sharp pins to the girls sitting next to the dance floor. One by one they gleefully popped the balloons as he danced around the very edge of the floor, only inches from the audience. Taking careful aim, Martie popped

31

the most strategic balloon, exposing a sequined red jockstrap.

Some of the men seemed self-conscious, but most were self-assured, confident of their sexuality, and appeared to be enjoying themselves immensely. They revelled in the attention—like young, precocious children, they loved showing off. What amazed Ginny was the reaction of the other women in the audience. They giggled and squealed, generally acting like schoolgirls, while the men teased them good-naturedly.

"It's fun in a way, but I can't imagine that anyone takes it seriously," Kate said as the music faded away and the last dancer disappeared to enthusiastic applause.

"I don't know. It's nice seeing different bodies. You get so tired of the same old thing," Joan responded lightly.

Martie admitted easily, "*I'm* taking it seriously. I stuck one of my cards in the balloon guy's jockstrap. I just hope he isn't gay."

Ginny laughed along with the others, but she was secretly disturbed. She understood everyone else's response to the unabashed, happy-go-lucky sexuality they had just witnessed. What she didn't understand was her own lack of a response. She felt curiously empty, unmoved, as if a vital part of her that should have responded on an elemental level was dead somehow. These young men were attractive, engaging, filled with an infectious joy in their own sexuality.

It would have been easier if she could pretend that she objected to the performers on moral grounds. But the truth was that she saw nothing wrong with what they were doing. It was silly, perhaps, and a bit boring after awhile, watching man after man awkwardly shed his clothes. But the sight of those well-muscled arms, broad chests, and trim derrieres should have struck a chord somewhere inside her. Instead she felt nothing.

4.

Ginny suggested their favorite restaurant, Alice's, for dinner after the show, and the others agreed. Located on the old Malibu pier, it was small and intimate, filled with lush green plants. The ocean view was gorgeous; at night floodlights lit the beach below, turning the softly breaking waves silver.

Normally casual and quiet, tonight Alice's was filled with happy, noisy people intent on celebrating the end of one decade and the beginning of another. There was the usual Malibu crowd, a variety of show business people, plus struggling young people blowing what was to them a substantial amount of money to party in the laid-back atmosphere of the good life, Malibu style.

"What did you think of the show?" Joan asked as she and Kate settled back in a booth.

"Pretty boring, actually."

"Well, *I* thought they were damn sexy," Martie interjected firmly.

"I don't know. I've never been able to separate sexual attraction from emotional attraction. I mean, I don't get turned on by those pictures in *Playgirl* because I don't know what the men are like."

"I know what you mean," Joan agreed fervently. "It isn't just sheer physical attraction that draws me to a man. There's something more . . . an aura of masculinity, of confidence. I can't really explain it, it's just a very *male* thing that has very little to do with how the man actually looks."

"I think it matters a lot how a man looks," Martie interrupted stubbornly. "I always look at a man's hands first. I just *love* long fingers, they're so sensuous. God, I would give anything for one night with James Coburn!"

"Who *are* you spending your nights with now?" Kate asked. "Anybody serious?"

"All the men I meet are married, of course," Martie answered. She clearly didn't want to say anything more, and Kate tactfully didn't pursue the subject.

"How's Betsy?" Joan asked, trying to draw the unusually silent Ginny into the conversation.

"Oh, you know, concerned about clothes and boys, in that order."

"Some things never change, I guess," Kate laughed. "Remember how we were our first year in high school? Idolizing all those older, infinitely mature and attractive junior and senior boys, and being pathetically jealous of the older, more sophisticated girls. We used to call each other every morning to find out what we were all wearing that day. God, it was so silly."

"Hey, our fifteenth reunion's coming up in June," Joan reminded them cheerfully.

"Oh, God, *fifteen years*," Martie groaned. "I don't want to think about it."

"You're gonna go, aren't you? We've all got to go. It will be so interesting to see what happened to everyone."

"I can't think of *anyone* I want to see again," Martie said bluntly.

Kate said nothing, but her mind went back fifteen years to graduation day and the last time she saw David Hanson. She hadn't thought about him in months. But now she could see him clearly, tall, thin, rather awkward, as basketball players so often are off the court. His brown hair shone red-gold on that hot June day as he strode across the field and out of her life forever. David . . . there was something immensely shy and appealing about him—his gentle strength, his kindness that prompted him to talk sometimes to Kate, who was intensely uncomfortable with her height then, convinced that no boy could possibly find her attractive.

David . . . she had tried desperately for days to work up the courage to ask him to the Sadie Hawkins dance, only to lose her nerve at the last minute. It was strange how he had stayed in her thoughts all these years, coming back to pique her curiosity sometimes as she lay alone in bed late at night or when she watched a basketball game and was reminded of his powerful grace on the court . . .

Her attention was brought back to the present when Ginny asked her, "What have you been doing with yourself, Kate? None of us have heard from you in weeks."

"Chasing Scottie mostly," she answered ruefully. "It's amazing how much energy that littly guy has. He's only four but he can outrun me already. It's

36

funny, I can actually see his big brown eyes light up with fiendish pleasure when he thinks of some new catastrophe to cause. He smeared peanut butter all over the cat yesterday, then proudly told me he'd made a sandwich."

"You should be chasing *men*, not your son," Martie said bluntly.

"Sure, I can do what every other divorced mother I know does: Have an endless parade of strange men through my bedroom so that my son inevitably will walk in on us when he has a nightmare and comes to mommy for a little love. Or go to a hotel and feel like a prostitute. Or go to the man's place and leave immediately after making love, instead of relaxing, because my babysitter has to get home. No, thanks."

"Well, if you insist on thinking only of Scottie's needs instead of your own then look at it this way—how are you gonna find him a father?"

"He *has* a father. One who couldn't care less about him, *never* sees him, and thinks his responsibility begins and ends with writing out the support check every month." Kate's voice was bitter now as she finished curtly, "Scottie had the misfortune to get stuck with a father who doesn't want to be one. I'm not gonna saddle him with a stepfather who'll resent him and constantly fight him for my attention."

"Are you convinced it has to be that way?" Ginny asked softly.

"When a family breaks up, you can't put it together again. It's like Humpty Dumpty."

"Well, I certainly hope you're wrong," Joan interrupted cheerfully, "because I intend to be part of a 'reconstituted' family soon. In other words, I'm going to remarry."

There was a stunned silence.

Martie recovered first. "I don't believe it. When did this happen?"

"I've known him for several months. I didn't actually leave Stan because of him, but he was definitely on my mind." Her hazel eyes narrowed in embarrassment. Clearly bracing herself for the expected impact of her announcement, she continued reluctantly, "And I may as well tell you now, I'm quitting my job. Alan wants a full-time wife. With his two kids and my two, I'll be pretty busy just being a mother."

"You tried being a wife and mother for a long time, and the last I heard it made you bored and angry," Martie said shortly.

"That was different," Joan answered sharply. "My marriage to Alan won't be like my marriage to Stan. He's all I need to be really happy."

"Don't you think you're rushing things just a bit?" Kate asked slowly.

"I knew you'd feel that way, but I'm convinced I know what I'm doing. It's *definitely* the right thing."

"Joan, you don't have to have a husband to be happy," Martie said sharply.

Joan's hazel eyes turned dark with anger. "I suppose you think I should follow the feminist example—sleep around, pretend that sex has nothing to do with love, *use* a man instead of making a commitment to him. If liberation means loneliness, then I don't want it."

Ginny knew that Joan was making a thinly veiled attack on Martie, who was the most radical feminist of the bunch. Joan had always firmly believed that a woman was happiest when she was being supported by a man and caring for him in return.

Stepping in to stop what was obviously shaping up to be a real cat fight, Ginny said calmly, "Tell us about this guy. Where did you meet him, what's he like, all that."

"Well, he's a lawyer and a widower. He knows Ross, as a matter of fact," Joan began happily. As she talked about her fiancé, who sounded more and more like her ex-husband, Ginny and Martie exchanged a wry look.

Ginny realized that for Joan, it was as if the tumultuous changes and progress women had known during the past decade had never happened. She continued to fiercely clutch the promise of happiness that everyone had held out to her when she was growing up—*find the right man and he will make you happy. You need nothing more in your life.* Despite strong evidence to the contrary, despite her own sense of emptiness and anger, she refused to be disillusioned. Instead of asking the obvious question—If I'm doing what I'm supposed to do, why aren't I happy?—she simply exchanged one man for another.

"I don't know about you guys, but I'm going to say to hell with diets and order a ton of food." Martie announced gaily when the waiter arrived. "And a bottle of the best champagne in the place to go with it. One of my clients just signed a big deal with

Paramount and I intend to celebrate. Today I made ten percent of an obscene amount of money."

"Martie, it's a constant amazement to me that anyone who has always been as flaky as you could be such a terrific agent," Kate said good-naturedly. "I remember when you nearly flunked out of college because you couldn't force yourself to get up in time for your morning classes. Beneath that madcap exterior must beat the heart of a ruthless capitalist."

"I live by one philosophy," Martie responded with mock seriousness. "Money talks and bullshit walks."

She eyed Kate. "You should have let me handle you as an actress when I wanted to years ago, you know. You had the looks and the connections through Kevin. With my help, you could have made it. Actually, you still have the looks."

"No thanks. When I said good-bye to Kevin, I said goodby to Hollywood, too, *happily*. I couldn't stand that whole scene. I'm much happier being a harried mother. The high point of my life is taking Scottie to the zoo, and I like it that way." Then, "Well, now we know what you've been up to, wheeling and dealing with moguls and superstars. What have you been doing with yourself, Gin? Every time I call, you're out."

Her eyes glinting mischievously, Martie interrupted. "Hey, is there a man, perhaps, inspiring you to look so terrific?"

"No man, Martie, just plain hard work. I've been painting all day, every day, out on the beach, doing seascapes and portraits. I've got to get together a portfolio to start showing to galleries. I'm a self-

supporting, working artist now." She added doubt-
fully, "At least, I hope I am."

"If I can help . . ." Martie began.

But Ginny cut her off quickly. "Thanks, but no
thanks. It's sink-or-swim time. A long time ago I
liked to think I had some talent. Now I'll find out if
I was right or wrong. Next week I start hawking my
work."

"You don't have anything to worry about," Martie said confidently. "You're going to be incredibly
successful, and I'm going to sell all of those paintings you gave me and make a fortune."

"Martie's right, Gin," Joan added reassuringly.
"You know we've always thought that you're *very*
talented. Just don't get so caught up in your career
that you forget you're a woman, too. A career is
nice, expecially when you're in a position where you
have to support yourself, but a good marriage is better. And don't wait until your divorce is final to
start looking around, either."

"Oh, Joan, don't start that," Martie began angrily. "This isn't the fifties, it's almost nineteen-
eighty. A career is a damn sight more dependable
than a man. As far as I'm concerned, true love went
away somewhere back in the early seventies, along
with miniskirts, Vietnam, and liberalism."

"Stop it, both of you," Ginny insisted firmly.
"Every time we get together it's the same old argument."

"Well, Joan's right about one thing," Martie con-
ceded. "I hope you're not falling into that all-work-
and-no-play syndrome. Don't let that terrific new
body go to waste, kiddo. You know, if you go with-

41

out sex long enough, you become a virgin again."

"Martie!"

"Ignore her, Gin," Kate said dryly, "We all know she's never gotten past puberty."

"Seriously, Ginny, are you dating anyone?" Joan asked.

"Nope," Ginny answered succinctly, "And I don't want to, so forget about setting me up with a blind date. I know that's what you were leading up to."

"God, now we have two spinsters in the group," Martie groaned.

"I'm not being a spinster. But right now my work matters more than anything, except for Betsy. Believe it or not, that's not a bad feeling to have."

"That's just an excuse, Ginny. You spent your entire adult life with Ross, so now you're afraid of other men. The truth is they're all the same, you know. Self-centered, insensitive bastards, basically. But they do have their uses."

"Don't make it sound so romantic and sugarcoated, Martie," Kate interrupted dryly.

"There's nothing wrong with looking at things realistically, Kate. If there's one thing that women should have learned during the past decade it's that we have sexual needs. That's normal, natural, and we shouldn't feel guilty about satisfying those needs. What women should be nowadays is the feminine version of macho; enjoying sex and not infusing it with seriousness and responsibility and all that crap."

Except I don't need or want sex, Ginny thought unhappily. *I almost hated having sex with Ross to-*

42

*ward the end, and now I have no desire to go to bed
with anyone, period.*

Ginny couldn't look at Martie; they knew each
other too well. She was sure her old friend would
sense somehow that she was that pitiful creature, the
frigid woman. Then, instead of sympathizing with
her as she had done, Martie would back off, thinking, "Now I see why Ross left—you couldn't satisfy
him." Being seen as a failure as a woman would be
infinitely harder to bear than simply being seen as
one of many women whose shallow husbands have
left them for younger women.

"But it's got to be more than just a physical
thing," Kate was insisting stubbornly. "There has to
be some feeling involved, or it's empty, not really
satisfying at all."

"What you're talking about is romance. What I'm
talking about is filling a need. I think I'm a hell of a
lot more likely to find what I'm looking for than
you are."

"I'm not looking," Kate said briefly.

"The same old argument goes on and on. Marriage versus career, romantic love versus no-strings-
attached sex." Martie turned to Joan. "You like to
think you've found the answer, simply by holding on
fiercely to the past. And maybe you're right. For
you. I sincerely hope so. But for the rest of us, that
happy-ever-after, stand-by-your-man stuff just
hasn't worked."

"Well, I'm going to try it again next week. And
I'm foolish enough to think this time it *will* work.
Maybe I'm not entirely right," she admitted reluc-

43

tantly. "Being so disappointed by my first marriage certainly shook me up. But I don't think your answer is the right one. That's just standard Gloria Steinem liberation stuff. She's alone. Most feminists *are* alone. I just don't want to be that way."

"Look, all of us want a man to be with, even me." Kate said unexpectedly. "The question is, on what basis? In a traditional marriage where he's the boss, you're completely dependent on him, and you hope he doesn't die or leave you?"

Ginny felt a sharp pang at that last barbed remark, though she knew Kate wasn't referring specifically to her and certainly never meant to hurt her. *When will it stop hurting*? she wondered.

Kate continued passionately, "Or is Martie's way right, sleeping around, never making a commitment? Most of us went through that in the seventies, that stupid 'me' decade, where all that mattered was experience and performance, not love or intimacy. 'If it feels good, do it.' If you can't be with the one you love, 'love the one you're with.' That didn't give us what most of us really want—a relationship."

At that moment the waiter interrupted what was rapidly turning into a maudlin discussion instead of a celebration. Holding a bottle of Dom Perignon, he poured a generous amount of the clear, sparkling liquid in each woman's glass.

"I want to propose a toast to this dying decade," Kate said recklessly, raising her glass. "To the ten years when we grew up, got married, got divorced, and somehow survived. Thank God it's over!"

Laughing, they drank deeply of the wine.

"Good-bye 1970s, hello 1980s," Martie added. "I

hope to hell this is a boring, thoroughly uneventful decade."

"I don't know. It hasn't been all bad, certainly," Joan insisted thoughtfully. "Maybe this is a good time to stop and look at where we've been and where we're going. Ten years ago everything seemed so certain, so simple. We each knew what we wanted out of life and who we wanted to spend our lives with. Now there are so many questions . . ."

"Like what happened to marriage?" Kate suggested. "Or, more specifically, what happened to *wives*? What do we want from marriage now, what do we need from a husband?"

"What about money, children, sexual dissatisfaction?" Martie added.

"Or disillusionment about love and romance," Ginny continued.

"The fear of being isolated, lonely," Joan finished softly.

They looked at each other, aware that they had shared a momentous time together. There had been sad times and happy ones; surprises, both good and bad; small miracles and minor tragedies; they had learned, loved, lost, gained. And they knew that whatever happened, they would continue to share the same fears and hopes and dreams.

After a great deal more champagne and a delicious dinner, Kate and Joan got up to leave.

"You can't go yet, it's not midnight," Martie insisted.

"I promised Scottie I'd wake him up at midnight

so he could see the New Year everyone's been telling him about," Kate explained smiling.

"And I have a million things to do for this wedding," Joan said apologetically. "My mother handled my first one and I had no idea how difficult and time-consuming it must have been. Well, I'll see you all at the wedding."

As soon as Kate and Joan were gone, men began approaching Ginny and Martie. "Apparently," Martie said slyly to Ginny, "four women are formidable, but two are inviting." She had just quickly, expertly, turned away two very drunk young men who were at least ten years younger than them.

"I have nothing against getting it on with a young guy occasionally, but that would have been robbing the cradle. And I can't stand drunks. They can't perform."

"Martie . . ." Ginny began haltingly.

"Yes?"

Four glasses of champagne gave Ginny the courage to articulate what had been on her mind for some time. "I've never gone to bed with anyone but Ross."

"I know. That practically makes you a nun nowadays. Actually, I've always admired you tremendously for that. Loyalty is a rare virtue."

"What's it like? Being with different men, I mean."

"You'll find out soon enough. I know you're hurt right now, but your natural desire will take over eventually."

Except I don't seem to have any natural desire, Ginny thought miserably, looking away.

"Hey, it's no big thing, nothing to worry about."

"Do you really enjoy it? Making love to men you may never see again?"

"I prefer not seeing them again. It's easier that way. And the answer is, except for two or three times, no, I don't really enjoy it," Martie answered. "I feel a certain release afterwards, and that's nice. But it's almost like a duty, like flossing your teeth every day or going to the health club three times a week. Sometimes I force myself to try to make it a little more loving for the guy's sake. I tell myself that this guy is going to get me off and he deserves a little hug, some closeness, for that."

Brightening, she continued, "It's totally different with Michael, of course. I *care* about him. I could stay in bed with him forever. He's a terrific lover and I feel so . . . so secure when I'm with him. The problem is I hardly ever see him."

"That isn't going to change," Ginny said curtly.

"I know how you feel about him, Gin," Martie responded angrily. "But you just don't understand. What we have together is special. I think very shortly now he'll be leaving his wife. He wants me as much as I want him."

"That's what you kept telling yourself about Ed, and you know how that ended. You keep weaving fantasies around people and expecting them to fulfill them. It doesn't work." Feeling herself growing angrier by the minute, Ginny forced herself to stop and cool off. "Listen, I'm sorry. Forget it. I have no business telling you how to run your life when I've made such a mess of mine."

"That's not true," Martie disagreed vehemently.

"Just because Ross went crazy with male menopause, that doesn't mean it was all a waste. You had a damn good relationship for a long time. You have a terrific kid. Betsy's about the least neurotic teenager I know. And you have a lot going for you right now. You're still young, prettier than ever, and you're finally doing what you should have done long ago, pursuing your art career."

"Well, you're right about the last thing, anyway. I should never have dropped out of college and stopped painting seriously."

"Why on earth did you do it? Was money that big a problem?"

"No. My parents and Ross's parents offered to continue paying for our educations. My mother especially wanted me to continue. She'd always been interested in art, you know, but was too busy being a terrific wife and mother to do anything about it. She told me that she didn't want me to end up like her. That was the first time I had the slightest idea that she was anything less than blissfully happy with her life." Then, pensively, "I think the real reason was that I felt so guilty about Ross having to marry me that I felt I owed it to him to take care of him and sublimate my own needs to his."

"That must have made you pretty angry after awhile."

Ginny leaned back in the hard wooden booth, stunned. It was so obvious, yet she had never really thought about it before. Was that deeply buried anger what had eaten away at her love for Ross? She realized that Martie, quite casually, had given her something she would have to think seriously about.

"I guess it did. You know, over the past couple of years or so, things haven't been too great between Ross and me. Not that we were actually fighting a lot, but we seemed to be drifting away from each other, losing that . . . that eagerness we used to feel toward each other."

Martie frowned. "When we were young we all thought love would last forever. But it doesn't, at least not passionate, romantic love. I'm still convinced that if that little bitch hadn't come along, you and Ross would have stayed together always, and been as happy as any two people can be."

Though she didn't say so, Ginny disagreed. The more she thought about it, the more she believed that Ross's infidelity was the symptom of the problem, but not the problem itself.

Just then the crowd around them started to count down to midnight. There was a loud, collective cheer as the hour struck, and much hugging and kissing while a stereo somewhere in the background blared out "Auld Lang Syne."

"To us," Martie said, smiling, holding her glass high. "We've come a long way, baby. I just wish we knew where the hell we're going!"

At home, Ginny looked in on Betsy, who was asleep, her room a shambles as usual. She lay on her stomach, wearing an old T-shirt of Ross's that hung limply on her slender frame, her knees drawn up toward her stomach. The pose reminded Ginny of how Betsy slept as a baby, on her tummy with her little diapered butt sticking up. But she was far from being a baby now. Her breasts were already full and her hips, once as straight as a boy's, were now beginning to broaden. With her mother's dark hair and her father's soft blue eyes, she was quite pretty, with the kind of fine-boned loveliness that can easily become real beauty. At fourteen, she was caught between childhood and maturity, still pulled by little-girl longings but drawn irresistibly to the different, exciting, disturbing world of womanhood.

Ginny's heart ached for Betsy sometimes, for the fantasies and illusions that she was fast losing, for the hard choices that she was increasingly forced to make. *It's strange how intimately I identify with her in some ways, female to female. And yet in other ways, she's such a stranger, no longer the child who needed me so completely, who made me feel special by that need. And she's different than I was at her age—more knowing, harder in a way because the world is a much less innocent place now. Drugs, sex, career choices . . . it's so much more complicated now being a woman . . .*

Filled suddenly with the sense of protectiveness that she had known when Betsy was first born, Ginny went up to her quietly and gently covered her with a blanket. Then she kissed her forehead softly and went to bed. Alone.

5.

On her wedding day Joan woke up early after a restless night. As she lay there, tired and vaguely irritable from not getting enough sleep, she was bothered by the nagging thought that she was forgetting something important. Then she remembered—today she was getting married. In a few hours she would be repeating vows she had already said, and broken, once. For a moment she was frightened enough to consider calling it all off. One mistake was enough. She didn't want ever to go through another divorce. Her first marriage was a series of disappointments, with a growing feeling of unhappiness and unfulfillment on her part. She was a good wife and an excellent mother, married to a successful man who treated her well. But she was miserable. Finally, deciding that life wasn't supposed to be so dreary, she filed for divorce.

But she hated being single, and when she met Alan and immediately fell in love with him, she happily agreed to marry him as soon as possible. He was a good man, as successful as Stan but more thoughtful and sensitive in his personal relationships. Her children got along well with him, which mattered greatly to her.

She assured herself once more that marrying Alan was the right thing to do. The fact that Alan was as traditional as Stan in his views of women and their role in the world wouldn't be a problem, she told herself firmly. After all, she wasn't an ambitious career woman like Martie, who had always wanted so much out of life. All Joan wanted was love and financial security. With Alan she would have both, forever. This time, she told herself, there wouldn't be an unhappy ending.

Ginny looked through her closet for the third time, rejecting almost everything immediately. She had absolutely no idea what to wear to Joan's wedding. It was supposed to be a casual afternoon affair, reflecting the fact that it was a second marriage for both the bride and groom. But knowing Joan, who was used to the best and who couldn't be truly casual if her life depended on it, there would probably be more than a note of formality about it. Better to play it safe and be a little overdressed, than to show up in something casual only to find everyone else dressed in cocktail dresses and furs.

But Ginny's artistic sense made her lean toward comfortable, cleverly thrown-together clothes, not chiffon dresses or velvet slacks. She simply didn't have anything really appropriate to wear, and she wasn't about to buy an expensive dress for this occasion. Her present financial state wouldn't allow for that luxury.

She was nearly broke. Though Ross had given her everything, that didn't leave her with a great deal. Her car wasn't paid for, the house was expensive to maintain, food prices were rising all the time, and her art supplies cost a fortune. Though she had nearly exhausted her savings account, she refused to touch the child support Ross gave her for Betsy each month. That money was Betsy's—for her medical and dental expenses, clothes, school supplies, and all of the myriad, miscellaneous expenses teenagers have.

She couldn't turn to Ross. Her pride wouldn't let her and, besides, she knew he had very little money right now. Everything he had was going into his film.

Sighing, Ginny lay back on her bed, staring at the ceiling thoughtfully. Though she was trying hard to hide it from Betsy, she was increasingly worried about money. Over the last few months she had been working hard on her paintings, trying to quickly regain an ability that she had allowed to deteriorate. If those paintings didn't sell . . .

No, I won't let myself think about that. I've got talent, my professors told me that. I'm good enough to make a living with it.

"What are you doing home? I thought you were going to Mrs. Hoffer's wedding."

Ginny turned to find Betsy standing in the doorway. Was it just her imagination, or was Betsy losing weight, too? She had heard about teenagers who suffer from anorexia nervosa, losing weight to an extreme extent because of emotional trauma. Until the separation, she never seriously worried about Betsy going through that sort of thing. Now she thought about it constantly.

"I can't find anything to wear. By the way, you weren't home for lunch."

"You were out on the beach painting, and I didn't want to bother you. Didn't you see the note I left in the kitchen?"

"No."

"Well, I took the bus into the studio and met Dad for lunch. We had pizza. It was so *greasy*—I'll probably be a zit-face tomorrow."

Ginny laughed, as much in relief as at Betsy's humor. She had forgotten that at Betsy's age a person could eat like a horse and stay slender. But she was vaguely bothered by the fact that Betsy met Ross at the studio. The only contact Betsy had with her father was at impersonal places, like the studio, theatres, or restaurants. So far, she refused to go to the apartment he shared with his girl friend. Ginny sincerely wanted Betsy to continue having a close relationship with Ross. She felt guilty enough about having a failed marriage; she didn't want also to think she had deprived her daughter of a father.

"I'm glad you're back. Maybe you can figure out what I can wear."

"What about that new dress you made, the embroidered white cotton one? That's really neat."

"A little too casual, I'm afraid. I think this is going to be a traditional semiformal affair."

"How boring. I'll bet if Martie was getting married, she'd do something really wild and different."

"She probably would," Ginny responded, smiling wryly.

Betsy liked Martie best of all Ginny's friends; she was the only one whom Betsy called by her first name. Martie talked to Betsy as one intelligent person to another, not as a condescending adult to an immature adolescent. Ginny long ago had made arrangements for Martie to be Betsy's guardian if anything should happen to her and Ross. At first Ross had argued that Martie was too flighty for such a responsibility, but Ginny knew better. Martie looked on Betsy as the daughter she herself would probably never have, and she loved her deeply.

Betsy was looking through Ginny's closet. "What about this one?" she asked, pulling out a sleeveless, emerald-green silk dress.

"Too summery. The sun may be shining on the beach in Malibu, but in Beverly Hills this is still considered a mid-winter wedding."

"Hey, I've got it! Wear my white velvet blazer with it, the one you and Dad got me for Christmas last year. I'll bet you can fit in it, you've dropped a ton lately."

"Thanks. You're really a joy to an aging mother, you know that, kiddo?"

But Betsy was right. The blazer not only looked great with the dress, it actually fit, as long as Ginny didn't try to button it.

While Ginny dressed, Betsy watched her thoughtfully. Finally she asked slowly, "Mom, why didn't you just buy a new dress to wear?"

Ginny knew what Betsy was getting at. She really wanted to know if they were so poor that Ginny couldn't afford to go shopping. Ginny wanted to be honest, without unduly worrying Betsy.

"I didn't want to spend a great deal of money on a dress that I would probably never wear again," she explained casually. Then, looking directly at Betsy, she added quietly, "If you're wondering about our financial situation, it's difficult but not desperate."

"It's not that," Betsy responded, looking away in embarrassment. "It's just that I know you're not working. I mean, you're painting, but . . ." Her voice trailed off.

If my own daughter doesn't take my work seriously, why should anyone else? Ginny thought sadly, stung by Betsy's attitude.

"I'm not just an inexperienced housewife who's dabbling in art, Betsy. I studied it seriously in high school and briefly in college. I was tutored by one of the top artists in Los Angeles, a man who only accepted students with exceptional talent. But when your father and I got married we couldn't afford to continue it. Then later . . . well, later I lost interest." Ginny continued firmly, "I think I can make a living at what I'm truly interested in—painting. At least, I intend to give it my best shot. If it doesn't work out, I'll do something else to support us. Your father and I have never glossed over our financial problems with you. You know there have been times when things have been strained. But I've always managed."

"I know that, I didn't mean anything. I think you're a good painter. Stacey Kaufmann saw that portrait you did of me when I was twelve and she said it was better than the one her parents paid a guy five hundred dollars to do of her."

Ginny smiled, ridiculously elated by the small

compliment. But she sensed that there was something more bothering Betsy, as if their financial situation was only part of what was on her mind.

"Then what's the problem?" Ginny asked bluntly.

"You're *always* busy with your painting," Betsy burst out sullenly. "You used to be here when I needed you, and now you're busy painting."

"I'll always be here when you need me, Betsy," Ginny responded softly, profoundly disturbed by her daughter's accusation. She was thoughtful for a long moment, then continued hesitantly, "I'm sorry if it seems that I'm thinking more about myself than about you nowadays. That really isn't true, you know. In a sense, everything I do is for you. From the moment you were born, I put your welfare above my own. Gladly. But . . ." she searched for the right words to explain to her daughter feelings that she herself was only beginning to understand. "But, you see, right now I'm going through a lot of changes. I'm not a housewife any more, I'm a woman who has to support herself. And I think maybe it's good that I'm being forced to do that, because otherwise I would never find out what I'm really capable of accomplishing. Do you understand?"

Betsy stood there uncomfortably, not looking at her mother. Finally, she answered reluctantly, "Yeah, I guess so. I just wish that everything didn't have to change so much."

"I know. I wish that, too."

Ginny looked at her daughter, realizing for the first time how profoundly affected Betsy was by the upheaval in their lives. She and Ross were deeply hurting the person they each cared most about. And there was nothing she could do to stop it.

The wedding was being held at the home of Joan's parents, the Weiners, in Beverly Hills. A large white colonial-style mansion, it was decorated with comfortable, traditional Early American furniture instead of the priceless antiques or trendy designer pieces that the Weiners could have easily afforded. Ginny had always felt comfortable in that house, and she understood why Joan wanted to be married there. Though it was situated in one of the most exclusive areas of Beverly Hills, it had the ambience of a loving, family-oriented home. Joan's parents doted on their only daughter. Though they were surprised and disappointed by her divorce, they accepted her decision because her happiness mattered most to them. When she told them she intended to remarry, they immediately offered their home for the ceremony.

When Ginny drove up she wasn't surprised to find a valet service parking the dozens of cars that filled the street in front of the Weiners' house. As she had suspected, Joan's "modest" wedding was actually quite lavish.

Inside, the house was filled with fresh flowers and the soothing sound of a string quartet. Guests sipped champagne and nibbled on hors d'oeuvres. Looking around for someone she knew, Ginny was relieved to see Kate standing alone in a corner. Kate saw her at the same time and immediately came over to her.

"I'm glad I decided to change my dress at the last minute," Kate said, grinning. "What I was originally going to wear would have been distinctly out of place. But something told me that Joan would do another lavish production number."

"You know how she is. Joan is a born aristocrat. She loves what money can buy. And she does have extremely good taste."

"I know. Whenever I'm looking for a painting or a piece of furniture for my house, I always take her along. She automatically knows what's best. Although unfortunately it's also usually very expensive."

"How's Scottie?"

"Oh, terrific. My mother's watching him right now, which he loves because she always bakes homemade cookies."

"He's old enough for preschool now. Have you thought about that?"

"Not really," Kate said uneasily. Then, "Anyway, he's very happy staying at home. I think a new place with strangers would frighten him."

"Kate, you can't keep him home forever. Next year he'll be starting school."

"I know, Ginny, but there's plenty of time to think about that."

Ginny stopped herself from saying anything more, though for some time now she had been growing increasingly worried about Kate's relationship with Scottie. She spent most of her time with him and didn't encourage him to make friends his own age. It was as if she wanted her son to take the place of her ex-husband, assuming the role of the "man" in her life. As a mother, Ginny knew how important it is to teach a child to be independent so that eventually he can leave and start a life of his own. Kate wasn't doing that, and Ginny was very much afraid that it might have disastrous consequences for both her and Scottie.

Mr. Weiner came up then, looking proud and happy, and after giving both women a fatherly kiss on the cheek, he told Ginny that Joan wanted to see her for a minute.

"It's so good to see you girls, again," Mr. Weiner continued cheerfully in his slight German accent, as they headed toward Joan's bedroom. "Since Joanie left home, we haven't seen enough of you, Ginny. I remember when the whole house used to ring with the sound of you girls giggling and talking. Both Mrs. Weiner and I have missed that. This is such a silent, empty house with all of our children gone now."

"Today it's very full."

"Oh, yes, and that's very pleasant. We were so happy when Joanie agreed to have the wedding here. Another wedding," he continued, sighing. "Who would have thought, when you were her bridesmaid, that her marriage to Stan would end and she would marry again? Ah well, I know that she wasn't happy, and as I told her, life is too short to spend it being unhappy. Do what you must do to make your life what you wish it to be. After all, we never know what will happen to us in the future."

There was a special poignancy behind his words that Ginny understood. She knew that he had survived a Nazi concentration camp, the only member of his large family who didn't die there. After seeing so much of death, he worshipped life and happiness.

"You know, I'll tell you a secret. We're giving Joanie this house as a wedding present. It's much too large for us now. With her children and stepchildren, she needs the room. And who knows, Alan may want more children, too. He's very much a family man, you know."

"But where will you and Mrs. Weiner live?"

"Oh, there's a house just down the street that is for sale. It's small, just right for my wife and me. And close enough so that we can see our grandchildren frequently."

"That's such a generous gift. Does Joan know yet?"

"No, I'm saving it as a surprise, after the ceremony. But I know I can trust you not to reveal our little secret. Ah, here we are."

They were on the second floor, in front of Joan's bedroom door.

"I'll see you later, Ginny."

He left, and after tapping lightly on the door, Ginny went inside. Joan was sitting at a vanity table, putting the finishing touches to her makeup.

"Oh, Ginny, I'm so glad Dad found you. Have you seen him yet?"

"Who?" Ginny asked, mystified.

"Ross." At Ginny's look of confusion, Joan explained, "I mentioned to you once that he and Alan are friends. Well, Alan insisted that we invite him even though I told him I thought it would be awkward for you. I heard that he was going to be out of town today and wouldn't be able to come, but this morning he called Alan and told him he'd be coming after all. I'm really sorry about this. If you want to leave, I'll certainly understand."

"Don't be ridiculous. Ross and I aren't enemies. I can't say I'm glad he's going to be here, but it's really no big deal." Though Ginny's words sounded brave and sensible, she was actually going through tremendous turmoil inside. She hadn't seen Ross in weeks and had only talked to him briefly on the phone once to clear up a problem that had cropped up in the divorce proceedings. She felt both excited and anxious at the thought of seeing him now.

"But he may bring that *girl* with him," Joan continued worriedly.

"Well, it will certainly be interesting to meet her." *That much is true, anyway*, Ginny told herself ruefully. *At least now I'll know what she looks like. It's been kind of strange to know absolutely nothing at all about the woman who broke up my marriage. No, that's not true, she didn't break it up. She just took advantage of its weakened condition.*

"I must say, I'm relieved you feel that way. I was afraid you'd be really upset. I'm glad you're going to stay. I want you to meet Alan."

"Ginny had the feeling that she already knew everything there was to know about Alan. But she said politely, "I'm looking forward to that. By the way, you look terrific, you know."

In a calf-length fawn-colored velvet dress, with her pale blonde hair pulled back in an elaborate bun laced with thin gold ribbons, Joan looked softly pretty. But there was something missing—that special glow that brides are known for. Joan had it at her first wedding, but it was replaced now by a look of anxious hopefulness.

That's understandable, I guess, Ginny told herself. *Even Joan has given up most of her illusions by now.*

"Well, I'd better let you finish getting ready."

"Oh, I'm ready. I'm just sitting here being nervous." Looking around her bedroom, a pretty, feminine room done in lavender and pale green, Joan continued thoughtfully, "You know, I spent the happiest years of my life here. A lot of people complain about their childhoods, but mine was perfect. My parents constantly let me know how much they loved me. And their relationship with each other was so great, they obviously valued each other so much, that I thought the whole world must be that way. When I married Stan I expected to have the same kind of relationship my parents have. Do you know, Ginny, that every morning of their married life my father has brought my mother a cup of tea to drink in bed before she gets up?"

"Your father's an incredibly nice man."

"Yes. Somehow he and my mother have managed to stay in love with each other for thirty-five years. My father told me once that the secret was never taking each other for granted. He knows what it means to lose people you love, and because of that he never stopped appreciating my mother."

Thinking about this, Ginny realized that she and Ross had stopped appreciating each other long ago. Somehow the love that had seemed so precious when it was new had gradually lost its value.

"Anyway, things didn't work out the same with

Stan. All my life all I wanted was to fall in love and get married. Well, I married a handsome, brilliant attorney and spent ten years being a model wife and mother. Stan seemed quite content to let things gradually grow less exciting, less intimate. By the end, we were each in our own worlds. I was taking care of the kids and doing volunteer work, while he was traveling a lot in his work, spending all his energy trying to achieve a partnership in the firm. The only time we saw each other was occasionally at dinner, and then it was usually a business thing with a client or one of Stan's bosses."

"You always seemed so happy, Joan," Ginny said softly. "When you told us you were getting a divorce we were all flabbergasted. Stan didn't seem like the type to run around, and I knew *you* weren't having an affair. I couldn't imagine what else could break up your marriage."

"I know. Everything seemed fine on the surface. And you're right about Stan—he would never have been unfaithful. I thought about it, though, lots of times. I found myself looking at the young man who services our pool and imagining what it would be like to go to bed with him. He's got a terrific body and a gorgeous tan. When I realized how tempted I was to do something foolish, I decided to talk to Stan. I told him how disappointed I felt with my life, and you know what he said? He said that this is the way life is supposed to be, a lot of hard work, and if you're lucky, a little fun. He said that it was silly of me to think a relationship could stay romantic and exciting."

She finished matter-of-factly, "So I left him. I just

couldn't accept that this was all I had to look forward to the rest of my life."

"I know the feeling."

"Martie and Kate think I've been stupid. But what do you think, Gin?"

"Oh, Joan, I can't tell you how to live your life. Only you know if you truly love Alan, if he's right for you. But I will say one thing. I think your father is right—life is too short to spend it being unhappy. There's *got* to be more than that somehow."

As Joan hugged Ginny tightly, for a moment they were two teenage girls again, sharing hopes and fears, gaining reassurance from each other.

With tears in her eyes, Ginny finished, smiling, "Oh, Joanie, I really admire you. It takes a lot of courage to try for the best, instead of settling for less."

"Well, I just hope I make it," she answered lightly. But there was a worried, desperate look in her hazel eyes that belied her frivolous tone.

Later, back downstairs, Ginny was standing with Kate when Martie arrived.

"You nearly missed the wedding. It's due to start any minute."

"I know. I almost didn't come at all." Martie looked wretched, pale and upset; her clothes seemed barely thrown together.

"What happened?" Ginny asked in spite of herself, though she knew what the problem undoubtedly had been.

"Oh, Michael and I had a fight. The usual thing. I wanted him to come with me today. After all, his family lives in New York, it's not like he'd be flaunting our relationship right in front of his wife. And I get so tired of never doing anything *public* with him."

Ginny was listening only half-heartedly. She had no sympathy for Martie in this situation; and besides, she was busy watching the door for Ross's arrival. Since Joan had told her that he would be there, she had felt a tight knot at the bottom of her stomach, and a tremendous desire to just get the whole thing over with. She badly wanted to get past that first awful moment when she saw him with his girl friend.

"Anyway, I'm sure he's going to be leaving her soon, so why go on being so secretive?"

"If you insist on dating a married man, you have to accept the rules of the game," Kate said bluntly. "And that means, the wife comes first."

Martie was just warming up to an angry reply, when Ginny saw them——Ross and Lisa, standing in the marble foyer. Ross looked uncomfortable and ill at ease. Remembering how much he disliked formal occasions, Ginny wondered what had prompted him to come to Joan's wedding. It was the sort of thing he would gladly pass up at the slightest excuse. But the young woman with him looked supremely confident, as if she couldn't care less what anyone might think of her.

Ginny's first thought was that Lisa Lawrence wasn't what she had expected. The platinum hair and starlet figure were common enough. But she wasn't exceptionally pretty, and somehow Ginny felt disappointed by that. It was easier to think she had been rejected for a beautiful woman than one who was no better looking than she.

"What are you staring at?" Kate asked, interrupting Martie's furious tirade. Turning, she, too, saw Ross and Lisa. "Oh, I see. Did you know they would be here?"

"Yes, Joan told me earlier," Ginny explained, wishing her voice were a little less shaky.

"Well, I think it's pretty tacky of him."

"She isn't even that pretty," Martie added.

Ross, looking around casually, suddenly saw Ginny. He stiffened, then smiled politely. Ginny smiled back, then turned to Martie and began talking animatedly about the wedding. Martie, understanding, chatted easily in return.

Mr. Weiner asked everyone to be seated, as the ceremony was about to begin. Ginny took a seat at the front so that she wouldn't have to stare at Ross's back. But during the entire short ceremony, she was uncomfortably aware that he was somewhere behind her. And next to him was the woman who had made a fool of her in the most humiliating way possible.

While the rabbi was speaking, Martie whispered softly to Ginny, "Alan's just what I expected. Stan all over again."

Ginny said nothing, but she hoped Martie was wrong. For Joan's sake, she hoped Alan had as much love to give as Joan did.

When the ceremony was over, Joan and Alan mingled with their guests. Sitting forlornly in an out-of-the-way corner, Ginny downed glass after glass of champagne.

"You'd better watch it," Martie cautioned her. "You never could handle that stuff."

Ignoring her, Ginny took another glass of champagne off a tray that a maid was carrying past her.

Before Ginny could tell her to mind her own business, she found herself face to face with Ross. When she realized he was alone, she breathed a sigh of relief.

"Hello, Martie, Kate," he said formally.

After muttering polite greetings, they each drifted away, leaving Ginny and Ross alone.

"How are you?" Ross asked softly.

"Fine. And you?"

"Fine." Then, awkwardly, "I wasn't going to come today. Then I decided that was ridiculous. After all, we're still friends."

"That's a very mature attitude," Ginny responded sarcastically.

"I think so," he answered, surprised by the sharpness in her tone.

"I wanted to talk to you about Betsy," he continued, but before he could say more, suddenly Lisa was beside him, smiling broadly.

"Ross, I wondered where you'd got to." She ignored Ginny, whom she clearly didn't recognize.

"Lisa, this is my ex-wife," Ross explained simply, wishing more fervently every minute that he hadn't come to the wedding.

"Oh? Nice to meet you," she said casually, with a cool, superior air that infuriated Ginny.

"Nice to meet you, too—finally," Ginny responded, emphasizing the last word pointedly.

Turning back to Ross, Lisa said firmly, "We'd

better be going, babe, if we're going to catch that plane to San Francisco."

Ginny was stung by the offhand reference to a romantic getaway to San Francisco, a city where Ross and Ginny had gone frequently for brief vacations. Unhappily, she had vivid images of Ross and Lisa doing what he and Ginny had done so often— eating seafood on the wharf, window shopping in Ghirardelli Square, taking the ferry to Sausalito to spend the night on a friend's houseboat. Those had been extremely romantic, intimate times for Ginny and Ross in the early years of their marriage. Remembering them now, she felt herself collapse inside.

"There's plenty of time," Ross answered sharply. Then, to Ginny, "I'll talk to you later about Betsy."

As he walked away with Lisa, Ginny forced herself not to cry.

As soon as she was alone, Martie and Kate came up to her.

"What did he want?" Martie asked eagerly, not bothering to disguise her curiosity.

"Nothing, really."

Accepting another glass of champagne offered by a maid, Ginny drank it down quickly.

"Getting drunk won't help," Kate said firmly.

"It won't hurt," Ginny answered curtly. At that moment all she wanted was to get blind, falling-down drunk. She was about as miserable as she had ever been in her entire life. She had no money, no job, no husband. Her paintings would probably be rejected rudely by every gallery in town. She was a failure in every sense of the word.

She had another glass of champagne.

When Kate had to leave a half-hour later, she told Martie firmly, "Get her home and into a cold shower. And don't leave her. If I'm right, this is going to be her first hangover, and it's going to be a really big one."

"Ginny never did do things halfway," Martie answered, sighing, looking at the sad figure sitting slumped in a corner.

Eventually Martie managed to convince Ginny that they should leave. Outside it was dark, and Ginny stumbled clumsily on the lawn as Martie led her toward her car. Suddenly Ginny stopped and pulled free of Martie, who had been holding her arm to guide her.

"I'm not going anywhere with *you*," Ginny said furiously, slurring her words badly. "You're just like Lisa, breaking up a home. Can't find a man of your own so you take someone else's."

Martie stood absolutely still for a moment. She had a redhead's quick temper and was just barely holding it in check. Telling herself that Ginny was drunk and didn't mean what she was saying, she started to take her arm again. But Ginny pulled away roughly, glaring at Martie.

"You hurt people and you don't care, because all you think about is yourself!"

Martie slapped her full on the face and sent her sprawling on the ground. Ginny lay there, not moving. She had passed out.

Two hours later Ginny, wrapped in a warm robe, sat in front of the fireplace at her house, drinking hot coffee. She had spent a half-hour in a cold shower, then was force-fed coffee by Martie. At one point she roused herself enough to protest weakly, "But I *hate* coffee."

"I know," Martie responded blithely, handing her another steaming cup.

Martie had sent Betsy to bed, telling her frankly, "Your mother has just done what most of us did when we were sixteen. She's gotten dead drunk. She'll be horribly embarrassed tomorrow and it will help if she thinks you didn't see her this way."

Now Ginny was beginning to think clearly again, to feel that she might perhaps live, after all. Looking at Martie through glazed eyes, she said slowly, "I feel awful."

"You *should*. You drank enough champagne to launch a battleship."

"I can't remember an awful lot."

"Good. There's nothing much worth remembering."

"But I think I said some terrible things to you."

"Forget it," Martie said coolly. But she hadn't forgiven Ginny, and Ginny knew it.

"I can't forget it. I hurt you deeply and I'm sorry. My only excuse is that I was so miserable I didn't even care what I was doing."

"Was it seeing Ross and Lisa together that did it?" Martie asked, more sympathetically.

"That was part of it. Actually meeting her somehow made the whole thing more real. In a way, I think, I've been living in a dream world, not facing up to reality. I was going through a divorce but I didn't really feel like I was going through one. Deep

71

down inside, I kept hoping the whole thing would turn out to be a nightmare that would end. Ross would come back, and I would be safe and secure again. The stupid thing is, I don't want him back, at least not if things have to be the way they were. Today I finally accepted the fact that he's involved with someone else and I've got to get on with my life. But, Martie, that's so *scary*."

"I know, Gin. I felt the same way when Ed left. I had a job and was beginning to make terrific money. I knew I could support myself. Yet I was terrified when he left. For weeks I refused to do things he and I had done together, like going to movies and restaurants, because I couldn't face doing them alone. But you know, when I finally accepted the fact that he wasn't coming back—when I actually cleaned out his half of the closet and mailed him the things he had left—it all became easier. I knew then what I had to do and I did it. And it does get easier as time goes by."

"But it's not just Ross. I'm thirty-three years old and I'm starting a career that most people start when they're eighteen or twenty. I don't know if I can do it or not. I sit on the beach, trying to remember everything I learned so long ago, then when I actually put something on the canvas I just stare at it, wondering if it's any good."

"Would you like a job at my agency? It would solve your financial problems."

"No. I started out to be a painter a long time ago and that's what I'm going to do, if it kills me." She glared at Martie. "Look, I'm no fool. I don't expect the world to beat a path to my door at first. And I know it's going to hurt like hell when I get rejected. But I'm going to try."

"Now *that* sounds more like the old Ginny. You're a strong person, a lot stronger than you give yourself credit for."

"Oh, sure, a strong woman. But not a very sexy one."

"What do you mean? You look sexier than you ever have in your life!"

"I *look* sexy, but I sure don't feel it. Even if I get over Ross, even if I sell my paintings, there's still another problem. I don't feel like a woman, like a sexually fulfilled woman, anyway."

"You just need to get involved with someone else. The right man will change all that. Ginny, I *know* how important that is. Why do you think I'm so hung up on Michael? Earlier you accused me of being a homewrecker, of not caring who I hurt. But that isn't true. I feel guilty as hell about his wife and children. But I *love* him. He completes me in a way that no one else does. I *can't* give that up."

"We're all the same, I guess," Ginny said quietly. "You, me, Joan, Kate. We all need the right man to complete us. No matter what else we have in our lives, whether it's children or a career, it still gets down to that."

"Unfortunately, I suspect that women and men were meant to be together," Martie agreed. "But I must say, from my own personal experience I think it's a rotten system!"

6.

Ross sat in a lounge chair by the pool at Hugh
Hefner's Playboy Mansion West, wondering what
the hell he was doing there. The house, a beautiful
old Gothic-Tudor chateau, and the grounds, acres
of rolling, well-tended lawn and gardens, were filled
with the Beautiful People of L.A. Actors, politi-
cians, writers, and bunnies mingled happily, taking
advantage of the delicious food and expensive liquor. Some lounged in the large, pillow-strewn living
room; others swam in the rock pool, disappearing
into the stone grotto jacuzzi where they bathed in
the nude. Lisa was in the grotto now, having a wonderful time.

But this wasn't Ross's idea of a good time. He disliked the people and the superficial atmosphere that
was titillating in an almost childish way. Ross's
strength lay in his total commitment to his art and
his almost inexhaustible creative energy. When he
found himself among others who did not give themselves over as completely as he did, he was generally
bored and restless. As he was now.

The thing he admired most about Lisa was her
commitment to her career. She was a serious actress.

But she was also part of the New Hollywood. She did a little too much cocaine for his taste, talked a lot about guarding her "space," and thoroughly enjoyed the whole counterculture scene.

Ross was rapidly coming to the conclusion that the only time he enjoyed being with Lisa was when they were alone and there were no distractions to point up the serious age difference between them. He was twenty years older than she was, with a sense of morality and a preference for a lifestyle that was a generation behind hers. The sense of sheer fun he had originally experienced with her was no longer enough to make up for the other things that were missing in their relationship. More and more, Ross found himself thinking of Ginny. They had been so *right* for each other, yet at the end their marriage had been unsatisfying. He had rationalized that it was inevitable that he and Ginny would grow bored with each other after so many years. But sometimes now he wondered if it might have been possible, somehow, to stop that boredom, to rekindle the flame that had burned so fiercely once.

There was still something between them. For the hundredth time, he asked himself if perhaps the divorce had been too hasty.

Suddenly Lisa swam up to the edge of the pool near Ross's chair, splashing him playfully.

"Hey, come on in, it's really warm."

"No, thanks. Listen, I've got to get back to the office to do some more work on that script. We start shooting pretty soon."

"Oh, Ross, you can take one night off. All you ever want to do is work." She pouted prettily, and for a moment he was tempted to stay after all. But he changed his mind when she added playfully, "The people in the grotto are all taking off their swimsuits. Things are getting lively."

"Sounds terrific," he responded tightly. "I've got to get some work done. I'll leave some money in your purse for a cab. See you later."

She glared at him as he walked off, then, shrugging, swam back to the grotto.

Ginny sat on a towel on the beach, a small canvas stretched out before her on a short easel. Her brief shorts and halter top showed off the deep tan she had gotten from spending so much time outside. With her long hair pulled back in a simple pony tail, she could have passed for one of the teenagers who spent their entire summers on the beach in Malibu.

Painting at night was difficult, but Ginny enjoyed it immensely. The ocean was completely different, much more mysterious and interesting than during the day.

She was concentrating intently, trying to catch the light just right. Moonlight was tricky, and so far she was frustrated and unsatisfied with her efforts to capture it. One thing that didn't help was the noise coming from a house down the beach. Tall, stark, made of redwood and lots of stained glass, it reportedly had just been bought by a famous actor. Ginny didn't care who lived there; she simply wished he would throw quieter parties.

The music and the hysterical laughter finally got to her. Sighing, she put down her palette and lay back on the towel, staring up at the moon. *Oh, to be young again*, she thought, *with all of the confidence of the inexperienced. Then trying to paint moonlight would be an interesting challenge, not an exercise in futility.*

"I wish I was eighteen again," she said softly.

"Why? You don't exactly look over the hill right now."

Sitting up quickly, she saw a man standing nearby. The waves breaking on the beach had drowned the sound of his footsteps. Dressed in slacks and a turtleneck sweater, his face covered with a thick dark beard, he looked like he was probably one of the guests at the actor's party down the beach.

After sitting down on the sand near her, he asked, almost as an afterthought, "Mind if I join you?"

"Actually, I was just getting ready to leave," Ginny said coolly. The last thing she wanted right now was to have a difficult painting interrupted by a man who was undoubtedly looking for someone to pick up.

"It didn't look that way. It looked like you were contemplating the moonlight."

"I was *working*," Ginny answered pointedly.

"You must have a very interesting job if it requires you to lie on the beach, looking terribly romantic."

His voice was deep, self-assured. Somehow it sounded familiar, but Ginny couldn't remember where she had heard it before.

"I'm an artist," she explained, proud of the definite way she said it. Usually, she sounded unsure of herself, as if she wasn't *really* an artist.

"Oh?" He sounded genuinely interested, but Ginny was in no mood to talk. She began to gather up her things.

"Hey, you're not really leaving are you?"

"What does it look like?"

"You mean you're going to leave me alone out here, with nothing to do?" His tone was playful, appealing.

"What were you doing before you interrupted me?"

"I was being bored to death at that God-awful party down the beach."

She smiled slightly. "I'm sorry, but I'm really just not in a mood to talk. Good night."

As she turned, heading toward her house, he called after her, "Don't worry about the painting. It's going to be great."

She hesitated for a moment, then walked on. But she was secretly pleased.

The next morning Ginny awoke with a sense of purpose. This was the day she had arbitrarily chosen to start trying to sell her work. She still had enough money to get by for a month or two, but she didn't want to wait until the last minute. If she wasn't going to make it as a painter, she would need time to look for a job.

Unusually nervous, she found herself worrying ridiculously over what to wear. She didn't want to walk into a gallery looking like an amateur but she had no idea what a professional artist should look like. After trying on nearly everything in her closet, she finally said, "Oh, the hell with it," and put on a simple white linen skirt and peach-colored silk blouse. It was what she often wore when she went browsing through the galleries in Beverly Hills.

Parking her car on La Cienega Boulevard, a broad street lined with art galleries, she tucked her portfolio under her arm and began canvassing the street. At the first gallery they refused to even look at her work. At the second they suggested she make an appointment to see the manager. Finally, at the third they agreed reluctantly to see what she had done. The manager, a thin, middle-aged man, quickly went through her work.

"Very interesting," he commented in a tone that indicated he was totally bored but humoring her because she appeared to be well-off. "But I'm afraid we aren't interested in this sort of thing."

"Why not?" Ginny asked firmly, determined to at least get some idea why she was being rejected.

"We only deal with the most modern, avant-garde art. Abstract expressionism, pop art, that sort of thing. Your little pictures"—Ginny winced at the denigrating term—"are *nice* but just not our sort of thing."

"Thank you," Ginny said politely, gathering up her paintings. She was too angry at that point to cry, but by the end of the day, when she had been to dozens of galleries and had received more or less the same response at each, she was on the verge of tears. Everyone who condescended to look at her work said the same thing—she had talent but her work was dated, behind the times.

Finding herself near Martie's agency, she stopped by. She was in dire need of a reassuring pep talk.

Martie was with one of the biggest agencies in Hollywood, Latham-Reynolds-Newbrough. Though she was one of their younger agents, she was rapidly becoming one of the best. Enthusiastic and determined, she worked hard for her clients, who were often newcomers to the business. She was developing a reputation as someone who was very good at finding talented new writers and actors.

The walls of her small office were crowded with paintings that Ginny had given her.

"What a nice surprise," Martie said happily when Ginny walked in. "What brings you here?"

"I actually went out and tried to sell some of my stuff today," Ginny explained glumly.

"Uh-oh. It doesn't sound like it went too well."

"That's an understatement. It was a *disaster*. The general consensus among Beverly Hills art experts is that I'm old fashioned."

"What do you mean, 'old-fashioned'? Just because a person can look at your paintings and actually tell what they're about . . ."

"Oh, Martie, it's *hopeless*. I've just been kidding myself all these months, thinking I had some real talent, that I could actually make a living at it. These people know what they're talking about. They know who will make it and who won't."

"Stop that! This 'poor-me' stuff isn't like you at all, Gin. You're usually the one giving the pep talk."

"Well, having two dozen people turn me down directly, and another dozen or so refuse to even look at my work, has changed my thinking. I'm going to have to become pragmatic now and start looking for a real job."

"Listen, at least wait for a day or two. Give yourself a chance to get over this blow. Clearly today was bad, but don't give up your dream because of one day. For as long as I can remember you've wanted to be an artist. Remember when we were kids and you drew pretend wardrobes for us?"

"Yeah. That was fun." Then, "Right! No reason to panic simply because the entire Beverly Hills art establishment thinks I should burn my easel."

"Absolutely. Now you're beginning to sound more like your old self."

"Well, my old self may shortly be a saleslady at Magnin's."

"Not yet."

Ginny left feeling slightly better. But deep inside her confidence was still profoundly shaken.

As she was driving up the long, narrow, winding Pacific Coast Highway that ran parallel to the ocean, she noticed a new art gallery that had opened recently. She had meant to look through it many times, but had been too busy getting her portfolio together. *What the hell,* she told herself. *I might as well stop. I've been rejected by experts today; these people can't be any worse.*

The gallery was small but impressive, with a casual, comfortable atmosphere that invited people to browse and enjoy the paintings. Somehow it didn't seem as high-pressured as the more formal galleries Ginny had been in all day. Clutching her portfolio determinedly, she walked up to an elderly man in a business suit who sat at a desk in the rear. When he saw her, he rose immediately, smiling pleasantly.

"I am Maurice Moreau. May I help you?" he asked in a thick French accent.

"Yes. My name is Virginia Carlson, I'm an artist, and I have some paintings I'd like to show you." Ginny said the whole thing so quickly, in one breath, that the man seemed rather taken aback.

"Of course. I'd be happy to look at your work."

"You would?" In spite of her resolve to be businesslike and firm, Ginny's voice betrayed her anxiety.

"Please sit down." He motioned to a chair near the desk, where Ginny sat down gratefully.

After carefully removing her paintings from the portfolio, he looked at them slowly, examining them as closely as if they were newly discovered works by a great master. Sitting on the edge of her seat, leaning slightly forward, Ginny stared at him nervously.

"Ah, American romanticism. I haven't seen work quite like this in some time," he said casually. Ginny felt her heart sink to her stomach. He was about to tell her she was old-fashioned. Then he surprised her by asking, "Why did you do these particular paintings in just this way?"

No one had questioned Ginny's motivation as an artist in a long time. She answered defensively, "I love the ocean and I love children. The two together especially appeal to me."

When he didn't respond, Ginny assumed the worst. She started to gather up her paintings. "Thank you for your time."

"But one moment, madame."

Ginny stopped, perplexed. What could he possibly want?

"I like your paintings very much. If you agree, I would like to represent you."

"You would?" Ginny didn't even bother to pretend to be reserved. She was simply overwhelmed.

"Yes, I would. In fact, I would like to keep all of these and put them up for sale immediately. I'll have a standard contract drawn up. Could you return day after tomorrow to sign it?"

"Oh, *yes*. I . . . I . . ." Ginny burst into tears. And though she was horribly embarrassed, she couldn't stop.

The man smiled indulgently. Reaching into his pocket, he pulled out a handkerchief and handed it to Ginny.

"It is allowed to cry for happiness, madame. Do not be ashamed. Tell me, have your paintings been turned down before?"

"*Have* they!" Briefly, she told him about her day in Beverly Hills.

"Ah, I see. That is rather a different milieu, if I may say so. They have their own ideas about art, their own clientele. My ideas are quite simple. I like paintings that make me feel good about life. Your paintings, madame, make me feel very good. My patrons are the same. Though I hesitate to speak prematurely, I must say I think they will like your work as much as I do. There is beginning to be quite a market for American romanticism."

"Then you think they will sell?"

"Of course. I am enough of a businessman not to take on work that I think will languish in my gallery. For now I think we should price your work modestly, say two hundred and fifty dollars for the smaller ones and three hundred and fifty for the larger ones. If they sell quickly, as I expect, then we shall raise the prices. In the meantime, I would advise you to work hard. By next month I expect to buy more from you."

"Oh, Mr. Moreau, I'm *so* grateful."

He raised a hand in protest. "Do not be grateful to me, madame. It is you who possesses the talent. I am merely in the privileged position of making a profit from it."

"Well, I'm still very grateful. Thank you." She kissed him warmly on the cheek.

"I must say, madame, that is the nicest way of consummating a deal that I have experienced in a long time."

After parking her car in the garage, Ginny rushed into the house to tell Betsy the good news. But Betsy was gone, and a brief note explained simply, "I'm having dinner with Dad, will be home early." Ginny was intensely disappointed. She was bursting with happiness but there was no one to share it with. She was especially anxious to reassure Betsy that everything would probably be all right now, that there was no longer any need to worry about money. She considered calling Ross and speaking to Betsy there. It would be a good way to let Ross know of her success, without telling him directly herself. She was sure that Betsy would immediately tell her father the good news. But before she could come to a decision, the phone rang.

"Ginny?" It was Martie and she sounded excited.

"Where on earth have you been? I've been trying to reach you for half an hour!"

"I was at a gallery . . ." Ginny began, but before she could finish, Martie continued eagerly, "You'll never believe it, you'll just never believe it! Not five minutes after you left, Dan Demaris came into my office." Dan Demaris, Ginny knew, was an actor only slightly less successful than Burt Reynolds and even more attractive. But at this particular moment she wasn't interested in Martie's inside gossip.

"That's nice, Martie, but . . ."

"You don't understand. I'm not excited because I met him although he *is* incredibly sexy. I'm excited because of *you*."

"Me? What do I have to do with him?"

"He saw your paintings and liked them, especially the portrait of Scottie. The movie he's doing right now has a scene where there's a giant, full-sized portrait of him, and he's been looking around for an artist to do it. He wants something really good, that he can keep in his house. And he wants you to do it!"

"*What?*" Ginny was, if possible, even more stunned than she had been when Mr. Moreau offered to show her paintings.

"That's what I've been trying to tell you. You've just got your first commission! And I'm sure it's going to be huge. The studio will pay for it and if you let me handle it, I think I can get you at least two or three thousand. What do you think?"

"I'm not capable of thinking."

"Well, don't worry about it. Let me do the thinking, that's what an agent's for. Listen, I've got to call Dan and tell him you'll do it. And then I've got to call the studio and start negotiating your fee. That won't take long, because Dan wants you to start immediately. They need the picture in about a month. Oh, by the way, what was your big news?"

"Nothing much," Ginny answered casually. "A gallery here in Malibu just agreed to show all of my work."

"Why didn't you tell me?" Martie said unreasonably, forgetting that she hadn't let Ginny get a word in edgeways during the whole conversation. "That changes everything. Now when I negotiate, I can tell them you're an established artist whose work is being shown at an exclusive gallery. That means even more money. Listen, I've go to get on this right away. Don't make any plans for Saturday night. I'm taking you and Betsy out to dinner to celebrate. Bye."

If Ginny had been happy before, she was ecstatic now. A gallery was showing her work, she had her first commission (and a big one), and she had an agent. "I'm an artist," she said softly, to herself. Then, shouting to the empty house, "I'm an *artist!*"

She definitely couldn't wait to talk to Betsy now, and she quickly dialed the number of Ross's office. He answered the phone himself.

"Ross, it's Ginny. Is Betsy there yet?"

"No. Is she coming?"

Confused, Ginny asked hesitantly, "Isn't she having dinner with you tonight?"

"No. In fact, I've been wanting to talk to you

about that. I haven't seen her in three weeks. Every time I talk to her she seems to be busy."

"Didn't you have lunch with her last week?"

"No. Why?"

"She was gone for awhile, and when I asked where she had been she said she was having lunch with you." Ginny's happiness and excitement were totally gone now, replaced by a growing sense of concern about her daughter. She had always trusted Betsy completely, and Betsy had lived up to that trust. There was none of the lying and dangerous stunts that other parents of teenagers had to put up with. Until now.

"Apparently we have a problem on our hands," Ross said. "I'd better come over so that we can both talk to her when she gets home."

"Yes."

As Ginny hung up the phone, she felt immensely relieved that Ross was willing to share the responsibility for dealing with this disturbing new problem. She made some tea, then took it into the living room, where she curled up in a chair. What should have been one of the happiest days of her life had suddenly turned into a depressing and frightening nightmare. Why had Betsy lied? Where had she really been when she was supposed to have been with Ross? Ginny's overactive imagination conjured up the worst possible images—Betsy taking drugs, Betsy with a boy too immature to even think of birth control.

And in all of it, Ginny kept thinking that it was she and Ross who were to blame. Betsy had been a happy, healthy, well-adjusted girl before her parents' divorce. Now, Ginny knew, she was moody and depressed, no longer able to confide in either parent. She had become a liar. What else had she become?

When Betsy finally came in two hours later, she was surprised to find both parents waiting for her, their faces grim. Realizing immediately that her lie hadn't worked, she began simply, "I guess you're both wondering where I've been."

"Yes. And not just tonight," Ross answered firmly. "I understand this isn't the first time this has happened."

"I wasn't doing anything wrong," Betsy insisted anxiously.

"Then why did you lie to me and tell me you were with your father? And why have you been lying to him?" Ginny asked, hating this whole inquisition but knowing it couldn't be avoided.

"I . . . I had things to do. It just seemed simpler to tell you I was with Dad. I knew you wouldn't worry then."

"Telling your mother the truth would have worried her a hell of a lot less than lying has done. Now what have you been up to, Betsy?"

"What business is it of yours?" she asked angrily. "You aren't even around here any more. You're busy with your teeny-bopper girl friend!"

"Betsy!" Ginny was amazed at this uncharacteristic outburst.

"Well, you can do whatever you want to me, I'm not going to tell you anything!" Betsy yelled hysterically, then ran sobbing to her room.

Stunned, both Ross and Ginny sat silently for a

long moment. Neither had ever seen their daughter this way before.

"Well, I've certainly been a big help tonight," Ross said sarcastically. Never in his life had he felt more impotent, more like a failure. The little girl he adored resented him bitterly, perhaps even hated him. And not without reason. He realized that he had a great deal to think about.

"I'll talk to you later, Ginny," he said absently, then left.

Ginny, as profoundly disturbed as Ross, sat in the chair for a long time, thinking. Her tea grew cold, and to her surprise she realized she was hungry. She knew that Betsy, too, was probably ravenous. She fixed two thick peanut butter and jelly sandwiches and poured two tall glasses of ice-cold milk, then took them on a tray to Betsy's room.

Betsy lay sprawled on her bed, her hair a mess and her eyes red from crying. She looked, Ginny thought lovingly, as miserable as she had when her first puppy died. Now, as then, she wore a look of utter dejection and hopelessness, as if nothing in the world could ever again be good.

Ginny set down the tray on the nightstand, then handed a sandwich to Betsy. Accepting it gratefully, Betsy began eating. For a couple of minutes, they both ate in silence. When Betsy drained her own glass of milk, Ginny offered her some of hers. Finally, Ginny asked slowly, "Do you want to talk about it now?"

"Mom, I can't. Believe me, I just can't."

"I see. You know, you hurt your father very deeply tonight."

Ashamed, Betsy looked down, absently picking at her sandwich. "I know. I'm sorry."

"I think you should tell him that."

"Yeah. I will." Then, "I promise."

"I got a job today."

"You did?" Betsy was genuinely excited, and Ginny felt some of her own excitement coming back.

"A commission to paint a portrait of the actor, Dan Demaris. And that gallery on Malibu Canyon Road has agreed to show some of my paintings."

"Oh, Mom, that's terrific!" Betsy seemed really proud of Ginny. She added thoughtfully, "I'm sorry I messed up your big day."

"I'm sorry, too. Are you sure you don't want to talk to me about it?"

"I can't," Betsy repeated listlessly.

"Okay. If you change your mind, let me know. In the meantime, from now on when you're supposed to see your father he will pick you up here and bring you back again. And you're grounded for a month. No movies, no dates. Your friends can come over here, but you can't go to their houses. Understand?"

"Yeah."

The fact that Betsy didn't even protest bothered Ginny. Whatever was going on must be even more serious than she had feared.

7.

Two days later a jubilant Martie completed negotiations for Ginny's fee.

"It's three thousand," she told Ginny proudly.

"Dollars?" Ginny asked, stunned. Overnight, she had gone from being a starving artist to an extremely successful one.

"It's not rubles. I must admit the studio was very reluctant to pay that kind of money to an artist no one has heard of, but fortunately Demaris insisted he wants you and no one else. So we had them over a barrel. By the way, here's his address. He wants to see you right away."

When Ginny heard the address, she was surprised to find that it was the new redwood house just down the beach from her own house. *Well, I won't complain about his parties any more,* she thought wryly.

As she stood in front of his door an hour later, loaded down with her easel and other painting paraphernalia, she wondered what he would be like. She knew very little about him. Uninterested in the type of movies he did, she had seen only one or two. And since she couldn't care less about the Hollywood social scene, she was basically ignorant of his highly touted love life. Occasionally she saw his picture on the covers of various magazines, and from the cover blurbs she got the idea that he was quite a ladies' man.

Even now, as she was about to meet one of the biggest male sex symbols in the country, she still didn't care about him as a person. She wondered only what he would be like as a subject; whether he would be difficult to work with, if his undoubtedly huge ego would present problems. The more Ginny thought about it, the firmer became her resolve to let him know that she was the artist and he was the subject. She simply wouldn't stand for any unreasonable demands on his part . . .

And then the door opened . . .

Ginny had expected a servant to answer, but it was Demaris himself who greeted her. Dressed in tennis shorts and a T-shirt, he had obviously just come off the courts. His black hair, still slightly damp from perspiration, curled around his forehead and ears, one lock falling rakishly over his deep brown eyes. His look was friendly, casual, slightly amused, as if he was constantly laughing at some private joke. Ginny had the odd feeling that she had met him before, but she decided that the sense of familiarity must be simply from seeing him in movies.

"I'm Virginia Carlson, the artist the studio hired," she began formally, but he cut her off abruptly.

"My moon nymph! You know, when I came back to the party that night and told everyone I had been talking to a beautiful moon nymph, they thought I was high on something. I began to doubt it myself later. It's nice to see you're for real."

Intensely embarrassed, Ginny realized where she had seen him before. "But you had a beard," she protested.

"Yeah, I grow one sometimes when I'm between pictures. Nobody recognizes me in a beard. That way I can actually live like a halfway normal person for awhile. Well, come on in."

He led her through the red-tiled entryway into a large living room with floor-to-ceiling windows overlooking the ocean. Ginny had somehow expected a movie star's home to be more opulent. Demaris had chosen simple, functional furniture in leather and brown corduroy, with heavy wood tables scattered around the room. It was very straightforward and masculine, just like Demaris himself. There were no feminine touches to indicate that women spent more than fleeting moments here. The only clues that revealed an actor lived here were framed photographs of Demaris with many of the top movie stars and an untidy pile of scripts on a table.

Ginny was especially interested in his taste in art, which she was surprised to find was much like hers. He had few paintings, but they were all in the category of primitive, or naive, art. She could see why he liked her work enough to have chosen her to paint his portrait.

"There's plenty of light in here," he continued easily. "I thought we could work here, if it's okay with you."

He was polite and deferential, and Ginny realized

with relief that he would be easy to work with—if she could get over the awkwardness she felt due to their first meeting.

"I, uh, I want to apologize if I seemed rather rude that night," she began slowly.

"Forget it. You were working and I interrupted you. I hate it when someone does that to me. Though the critics think what I do is easy, it isn't. And I get really mad when someone blows my concentration. I'm sorry I bothered you, but I was a little crazy from that stupid party. It was my publicist's idea, and I was bored to death with the people he invited. When I saw a beautiful, interesting woman to talk to, I couldn't resist."

That was the second time he had called her beautiful, and Ginny's head was beginning to spin. Suddenly, unexpectedly, she was beginning to understand Dan Demaris's appeal—the rugged masculinity, the disarming openness, the seemingly sincere compliments. He made her feel like a woman, a highly desirable one. *Is every other woman he meets as easily charmed as I've been?* Ginny wondered, a little angry with herself for being so gullible.

"If you don't mind, I'd like to get to work immediately," she said, trying to sound businesslike. "I don't really have much time to finish this."

"Sure. Just tell me what to do."

"I'll do some preliminary sketches first. Do you have the clothes the studio wants you to wear in the portrait?"

"Clothes?" he asked, surprised.

"Yes. You'll have to wear the same outfit they want you to wear in the painting."

"I think there's been a lack of communication here," he began, his eyes twinkling merrily. "You see, I don't wear any clothes in the painting."

"What?"

"I guess they didn't tell you. This is supposed to be a life-sized portrait of me *nude*."

Ginny stood tranfixed for a moment. Then, trying not to appear flustered, she responded slowly, "You mean, you don't wear *anything*?"

"Not a stitch," he answered, clearly amused. Then he explained, "In the movie I play a guy who's a nude centerfold. And in one scene there's supposed to be a nude portrait of me hanging in the magazine editor's office."

"I see."

"Have you done many nude studies?"

"Well . . . no."

"But the picture I saw in your friend's office that impressed me so much was a nude male."

"Yes, but that nude male was two years old."

"Well, the only difference is that I'm forty years older and about four feet taller."

"Somehow, I don't think that's the only difference," Ginny responded, smiling in spite of her awkwardness.

"Don't worry about it," he said slyly. "While you're painting me, just pretend I'm that little boy. All you have to do is make everything slightly larger."

Deciding that the conversation was quickly getting out of hand, Ginny said matter-of-factly, "Well, we'd better begin before we lose the light. Why don't you, uh, get undressed and put on a robe, and then we'll try some poses."

"Okay. I'll be right back."

Ginny quickly set up her easel and drawing paper, all the while reassuring herself that this was still just a job like any other. She decided to pretend that she was back in her drawing class in college, drawing nude models who were too bored and professional to be seductive.

When Demaris came back a moment later, wearing a brown terrycloth robe, Ginny began curtly, "Please sit over there, Mr. Demaris."

"Don't you think you should call me Dan? After all, we're going to be seeing a great deal of each other."

"Very well, Dan . . ."

"And what do they call you? Somehow you don't look like a Virginia."

"Ginny."

"That's very pretty. Okay, Ginny, I'm putting myself completely in your talented hands. Just tell me what you want."

If his deep brown eyes continued to look at her in that bold, playful way, and if his conversation continued to be filled with sexy double entendres, Ginny knew she would have a hard time concentrating.

"If you don't mind, I work better in absolute silence."

"Sure."

He didn't say another word, but he continued to watch her carefully, as if he was intensely interested in her.

After asking him to try different poses, Ginny decided on one that she thought would work. Still trying to sound professional, she said coolly, "Please take off your robe now."

He slipped out of it quickly, unself-consciously, without saying a word. Immediately, Ginny began sketching him.

He had a marvelous body, long and lean and dark. His chest was broad, covered with a thick mat of black hair, his hips slim, and his thighs muscled and sinewy.

As Ginny stared intently at him, carefully noting every plane and angle, trying to transfer them accurately onto paper, both the artist and the woman in her began to merge. The artist admired his body as a thing of beauty, while the woman saw it as an object of desire and pleasure. His face, handsome, hard, yet beguilingly soft at times; his shoulders, strong, well-muscled; his torso, with the classic lines of the young David; his hands, large yet somehow elegant, with long, graceful fingers that looked as if they could play an instrument—including a woman's body—well; and his legs, strong enough to carry him swiftly to her if he chose . . .

The figure on the paper was coming to life now, a man whom the artist had invested with an aura of sensuous appeal. As always, Ginny was falling in love just a little bit with her creation. She examined the drawing in every minute detail, her eyes flitting quickly back and forth from Dan to his likeness. The drawing was a part of her; in a sense, *he* was a part of her. They were joined now, artist and subject, almost as intimately as a man and a woman join together.

For an hour she had worked in absolute silence. She had said nothing, while Dan watched her with growing interest. But in the silence there was a growing tension between them, building toward a climax.

Ginny sighed deeply and laid down her pencil, closing her strained eyes for a moment. The light was gone and she was too tired to concentrate any longer.

"May I leave this here?" she asked.

He nodded silently.

As she turned to leave, he said quietly, "I'll see you tomorrow, Ginny."

"Of course," she answered, a little breathlessly, then hurried away like a frightened animal fleeing a predator.

That evening Ginny cooked Betsy's favorite dinner, lasagne and garlic toast, throwing herself wholeheartedly into the elaborate preparations as if she was commencing a painting. She was still filled with the same disturbing feelings that had come over her so unexpectedly at Dan's house. And try as she would, she couldn't make them go away. Trying to keep her mind on the food and on Betsy, she ate ravenously and talked animatedly. But Betsy was strangely quiet and uncommunicative, and the entire effort was a failure.

When Ginny reluctantly went to bed that night, she was plagued with a sense of fear and yet at the same time felt a thrill of anticipation.

The next day she purposefully wore her dullest,

least attractive clothes, and maintained an icy reserve as she began to draw Dan. But, as usual, her artistic drive took over, and gradually she began to concentrate intently on the work. Once more, she was caught up passionately into transferring Dan to paper, capturing the heavy, masculine lines of his body, the aura of unabashed maleness. When she finally finished, she felt drained, weak, almost passive, as if all of her energy had been invested in the figure on the paper. Sighing deeply, she laid down the pencil.

Dan rose and walked over to her without bothering to put on his robe. Looking at the drawing, he smiled, pleased. Then, turning to her, he said huskily, "You've captured me. Now I'll return the compliment."

Picking her up easily, as if she weighed no more than a rag doll, he carried her up the stairs, unprotesting.

His bedroom was huge, running nearly the entire length of the second floor. A giant aquarium filled with breathtakingly beautiful tropical fish divided the room in half. On one side was a sitting room with a desk, sofa, and fireplace. On the other side was a king-sized bed on a raised dais. Two steps led up to the bed, and above it on the ceiling were mirrors.

Mounting the steps, he laid her down gently on the velvet bedspread, his brown eyes scanning her face intently for a brief moment.

"You don't have to do this, you know," he reassured her candidly. "It's not part of the deal."

"I know," she whispered.

He began to undress her then, his fingers working slowly, carefully, as if she were a precious package that was a joy to unwrap. When she was naked, he lay down beside her. They looked at each other, knowing that the fierce attraction that was dominating them now was a rare and special thing. Neither wanted to rush it, both wanted to savor the moment, the delicious anticipation. He kissed her gently, and then, unable to wait any longer, he took her in his arms, nearly crushing her in his powerful embrace. She shivered as he kissed her lips, then his mouth travelled over her entire body, waking it from a long, deep sleep, leaving nothing untouched. For the first time in a very long while, the deep hunger that she had tried to deny was satisfied. He took her passionately, and they both trembled as they came together.

The restlessness that had tormented her was gone. Now there was only a deep peace . . .

When Ginny got home, she took a quick shower; then, wrapped in a giant towel, her hair hanging limply against her back, she sat down in the living room, staring out at the ocean. It was night now; only minutes earlier she had left Dan sleeping peacefully in his bed, unaware that she had slipped away. She couldn't face him somehow. She wasn't sure she could face herself. She was simply relieved that Betsy was with Ross, because she badly needed some time to think. She had just done something she thought herself incapable of—having sex with a man she had known only a short time, whom she didn't love and could never expect to have any kind of meaningful relationship with. The feeling of incredible satisfaction only barely outweighed her sense of shame. The worst of it all was her conviction that as far as Dan was concerned, she was only the latest in a long line of easy conquests.

And yet, despite her deep misgivings, she couldn't help feeling a tremendous sense of relief. She had just learned two important things—she wasn't frigid, and sex could still be as exciting and passionate as it had been when she was a newlywed.

As Ginny was mentally stacking up the pluses against the minuses, there was a firm, almost angry knock at the door. Forgetting that she was wearing only a towel, she went to the door and opened it.

It was Dan.

"You might, at least, have said good-bye," he began furiously. "Or do you always treat your lovers so casually?"

"Me? I've never done anything like that before in my life! I thought . . . I thought you got what you wanted and would be quite happy to have me simply disappear."

He let out a deep sigh of relief. "I was hoping it was that, just my stupid reputation again."

Taking her by the shoulders, he pulled her to him, looking directly into her eyes. "Listen carefully, Ginny. I don't automatically go to bed with every woman I meet. I thought you were very unusual, very special. When you wanted me as much as I wanted you, I knew that really meant something. So from now on, let's try talking to each other, okay? That will prevent these stupid misunderstandings."

"From now on? You mean . . ." Ginny didn't quite know what to say.

"I mean, I'd like to get to know you a great deal better. Now, I don't know about you but I'm starved. How about some broiled lobster dripping in butter?"

An hour later they had finished a delicious dinner. Ginny couldn't remember when she had enjoyed food more. Her appetite was tremendous, as if she had been half-starving herself for months. Now, as she lingered over dessert, she felt completely satisfied, in every way. She knew she would sleep very well indeed that night.

"I know about Ginny Carlson, the artist," Dan began quietly. "Your work reflects a deep joy in life, a very healthy, positive outlook. But what about Ginny Carlson, the woman? I noticed you're not wearing a wedding ring."

She told him about herself in a light, superficial way, dwelling on Betsy and her life since the divorce. Then, she continued hesitantly, "I hate to sound ignorant, considering the amount of material that's been written about you, but have you ever been married or had children?"

Dan laughed. "Don't apologize. It was the fact that you didn't recognize me that first attracted me to you. You don't know what a relief it is to meet someone who's not impressed with Dan Demaris, the actor. It's extremely important to me that you like *me* and not my image. But to answer your question, no I've never been married. And as far as I know, I have no children."

"You don't know what you're missing, not having children."

"Actually I do. I came from a big family—five older sisters who spoiled me rotten. I guess that's why I love women so much. And why I've never been able to bring myself to get married. I can't imagine giving up all the beautiful, loving women I would miss if I committed myself to one woman."

"Well, I can say from personal experience that you're making a lot of women very happy."

They both laughed. After the waiter poured more coffee, Ginny continued slowly, awkwardly, "Dan, I want to say something to you, and I'm not sure how to do it."

He watched her intently, with great interest.

"You see," she explained, "before tonight, I was beginning to be afraid that I . . . well, that I would never enjoy sex again. That part of me didn't seem to be functioning very well by the end of my marriage. Now, for the first time in a very long while, I feel that I'm still capable of very romantic, very sexy feelings."

"Let me assure you," he responded, taking her hand and looking deep into her green eyes, "the woman I made love to tonight was exciting and passionate." Then he continued soberly, "Sex should always be that way, not a boring, routine duty as it becomes inevitably in marriage. I believe in romantic love. It's the greatest adventure, the greatest challenge in life. Ecstasy should be something we all experience frequently. But as far as I can see, that dies in marriage. There's no adventure, no challenge—no ecstasy."

"Well, I can't argue with you. Unfortunately, that's what happened in my marriage."

His voice grew husky as his fingers gently stroked her hand. "In case you have any lingering doubts about your enjoyment of sex, perhaps we should work on this area a little further."

A slow, wicked grin spread across Ginny's face. She nodded.

She didn't get home until dawn.

8.

Martie walked into her office on that Monday morning feeling exceptionally happy and optimistic. Michael had spent the entire night with her, something he rarely did, and she interpreted this as another sign that he was nearly ready to make a commitment to her. She was convinced that it was only a matter of time before he would leave the wife whom he described as boring. Martie had never met Michael's wife and knew nothing about her, preferring to accept Michael's withering assessment of her as a sexless nonentity. She knew that if she let herself think of this other woman as a human being who was vulnerable and perhaps likeable, she would forever be plagued by feelings of guilt.

"You're late," her secretary, Denise, said, as she passed her desk. "But the way you're glowing, it looks like it was worth it."

"It *was*. What's up today?"

"You've got about a dozen calls to return. They're on your desk, and I've marked the urgent ones. Mr. Latham wants to see you at eleven to discuss packaging the Anderson book project, and Mr. Reynolds wants you to take over his lunch meeting with those network people. He's hung over again and doesn't feel up to it. There's that new Redford movie premier tonight, with a party afterwards. And there are three scripts on your desk that Mr. Latham wants you to read and comment on as possible projects for Dan Demaris."

"In other words, I don't even have five free minutes all day."

"Right. It's a dirty job, but somebody's got to do it."

"Okay. Tell Reynolds I'll take the lunch meeting, and try to find out from him what the hell it's about."

"Oh, by the way, that writer you wanted to see is waiting for you in your office. You know, Stuart Mendoza? He did that script on spec for 'Little House on the Prairie.' "

"Oh, yeah. I do want to talk to him, but God, today is such a hassle. Well, I'd better get to it."

Hurrying into her office, Martie found a tall, slender, rather attractive young man waiting for her. His Latin ancestry was obvious in his dark hair and eyes and olive complexion, but when he spoke it was without a trace of an accent.

"Hi, Stuart, I'm Martie Bass," she began quickly.

"You're a woman," he responded abruptly.

"Well, yeah," she answered, taken aback. "Don't look so surprised, there are a lot of us around, you know."

"It's just that when your secretary called and said Martie Bass wanted to talk to me, I assumed it was a man. I'm sorry, I don't mean to be rude, but . . ."

"But what?" Martie asked bluntly, sensing an unpleasant punch line coming.

"I know some people in the business, and they told me not to go with a woman agent."

"I see. Did they say why?"

"Well," he began hesitantly, clearly uncomfortable, "the general consensus seemed to be that women agents are too abrasive."

"*All* agents are abrasive," Martie interrupted angrily. "It's one of the requirements for the job. Doctors are known for their bedside manner. Not agents." She was shaking with fury now. Unknowingly, Stuart Mendoza had touched a deep sore spot within her. "And I'll tell you something else, you chauvinist Chicano, most beginning writers would give their right arm to be talking to one of the top agents with one of the top agencies in Hollywood—"

Gently but firmly he placed his hands on Martie's shoulders and ordered authoritatively, "Calm down. Just . . . calm down."

The effect of the physical restraint and his nononsense tone was immediate. Stopping in midsentence, Martie stared at him, stunned.

"First, my parents came from Argentina, so I'm not a Chicano. Second, I apologize for insulting you. Believe it or not, I really didn't mean it. I admit freely that I know nothing of Hollywood and am inclined to take at face value any advice that's given to me. Now, since we've gotten off to an unfortunate start, I suggest we begin all over. I want to be a writer. Will you help me?"

Damn those eyes! Martie thought angrily. Those big brown cow eyes that look absolutely guileless.

"All right, I'll help you, but only because you happen to have a marketable talent that could make the agency, and me, a great deal of money. From now on there's to be no more of this me-woman, you-man stuff. I'll be your agent, I'll handle your business, but I'll leave it to you to work out your mid-Victorian prejudices against women."

"Fair enough. And I'll leave it to you to work out that chip on your shoulder against men."

His amused, ironic tone was infuriating, and Martie nearly started shouting again. But there was no time to be drawn into a lengthy argument with a man who clearly had never heard of Gloria Steinem or the ERA.

"The people at 'Little House' liked your script a lot, which rarely happens with unsolicited material. They can't use it because they're already doing a similar show, but the story editor wants to talk to you about any other ideas you might have. I'll have my secretary set up a meeting. Now, do you have any other scripts that you've written?"

"No, that was the first time I tried anything like that. But I do have a book manuscript. Could you handle books?"

"I can handle anything," Martie said firmly.

Stuart laughed, a pleasant, deep-throated sound that Martie found surprisingly appealing. "I imagine you could, Miss Bass."

"*Ms.* Bass. What's the book about?"

"Argentina. It's a generational story. It's fifteen hundred pages long."

Martie groaned. "Oh, God, another magnum opus that no publisher in his right mind will take the time to read. Well, send it over to me anyway. You never know. Now, Mr. Mendoza, I . . ."

"Stuart."

"Stuart. I really have to get on with some other things, now. You'll be getting some contracts from us in the mail this week. Sign them and get them back to us immediately, because I can't start making you rich and famous until you're legally our client."

"Don't worry, I'll bring them by personally." Rising, he took her hand and leaned toward her, his face only inches from hers. "Thank you, *Ms*. Bass." And he kissed her hand. Then, grinning, he finished, "I hope that old-fashioned continental touch doesn't offend you. In Argentina, it's merely considered good manners."

As he turned to leave, Martie said suddenly, almost without thinking, "If you're not busy tonight, would you like to attend a premiere with me?"

"Yes," he responded eagerly, clearly surprised by the invitation. "That would be great."

"Don't get the wrong idea—this is purely business. I have to go and my boyfriend is busy. This will be a good way for you to start meeting the right people and learning how things operate."

"I see. Don't worry, I won't make the mistake of thinking this is supposed to be enjoyable." His tone was once more ironic, and Martie found herself in the unusual position of not knowing what to say. Really, he was a very exasperating man. If he wasn't such a good writer, she would have nothing to do with him.

As soon as Stuart left, Martie called Ginny. She was anxious to find out how things had gone with

Dan Demaris. Knowing how important this assignment was, she hoped that Dan and Ginny had gotten along well.

When Ginny answered, her voice sounding tired and sleepy, Martie began without preamble, "So how did it go? Did you completely charm The Hunk?"

"The who?"

"The Hunk. That's what the secretaries around here call Dan."

"Well . . ." Ginny drawled lazily, "I think it's safe to say we got along fairly well. He's different than I expected, much nicer and more real somehow."

"I *knew* it. He charmed you, obviously. Well, don't be coy, I know you too well for that, Ginny Carlson. Tell me every sordid detail."

"No way, José. I don't kiss and tell. Neither you nor *National Enquirer* are going to get a word out of me about Dan Demaris."

"Wait a minute! You mean . . . Ginny! You went to bed with him, didn't you?"

Feeling like a giggly teenager talking about her first heavy make-out session, Ginny laughed and admitted happily, "Yes. And you can forget all of my complaints about my sex life. They're no longer accurate."

"Boy, Gin, when you jump back in the water you really do a high dive. Most of us divorcees start out with a discreet affair with an accountant or a shoe salesman. You picked the sexiest man in America. So what's happening—are you gonna see him again?"

"Of course. I'm painting his portrait, you know. Which you neglected to tell me is in the nude."

"The *nude*? Hey, I didn't know that. Now I see how he got to you. All he ever bares in his movies is that gorgeous hairy chest. If the rest of him is that terrific, you must have been overcome with terminal lust by the end of the first sitting."

"Something like that," Ginny laughed, embarrassed but happy. "But, Martie, it wasn't just a roll in the hay. He says he wants to get to know me better—an idea that I don't mind one bit."

"Are you falling in love with the guy?" Martie asked pointedly.

"No. Definitely *not*. I hardly know him well enough for that, and besides I'm sure you know even better than I do the odds against us ending up together. But I like him—a lot. He's just what I needed right now. I haven't thought about Ross in two days, a definite improvement over the depressed, mopey way I've been feeling."

"I'm glad to hear that. And, to be frank, I'm glad you are going into this thing with a realistic, healthy attitude. I think a lot of Dan—he's immensely charming and attractive and much kinder than most people in his position. But he goes through women the way most of us go through toothpaste. He makes no secret of the fact that he enjoys variety and grows bored easily."

"Martie, I know all of that. Believe me, I'm not some starry-eyed fool. I'm accepting this relationship for what it is without expecting, or even wanting, more. I made a commitment to Ross and it didn't work out. I'm not ready to do that again, even with Dan."

"Okay, I'll back off and stop offering unwanted advice. Except for one final thing—I don't think it's in your nature to have a superficial relationship for long. You were meant to be a wife."

"Perhaps. But I just don't see that happening again. I never wanted more than one marriage in my life. Some people feel that if you don't get it right the first time, try, try again. I can't do that. I can't keep giving what you have to give in a committed relationship, getting to know a man intimately, opening up and being vulnerable. No, I really think that's all behind me now."

"Look, Gin, I expected you and Ross to stay together forever, too. You seemed to have something special going for you, almost as if you were a matched set that didn't look right apart. But it's over. You can't let that stop you from trying to find the same thing with someone else."

"You don't understand, Martie. I don't *want* to find the same thing with someone else. That phrase 'one-man woman,' definitely applies to me. I fell in love once, deeply, completely, and I just can't imagine doing it again."

"Okay, I give up. For now. But I gotta tell you, I expect to be your matron of honor one of these days. I missed out the first time because you didn't have a wedding. But this time I intend to be there."

Ginny laughed deprecatingly. "Sure. I've got to go now, Dan's waiting."

"Yeah, you'd better hurry, I wouldn't want him to catch cold sitting there in front of the easel."

As she walked down to Dan's house, Ginny thought about what Martie had said. She appreciated her friend's concern, but she still felt that Martie was wrong. Though her love for Ross had died, she couldn't imagine falling in love with anyone else—even Dan.

After learning that Stuart drove a ten-year-old Volkswagen, Martie told him that she would pick him up at his place, and drive them both to the premiere in her new BMW. She understood as well as anyone how important appearances were in Hollywood. A Volkswagen would be distinctly out of place among Mercedes, rented limousines, and expensive foreign sports cars.

Stuart lived in a small guest cottage behind a large house in Pacific Palisades, a pleasant, hilly area near the ocean, famous primarily as the home of Ronald Reagan. Stuart answered her knock immediately and invited her in while he finished dressing. Martie was surprised at the smallness of the place—just a combination bedroom and sitting room, with a tiny bathroom and no kitchen. In a corner near a window was an old typewriter and a delapidated desk piled high with papers and books.

"A typical writer's residence," Martie observed sarcastically. "Dirty, messy, and cramped."

"But cheap. And my landlady occasionally takes pity on me and invites me to dinner."

"Where do you eat normally?"

"There's a deli down the street. And when I'm really broke there's a McDonald's in Santa Monica." Grinning broadly, he continued, "But you're going to change all of that, remember? You're going to make me rich and famous."

"I have to now. My conscience will bother me forever if I don't get you out of this place."

"It isn't that bad. I mean, I can't honestly say I love it. It would be nice to at least have a refrigerator to keep cold beer in. But I'm doing what I want to do—writing."

Martie had been watching Stuart struggle awkwardly with the tie on his rented tuxedo. Finally, unable to sit quietly any longer while he bungled the job, she stood up and did it herself, quickly, expertly.

"You really should learn how to do this. You'll have to wear a tux at the Academy Awards next year when you win an Oscar for best original screenplay."

Cocking his head to one side, Stuart eyed her carefully. "I can never tell when you're being sarcastic and when you're really sincere. Tell me honestly—do you think I'm that good?"

"Yes," Martie answered simply. "You're better than any beginning writer I've ever known." Then as she stood close to him, she was overcome by an inexplicable and uncharacteristic attack of shyness. Stepping back she finished brusquely, "But it takes more than talent. You've got to learn how the business operates so that you won't get eaten alive."

"I'm afraid I'm hopeless at that. As you can see, I couldn't care less about money and couldn't understand a contract if my life depended on it. So, I guess that I'm very lucky that I met you."

His brown eyes had an amused glint in them now

that Martie found disconcerting. He had an annoying way of making her feel self-conscious.

"Right. Let's go."

The premiere went by in a blur for Martie, who spent most of the time talking shop, while Stuart stared wide-eyed at the famous people surrounding him. The movie was good, as Redford's usually were, but Martie paid little attention to it. She was too busy digesting the information she'd learned from her quick conversations with various people, planning the work she must get done the next day, and formulating long-range plans for some of her clients. In the frenetic, fast-paced world of Hollywood deal making, an agent couldn't afford to slow down for a minute. Martie was constantly planning strategies, evaluating properties, weighing career decisions for her many clients. If she let up for just a moment, one of them might lose a big opportunity. Lately, as the pressure had grown in direct proportion with her success, she had found it more and more difficult to keep up the pace. The answer was pills. Her "little friends" as she called them, the multi-colored antidotes to fatigue and nervous tension. She told no one of this, least of all Ginny, whom she knew would disapprove.

After the movie, Martie slipped into the women's restroom to surreptitiously swallow a couple of her "little friends" to counteract the tiredness that was beginning to overtake her. She had to be at her best and brightest for the party that was to follow. If she tried hard enough, and was lucky, she might be able to set some big deals in motion.

The party was held in the private banquet room

of a chic Beverly Hills restaurant. Though the room was large, it was packed with industry people and their guests. Stuart fought his way through to the crowded bar to get drinks for himself and Martie. But in the crush he lost her, and by the time he finally found her again, she was deep in serious conversation with a network executive. Realizing that she was not relaxing but working, he decided not to bother her. Instead he found an empty chair in a corner and, sipping his drink slowly, observed the fascinating variety of people around him. Inexperienced as he was, he could still recognize the different types—the ones on the way up, distinguishable by an almost tangible air of the "killer instinct," and the ones on the way down, trying desperately to hide the naked fear in their eyes. The atmosphere was full of deception, shallowness, a superficial bonhomie that didn't quite mask the overwhelming self-preservation. Stuart wondered how Martie could take dealing with these people every day. He knew that he couldn't force himself to do it, no matter how great the rewards.

When Martie finally rejoined him an hour later, he had decided that, assuming he was lucky enough to become a successful writer, he would never, under any circumstances, attend another party like this one.

"I'm afraid the ice melted a long time ago," he said pointedly to Martie as she eagerly clutched the drink and downed it thirstily.

"I don't care. I'm about to die of thirst. And if that's your way of telling me that I abandoned you, I'm sorry. But I told you this was business, not pleasure. And if it will make you feel less rejected, you must know it was your business I was working on."

"My little deal maker at work already?"

"Yes. Maybe you don't mind starving in a garret for your art, but I intend to see you well fed in a Marina del Rey condo. The guy I've been talking to is the executive in charge of a big new mini-series ABC's doing. It's a classy project and they want real writers, not hacks. I finally managed to persuade him to read what you've done. I told him you're Shakespeare reincarnated. I'm sending him your 'Little House' spec script tomorrow and I'd like to include that book manuscript you mentioned. Don't let me forget it when I drop you off."

"Martie . . . thanks. I appreciate what you're doing."

"Forget it. The only thanks I want is ten percent of a big fat fee for you. Now let's go. I've got to read that book of yours before I send it to him tomorrow."

"Fifteen hundred pages in one night?" Stuart asked skeptically.

"I won't actually read every page. I'll just skim through to get the highlights."

"Well, to save you some trouble why don't I just write down the important pages, like twelve, forty-nine, etc."

"Don't be bitchy. That's my role."

Later, as Stuart handed Martie a thick binder, he said softly, once more flashing his disarming smile, "By the way, I meant to tell you earlier—you look lovely tonight."

"Oh . . . well, thanks."

As she drove off, Martie wondered why the simple compliment had pleased her so.

At five o'clock in the morning Stuart was awakened by the persistent ring of the telephone. Groping awkwardly for it in the dark, he finally found it and hugged it to his ear.

"Hello."

"Why didn't you tell me this was good!"

The voice was unmistakable, even if the words made no sense at all.

"Martie, do you know what time it is?" he asked sleepily, yawning deeply into the phone.

"This is another *Thorn Birds,* at least. Maybe *Gone With the Wind.* Stuart, this is terrific!"

Now he understood what she was referring to and he shook himself awake. "Wait a minute. You mean you like the book?"

"*Like* it? Listen, idiot, I'm not sending it to that guy at ABC. I'm sending it to a senior editor at Random House who owes me a favor. I'm going to ask her to read it immediately, and unless my judgment totally disappeared sometime in the wee hours of this morning, I'll bet they'll snap it up. And if you don't get a six-figure advance, my name is not Martina Camille Bass."

"Martina Camille?"

"My mother was a hopeless romantic. Now you know why I use Martie. Meet me for lunch at one o'clock at Ma Maison. Don't worry, I'm paying. We've got to talk about this."

"Wait a minute. *I'm* paying."

118

"Don't be ridiculous, you can't afford Ma Maison, and I refuse to go to McDonald's. Don't get your fragile little male ego ruffled. Agents always pay for lunches with clients."

"All right. But when my first check comes in, I'm taking you to *dinner* at Ma Maison."

Martie sighed in exasperation. "Okay. See you later."

Leaning back against the pillow, Stuart smiled warmly. Martie was really something. In more ways than one.

They had finished a delicious, expensive lunch, and were relaxing over coffee. Martie explained eagerly, between quick sips, "So I told her that I was giving her the opportunity of a lifetime only because she was a friend. And if she didn't get back to me on Monday with a response, I'd start sending it elsewhere."

"And she agreed to it? She agreed to read a first novel by an unknown writer?"

"Of course. You should have realized by now that I'm a *very* good agent. I'm telling you, Stuart, you're gonna be in that Marina del Rey condo next year."

"Actually, that isn't quite my style, you know," he responded easily. "I'd prefer a two-story colonial in Pacific Palisades with a white picket fence and a basketball hoop over the garage door."

"Wouldn't that be a little big for you?"

"Not when you add five kids and a wife who's a terrific cook."

119

"Five kids?"

"Enough for a basketball team. I'm crazy about the game."

"I think in this day and age you might have trouble finding a woman willing to supply five kids."

"I don't know. Producing happy, healthy children is still the greatest accomplishment for a woman."

Martie groaned. "You've gotta meet my friend Joan sometime. You have a lot in common."

"Don't you want to have children some day?"

"Not really," she answered coolly, which was a lie. She had always assumed she would have at least one child. In her imagination she pictured him as a red-haired, freckle-faced little boy who would grow up to be very successful doing something worthwhile. At the beginning of her marriage she thought she could have it all—a career, a husband, a child. But now she had come to the bitter conclusion that the only thing she could expect to have was her career and a free-form relationship with Michael.

"I imagine you would be a very good mother—responsible, loving, and a lot of fun."

"Sure. I could schedule lunch meetings with the kid once a week so we could stay in touch. Look, Stuart, you can see how busy I am. There's no time for motherhood in my life."

"Does your career mean that much to you?"

"Yes. And don't expect me to feel guilty about it. I enjoy what I do, and I love making money. It's important to me to be independent and self-sufficient. If I had to stay home all day watering plants and asking my husband for money, I'd go crazy."

"In other words, you're the 'new woman,' on your own and loving every exciting minute of it?" His tone was clearly skeptical.

"Yes. And if men can't handle that, it's their problem. I think what bothers you men is that you're afraid and you don't want to admit it. In the past women were so dependent on men that they were terrified of being abandoned by them. A woman whose husband left her had nowhere to go, no way to make a full life for herself. Now we can go to a job or another man, even a younger one, or just be by ourselves. Now it's the men who are afraid of being abandoned, and unlike women, they haven't been taught how to hold onto someone."

"That's a pretty grim picture of male-female relationships."

"That's reality, 1980s' style."

"You're wrong, you know," he insisted quietly but firmly. "Reality is that men and women need each other. We always have and we always will. You take an all-or-nothing attitude, but what about compromise? Why can't we each give a little? Perhaps in the process men and women could become intimate in every way."

"You're just talking about sex now."

"No, sex is only a small part of what I'm talking about. I'm an optimist by nature, and I like to think that we're entering a time when men and women can be truly intimate with each other in every way, sexually, emotionally."

"But you still want women to stay in the kitchen."

"I admit I like good cooking and would rather have a wife doing it than try to do it myself. But I do understand that most women need more than that to feel happy and fulfilled."

"Thanks. That's very generous of you." Now Martie was the one who was being sarcastic.

Stuart frowned. "You try to act so tough. But nobody with eyes as open and vulnerable as yours could possibly be so hard inside. Someone must have hurt you very deeply to make you put on this act."

He was staring directly at her now, all trace of amusement gone from his voice.

Damn him! Martie thought furiously. *In the space of five minutes he's made me think of the child I'll never have, the loneliness of an all-enveloping career, and my tough-bitch facade that I feel so uncomfortable with. If I didn't know better I'd swear he's a psychiatrist masquerading as a writer. He brings up all of the painful things that I don't want to think about.*

When she got back to the office, she immediately called Michael and told him she badly needed to see him. But he insisted he was busy.

"I know how busy you are, but I've had a pretty rough day and I really need a little stroking right now." Martie tried unsuccessfully to keep the pleading sound out of her voice.

"I've had a rough day, too, love, and it's not over yet. Go have a drink or something, and I'll see you tomorrow night. Bye."

Martie held the telephone to her ear for a long moment after Michael's abrupt sign-off. She had told him as frankly as she knew how that she needed him. And his response had been a casual rejection.

122

That night Martie went to bed with an obnoxious, overbearing fellow agent from her office named Doyle who had been after her for months. Afterwards, when he left, she cried into her pillow for the young woman she had once been who thought sex involved love and caring.

9.

Ross lay in bed, listening to Lisa in the next room. She was singing in the shower, her voice floating high and lilting into the bedroom. Her perennial cheerfulness was one of the things he liked best about her. She seemed to view everything in life as an exciting adventure and almost always looked on the positive side of any experience. Of course, she hadn't really been tested by the world nor had to face its harsher realities. Ross realized that at least some of her youthful optimism was bound to diminish in time, but that didn't lessen her appeal.

After several months with her he was beginning to understand what had drawn him to her. She let him know in many different ways that she enjoyed him sexually, something Ginny hadn't done in years. She admired him tremendously, and at a time in his life when he was beginning to doubt that he would ever achieve his ultimate goals, that was extremely reassuring to him. But even more important, he didn't have a shared history with her. She knew nothing of his failures and mistakes, hadn't seen him struggle during the early, difficult years. Whereas Ginny knew him disturbingly well and was aware of every embarrassing fault, to Lisa he was simply a brilliant film maker and terrific lover.

At first his ego had needed this blind adoration and simple enjoyment of life. Now he was beginning to chafe at the superficiality of their relationship. More and more he thought of Ginny, of the bond between them that he knew he could never build with Lisa.

Lisa came out of the bathroom, wearing a short blue terrycloth robe, drying her long platinum hair with a thick towel.

"Hey, you'd better hurry, Ross. We're supposed to meet the others in half an hour."

Flinging the towel at him playfully, she began to dress.

"Lisa, I don't think I'll go today," he began slowly. Then, more firmly, "Look, your friends are all at least ten years younger than I am, and I'm sure they feel just as uncomfortable around me as I do with them."

"That's not true. They love talking to you."

"Only because they suspect they might be able to learn something about the film industry from me. Let's face it, they're your peer group, not mine."

Sitting down on the edge of the bed, she stared at him thoughtfully. "This is the second time this week you've commented on the difference in our ages. Ross . . . it's over between us, isn't it?"

He was surprised at how quickly she got to the point, but he didn't bother to deny that she was right.

When he said nothing, she continued soberly, "It's all right. I've been expecting it for some time.

You're not happy living the kind of life I live. And you miss your wife, don't you?"

"Yes," he admitted heavily.

"Don't look so miserable and guilty," she said softly, her voice trembling slightly. "Deep inside I always knew it would come to this. I know you think I'm pretty empty-headed and don't know much about the world, but even I could see that we're just different. Okay, so we had a few months together instead of a lifetime, that doesn't make our relationship a failure. You gave me something nourishing, something I'll never forget. You taught me so much that I needed to learn, about film, about life, about myself. I only hope I've given you something in return."

"You have, Lisa, more than you could possibly appreciate right now. You gave me something beautiful, a renewed faith in myself. I was feeling so low when I met you and now I feel like taking on the world again."

"Will you go back to your wife?"

"She's no longer my wife. And I don't know if she'll have me."

"She's crazy if she doesn't. You're worth more than every guy I've ever known all put together."

"That's nice of you to say, but Ginny may not feel that way. I hurt her very badly, you know."

"We all make mistakes; hopefully we learn by them." She smiled. "Doesn't that sound mature? See what a positive influence you've been on me?"

Leaning toward him, she kissed him warmly. But there was friendship, not passion, in his response.

Quickly packing his few possessions, he threw his

suitcase in the car and headed toward Malibu. Right now, more than anything else in the world, he wanted to see Ginny.

The painting was nearly finished, and Ginny could afford to relax now after the first hectic weeks. She and Dan had settled into a pleasant routine of working hard each day for three or four hours, then going up to his bedroom where they remained until Ginny left to make dinner for Betsy.

"I have a surprise for you," he said happily as they climbed the stairs together.

"What?" Ginny asked eagerly.

"I won't tell. All I can say is that it involves doing something very different in bed."

"That sounds interesting," she responded slyly.

They were at his bedroom door now. "Close your eyes."

She closed them, and he picked her up and carried her inside. As he put her down, he said, "Okay, open them."

Opening her eyes, Ginny was amazed to see a bucket of chilled champagne next to the bed. "You don't have to get me drunk, you know," she teased.

"That's only part of it. Look."

On the bed was a small package wrapped in red foil paper, tied with a gold ribbon. Ginny looked at Dan, and he smiled broadly. "For you," he confirmed. Then, impatiently, "Well, don't you want to know what it is?"

Laughing, Ginny responded, "Of course!"

Nervously her hands unwrapped the present. She hadn't expected anything and felt at once embarrassed and excited. When she opened the small leather case and found a delicate gold neck chain with a large, perfect diamond hanging from the center of it, she was stunned. She could only guess at how expensive it had been, but she knew it must be extravagant.

"You shouldn't have," she said stupidly, too confused to be clever.

"Why not? You have no idea the pleasure it gives me right now to see the look of surprise and delight on your face."

"Well," Ginny responded happily, wrapping her arms around his neck, "I'll just have to share some of this pleasure . . ."

Dan walked with Ginny down the beach to her house, his arm around her affectionately. Both were tired, relaxed, sated from two hours of lovemaking.

As they reached the back door, Ginny said easily, "Why don't you stay for dinner? It's about time you met my daughter. She'll be home any time now."

Looking at her quizzically, Dan responded, "I was beginning to think you didn't want her to know about us. So far you've managed to avoid letting us meet."

Frowning, Ginny admitted reluctantly, "I suppose I have felt rather uncomfortable about the situation. She's never seen me with any man other than her father. I don't know how she's going to take it."

"She has to get used to the fact that you're divorced now. She can't expect you to join a nunnery. Surely she realizes that you're too young and attractive not to develop another relationship."

"You don't understand, Dan. The divorce has been awfully hard on Betsy. She really hasn't adjusted to it yet. And to see me with someone else—well, I just thought it might be too much for her right now. But I don't like running around behind her back, so to speak, either. It's too dishonest and not fair to you."

"So we're agreed. Tonight I'll meet her, and I assure you I'll be at my most charming."

Kissing him lightly, Ginny responded, "Then she will certainly adore you."

"Just tell me one thing. Does she like my movies, or does she take after her mother?"

"Well . . . I'm afraid her taste runs more toward John Travolta."

"I knew it! I'm going to have to give you two a private course in the art of film appreciation."

Suddenly the doorbell rang. Still smiling from her banter with Dan, Ginny opened the door and was stunned to see Ross standing there.

He looked rather awkward but hopeful as he began eagerly, "Ginny, I have to talk to you . . ."

But before he could finish he noticed Dan standing in the background.

"Ross . . . well, come in," Ginny said reluctantly, feeling guilty for no reason at all. Reminding herself that Ross was no longer her husband, she introduced him to Dan, trying to make her voice sound light and casual.

From the first second that he saw them together, Ross knew—they were lovers. That special look of intimacy was too obvious to be misunderstood. As Ginny was introducing them, a myriad of conflicting thoughts and emotions went through him. He was stunned, jealous, angry, embarrassed, filled with an infuriating sense of helplessness because Ginny had the right to do as she pleased, to have any man she wanted. In that moment his fantasy of getting her back crumbled, and he knew that he had only himself to blame for losing her.

"Pleased to meet you," Dan said politely.

Ross responded in kind, and then there was an awful, tense silence.

Standing between the two men in her life, the one who had introduced her to love and the one who was teaching her to be an expert at it, Ginny felt ill at ease and yet also strangely exultant. She didn't want to hurt Ross—her bitterness toward him had dissipated as her relationship with Dan grew—but, being human, she couldn't help wanting him to see that she was doing quite all right without him.

"I'm familiar with your work," Dan continued evenly. "I've always admired its integrity." Then, with his typical self-deprecating humor, "As someone who sold out a long time ago, I respect people who don't."

"Thanks, but you have nothing to feel bad about. You're really underrated by the critics."

Ginny knew that Ross actually despised Dan's films and she admired his consideration in not revealing that.

"Well, listen, you two probably would like a private conversation, so I'll go. I'll call you later, Ginny."

Neither Ross nor Ginny protested. Ross was anxious for Dan to leave and Ginny was interested in hearing what had brought Ross out here so unexpectedly.

When Dan was gone, Ginny looked at Ross expectantly. He lied haltingly, "I . . . uh, wanted to talk to you about Betsy."

"Oh?"

"Yeah, I know she's been reluctant to spend much time with me as long as I was living with Lisa, and, well, I'm living alone now, so I thought maybe she'd spend the weekend with me. We've been pretty distant lately."

Though this wasn't the reason he had come to see Ginny, there was a great deal of truth in it. His estrangement from Betsy had been troubling him deeply and he wanted to start repairing the damage.

"But why didn't you just call?" Ginny asked logically.

"Well, uh, I was hoping she'd be here, and I happened to be in Malibu, so I thought I'd just stop by."

"I see." Ginny couldn't quite believe this somehow, but she didn't say so. She was glad that Ross was anxious to reestablish a close relationship with Betsy, and she was surprised that he was no longer with Lisa. Nearly bursting with curiosity, she wanted badly to ask him what had happened. But she couldn't. The only consolation was the obvious fact that he was jealous of Dan.

"She'll be home soon, why don't you wait?"

"No, that's okay, why don't you just tell her that I'll pick her up after school Friday."

"All right, if you prefer."

"Well, I'd better be going. As soon as I settle into

a new place I'll give you my new address and phone number. In case you need to get in touch with me for any reason."

"Very well." Ginny's tone was maddeningly cool.

Ross left hurriedly, suspecting that if he stayed a moment longer he wouldn't be able to resist taking her into his arms and ordering her to stay away from Dan Demaris.

That evening, after a typically silent dinner, Ginny decided that she should tell Betsy about Dan. She still had no idea what was bothering Betsy so intensely. If it was simply the divorce, she knew that this news would only make her more upset. But she couldn't avoid talking about Dan any longer. He had become an important part of her life, and she only hoped that Betsy would eventually be able to accept him.

Betsy was in the living room watching television. Standing near the set, Ginny began softly. "Do you mind if I turn this off for a minute? I'd like to talk to you about something."

Looking apprehensive, clearly expecting another "What's wrong with you?" interrogation, Betsy nodded reluctantly.

"Honey, my divorce from your father will be final next week. I know you've been secretly hoping that we'd get back together again, but that just isn't going to happen. You have to accept the fact, as your father and I have done, that our marriage is over. Holding onto a fantasy that somehow everything will go back to being the way it was can only hurt you even more deeply. Accepting reality is painful but at least it's a quick pain. Avoiding reality is a lingering pain that never goes away."

Seeing the familiar sullen, stubborn expression on Betsy's face Ginny realized unhappily that Betsy was not accepting anything she was saying. Sighing deeply, Ginny forged ahead determinedly. "We've been over this before and I know you would rather not think about it. The reason I'm bringing it up now is that there's been a, uh, further development."

God, I'm putting this so stupidly, Ginny thought, frustrated.

"What I'm trying to say is that I've started . . . dating . . . someone else and I'd like you to meet him."

As worried as Ginny had been about how Betsy would react to this news, she still wasn't prepared for the vehemence of Betsy's response.

"What? You're not even divorced yet and already you're running around with someone else?"

"I'm not 'running around' with anyone," Ginny responded evenly. "You know I've been painting Dan Demaris. We've become good friends and I enjoy his company very much. I'd like to have him come over for dinner to meet you. I think you'd like him."

"An actor, of all people." Betsy had clearly inherited her father's low opinion of actors. "Why couldn't you at least have chosen somebody normal?"

"Dan is intelligent and charming and quite nice. If you'd stop being so close-minded I think you'd realize that I would never be interested in someone who wasn't basically pretty decent. You might at least give me that much credit."

Ginny was angry now, her green eyes flashing.

Avoiding Ginny's eyes, Betsy continued curtly, "I suppose you're sleeping with him."

That was more than Ginny was willing to stand. Moving directly in front of Betsy so the sullen girl couldn't avoid looking at her, Ginny answered firmly, "My sex life is simply none of your business. I don't intend to be cross-examined as if you were the parent and I the child. You owe me a great deal more respect than that, young lady! Dan is coming to dinner tomorrow night and I expect you to treat him with the same courtesy you have been taught to show to any guest in our home. Is that clear?"

"Yes," Betsy replied in a voice so low that Ginny could barely hear it. Then, rising abruptly, she fled to her room.

Sighing, Ginny flung herself angrily into a chair. She had expected Betsy to be surprised to learn that she was dating someone, but she hadn't expected such bitter, intense resentment. Before tonight's conversation, she had hoped that Betsy would ultimately be captivated by Dan. Now she simply prayed that Betsy would tolerate him and not be openly rude.

Dinner was a disaster. Ginny prepared an elaborate, delicious meal, yet neither she nor Dan, and least of all Betsy, enjoyed a single bite. Dan tried gamely, showing a sincere interest in Betsy and asking intelligent questions about her school life. But she responded in monosyllables, clearly unwilling to volunteer any information at all. When Dan was funny, as he was quite often, Betsy bit her lip, making a determined effort not to laugh. She asked him no questions at all, though Ginny suspected that she was dying to know more about him. When he offered to let her visit the set of his new movie, she responded coolly that she had been on movie sets before with her father and found the experience totally boring.

Ginny was at a complete loss as to how to handle the rapidly deteriorating situation. She couldn't force Betsy to like Dan, even though she was convinced that if she would just give him half a chance she would like him a great deal. By the end of the seemingly endless meal, Dan had exhausted nearly all of his considerable charm and was resigned to carrying on a limited conversation with Ginny. When Betsy, explaining that she had a great deal of homework to do, asked to be excused, Ginny immediately gave her permission. All three were relieved that the strained, unhappy meal was over.

Dan and Ginny soon went into the living room, where Ginny poured each of them a large brandy.

"I thought you weren't much of a drinker," he commented dryly.

"Normally, I'm not. But normally I don't have to deal with a teenager at the height of her considerable ability to be obnoxious. Dan, I'm sorry for Betsy's behavior tonight . . ."

"Don't apologize. I'm not very good with kids, you know. And you can't really blame Betsy. Clearly she worships her father and resents what she sees as my attempt to take his place. Don't worry about my feelings in all of this. I'm just sorry I wasn't better at breaking down her resistance."

"Attila the Hun couldn't get past that wall she puts up sometimes. Aside from her father, she's the most stubborn person I know."

Smiling amiably, Dan said, "Hey, it's not that bad. She just needs time to get used to me. I'm not giving up, you know."

Ginny smiled at Dan in return. "I expected you to say that you never want to see her again."

"No way, lady. I know how much she means to you. She's part of your life, and I'm just gonna have to persuade her to accept me as part of your life, too."

"You have the patience of a saint."

"That's the first time anyone has ever compared me in any way to a saint. I know several producers and directors who would find the very idea ridiculous."

Grinning, Ginny responded softly, "They don't know you as well as I do."

They each sipped the strong, warm brandy, and were silent for awhile. Ginny's thoughts were entirely on Betsy, so she was startled when Dan suddenly brought up the subject of Ross.

"I didn't realize that your ex-husband was Ross Carlson."

"Why, does it matter?"

"No. But I can understand why Betsy is so strongly attached to him. From what I've seen and heard, he's a rather exceptional guy. Especially for people in this business."

"I have to tell you, it makes me feel rather strange listening to you compliment my ex-husband."

"Don't get the wrong idea. I don't want to give you second thoughts about going back to him."

"That's hardly likely to happen. *He* left *me*, remember?"

"Maybe, but unless I'm a worse judge of character than I like to think, he was plainly jealous when he found us together today."

"That's just residual possessiveness. He's never seen me with anyone else before. From the moment I first met him years ago, he was the only man in my life. Even though he doesn't want to be married to me any longer, he may find it hard to accept that I could be involved with someone else."

Ginny firmly believed what she was saying, but at the same time she was surprised at how flattered she felt that Dan had noticed Ross's jealousy, too.

"Well, anyway, I'm glad he's out of your life and there's room for me."

"Oh, there's definitely room for you!" Suddenly turning serious, Ginny continued soberly, "Dan, I've been wanting to tell you . . . these last few weeks have been extremely happy ones for me. Whatever happens, now that the painting is nearly done, I want you to know that I'll always be glad I knew you."

Narrowing his brown eyes in concern, he replied quickly, "Hey, that sounds suspiciously like a brush-off."

"No," Ginny reassured him immediately, "the last thing I want is to stop seeing you. I just wanted you to know that I'm not the clinging sort. When it ends I'll simply say it was fun while it lasted and genuinely wish you well."

Leaning back against the sofa, Dan looked unusually thoughtful for a long moment. Finally he said pensively, "You continually surprise me. I've never known anyone like you."

His brown eyes searched her face intently, as if he was looking for something rare and secret. Ginny began to fidget nervously under his close scrutiny. She put down her glass of brandy, then picked it up again, finally setting it down once more without tasting it.

"You're looking at me like I've suddenly grown a third eye or something," she said, laughing nervously.

"I'm sorry," he answered, pulling away, "It's just that I could look into those lovely green eyes forever." Then, smiling sheepishly, "That sounds like a line from one of my movies, doesn't it?"

"Well, if it is, I don't mind. It's awfully nice."

"You're awfully nice. You're intelligent and compassionate and lovely and sexy, and about a million miles removed from all the other women I meet."

"That's just because you're used to actresses. I'm no different from any other average woman."

"Ah, no, you're not average. You're special. You're . . . *Ginny*."

Suddenly he swallowed the rest of his brandy in one long drink, then set down the glass and rose abruptly. "And I'd better be going before this spell you've woven around me gets any stronger. Another five minutes and you'll have me talking about love and marriage." Bending down to kiss her quickly, he grabbed the jacket that he'd thrown over a nearby chair earlier and left.

For a long moment Ginny sat there, stunned. *Am I going crazy or did he actually mention love? And marriage.* Not once had she thought of Dan in those terms. From the beginning of their passionate affair she'd had no illusions about how it all would end eventually. Dan would grow bored, as he had with every other woman in his life, and would go on to someone else. In a way, it was rather comforting, really, knowing that it would never get serious, that it was all just for fun. Until now. Until Dan said the two words that Ginny had never expected to hear from him . . . *love* and *marriage*.

Strangely enough, though she cared for him deeply, she was neither excited nor happy now. She was worried . . . worried that he might start asking for something that she no longer had to give. She had no desire to fall in love again, and no intention of ever remarrying.

That night when she went to bed she found her thoughts dominated not by Dan but by Ross. She had known love and marriage with Ross but it all had ended in pain and disillusionment. She didn't want the same thing with Dan. That part of her was closed off, shut down. And she was determined that it would remain that way.

10.

One month after Ginny's paintings went on sale at the Moreau Gallery, they were gone. Maurice called, asking for more paintings and suggesting an increase in price. Ginny's lovely, affectionate portraits of children by the sea touched people deeply.

"You are taking off, as they say, very quickly," Maurice told her happily. "I expected you to do well, but even I didn't anticipate such a meteoric rise. Soon, I'm sure, the critics will take notice and will undoubtedly declare your work to be classic examples of American romanticism."

"I don't care about the critics," Ginny responded. "It's just so encouraging that people like my work. At first I wasn't at all sure that anyone would."

"People love your work. That is what makes you such a special artist. The people who buy your paintings aren't doing so as investments. They are buying them because they want them to grace their homes. Ginny, your warmth and reverence for life are reflected in your work. People always respond to such qualities."

Ginny was so thrilled by Maurice's effusive compliments and by the success that she once feared would never happen, that she forgot to tell Betsy that Ross would pick her up from school that Friday.

Ross waited in his car in front of the school for several minutes, until the stream of students leaving classrooms had shrunk to a few lolling on the lawn waiting for late parents. Growing impatient, he decided to go looking for Betsy. He was anxious to talk to her, to once more start communicating with the daughter who was now practically a stranger. He finally found her in an isolated corner behind a building. She wasn't alone. A young man was with her and she was handing him money as he handed her a polyethylene bag.

With a sickening jolt Ross realized that his daughter, whom he still thought of as a little girl, was using drugs. And from the impatient, desperate look on her face, she seemed to be heavily into them. Something inside him snapped and he was filled with a blind rage.

Rushing up to them, he grabbed the bag before they even realized he was there. Betsy, surprised and horrified, shrank back against a wall. Startled, the young man tried to bolt but Ross caught him easily, twisting his arm behind his back viciously. Ross was taller and stronger, with all the expertise of a former college wrestler. The boy was no match for him and immediately stopped struggling. Instead he started talking urgently, trying to argue his way out of the situation.

"Hey, man, if you're her father you'd better think about somethin'! If you turn me in, she goes, too."

Ross looked at Betsy cowering against the wall, looking ashamed and unhappy. He couldn't let her go to jail, or at the very least be suspended from school. But he wasn't about to let this crummy little drug pusher go free to ruin anyone else's life.

"Is he a student here?" Ross asked Betsy, his voice hard. She nodded wordlessly. "Okay, go to the car. It's parked out front. Wait for me there."

Betsy left hurriedly, glancing back once anxiously.

When she was out of sight, Ross continued, a deadly fury in his voice, "You'd better listen to this, because I'm only gonna say it once. You're leaving this school and you're never coming back. I'm gonna check next week, and if they don't tell me that you quit, I'm coming after you. And when I find you I'm gonna break both your arms."

He twisted the boy's arm harder, so that he screamed in pain. "That should persuade you that I know how to do it. And one more thing. I'm giving your name to the cops as a suspected pusher. They'll be watching you like a hawk from now on, so I suggest you think twice before continuing with your little business."

Suddenly letting go of the boy's arm, Ross turned him around to face him. "If you ever so much as talk to my daughter again, I'll see you go to jail, if I have to set you up to do it. Understand?"

The boy nodded tightly, rubbing his throbbing arm.

Ross strode purposefully back to his car, where Betsy waited, her eyes filled with tears and her face drawn.

He drove straight to his new apartment. There, while Betsy sat nervously on the sofa, he flushed the contents of the bag down the toilet. Then he sat down in a chair opposite her and stared at her wordlessly for a long time.

Finally he said quietly, "You used to be too smart for that kind of thing. What happened?"

She started to speak, then stopped. He could see a veil come over her eyes, as if she were shutting him out, and in that instant he realized how great was the gulf between them now.

"Okay," he continued heavily. "I'm taking you to the doctor as soon as possible. They'll run some tests to determine if you're on anything hard. Then you're going to join a drug program that I know about. I'm going to personally take you to every meeting. Until I feel I can trust you again, you'll be given no cash at all. Whatever you need, your mother or I will pay for."

"Are you gonna tell mom?" Betsy asked, frightened.

"Yes."

"I'm not some kind of junkie, you know," Betsy said defensively.

"Good. Then it'll be a lot easier for you to get clean again."

They were both silent for a moment, before Betsy asked curiously "What are we doing here anyway?"

"This is where I live now. I'm not seeing Lisa any more."

"You're not?" Betsy's expression brightened for the first time, and for a brief moment she looked like the happy, carefree young girl she had once been.

"No." Then, "There's just one more thing, Betsy." He left the chair and sat down next to her on the sofa. Cupping her chin in his hand, he turned her face toward his. It was almost like looking in a mirror, one that had stopped time in its tracks twenty-five years earlier. The same inquisitive, shrewd blue eyes, the same stubborn chin. There was intelligence and willfulness there, but also compassion and kindness. The softness that made the features feminine instead of masculine came from Ginny, as did the long chestnut hair. In that instant Ross felt moved as he had been when Betsy was born, realizing that he had helped to create this special human being.

"I love you more than anything in the world, Betsy. I think you've stopped believing that, so I'm gonna spend a lot of time from now on proving it to you."

Tears spilling from her eyes, Betsy buried her face in his shoulder and sobbed, "Oh, Daddy, I've missed you so much!"

Holding her, he rocked her like the baby she still was in some ways, whispering soothing words and patting her back.

That night when they had finished eating dinner at Betsy's favorite restaurant, Ross said to her quietly, "Tell me what's been bothering you so much, making you so unhappy that you turned to drugs."

"Everything," she answered, sighing. "When you and Mom broke up, I couldn't believe it at first.

And then when I saw that you weren't getting back together, it was like somebody pulled a rug out from under my feet. Everything was so nice before and then it all turned so bad. You weren't around and I didn't want to bother Mom with problems because she had enough of her own."

"What problems?"

"You wouldn't understand," Betsy answered hopelessly, looking away.

"Wait a minute, give me a chance. I *want* to understand. There's been more than enough silence between us. I want us to try talking to each other from now on."

Betsy hesitated, still unconvinced. Finally she said reluctantly, looking away, "It's Stacey . . ."

"Yes," Ross prompted encouragingly. He knew that Stacey Kaufmann was Betsy's closest friend.

"You won't tell anyone, will you?" Betsy asked suddenly.

"I can't answer that," Ross said honestly. "I don't know what the problem is. But whatever is wrong, I'll do anything I can to help Stacey."

Obviously weighing his words carefully, Betsy finally said slowly, "The problem is . . . she's pregnant."

Ross was shocked. Stacey was just Betsy's age, not yet fifteen. He hadn't seen her since his separation from Ginny, and his memories of her were of a giggling, highly excitable, very pretty little girl. Though he knew the statistics well—one out of ten teenage girls gets pregnant each year—he couldn't imagine Stacey in that predicament. Still, Ross had seen it all too often while making his new movie about unwed mothers—young girls old enough to have sex but not old enough to know how to handle it, a little girl's innocence and ignorance tragically combined with a woman's drives. Looking at Betsy now, he knew that their tenuous renewed closeness depended on how he handled this problem she was sharing with him.

"How far along is she?" he asked pragmatically.

"Three months," Betsy answered quickly, clearly relieved at her father's matter-of-fact tone. She had been worried that he would be shocked, critical of Stacey; instead he was approaching this as a serious problem requiring careful thought.

"Has she told her parents?"

"Yeah. Her father won't talk about it at all. Her mom says she's got to have the baby and raise it because it's her responsibility and she needs to learn a lesson."

Christ! Ross thought furiously, what an attitude for the parents to take. As if this was just another mistake requiring the usual punishment. And in the process, both Stacey's life and the life of her child would be ruined.

"What does Stacey want to do?"

"She doesn't know. There's no one she can talk to but me, and I don't know what to tell her. But, Dad, I just can't see her keeping the baby. I think about it all the time, trying to think of an answer, but all I can come up with is that it will totally mess up her life if she keeps it. You know how dingy she is sometimes. She just wouldn't be a good mother."

Poor Betsy, Ross thought with a mixture of concern and pride. She was clearly worried to distraction by her friend's problem, and trying desperately to think of a way to help her. It was a heavy load for a fourteen-year-old to bear. On top of everything else that was happening in her life, it was no wonder that she was turning to drugs.

"Has Stacey talked to a counselor or doctor, maybe someone at Planned Parenthood or a place like that?"

"No. She hasn't even seen a doctor. She took one of those home pregnancy tests, and that's how she knows she's pregnant. Her mother wants her to see their family doctor pretty soon."

"Stacey needs professional counseling to help her make the decisions that have to be made immediately," Ross explained slowly. "What she decides right now will affect the rest of her life as well as her baby's life. It's wrong for her mother to force her to keep the baby as a form of punishment."

"That's what I think, but when I tried to talk to her mother she got real mad at me." Then, cautiously, "Dad . . . would you talk to her parents?"

Ross frowned. He had a pretty good idea how Stacey's parents would react to his butting into their private problem. But it was apparent that Stacey needed help of a kind that her parents were simply unable to give. He thought of the many girls like Stacey whom he had interviewed for his film. The ones who chose to keep their babies were the most tragic. More often than not they were motivated by self-destructive impulses that they didn't understand, and both they and their helpless babies paid a heavy price. Child abuse was common as the girls began to resent the children who had changed their lives so drastically, forcing them to handle responsibilities they weren't ready for.

"Okay," Ross agreed finally. "But don't expect miracles. This is a mess and I don't think anyone, least of all me, can step in and clean it up. There are no easy answers."

"I know. But . . . thanks, Dad."

The look on Betsy's face—relief, the conviction that her father could handle anything—was reassuring to Ross. Betsy hadn't looked at him in that way for a long time.

The Kaufmanns were extremely reluctant to talk to Ross. Only after he told them that Betsy had confided in him about Stacey's problem did they finally agree to meet with him. But Mrs. Kaufmann was curt to the point of rudeness and Ross knew that she would be difficult to deal with.

Sitting in their living room that night, he came straight to the point. "I've been working for the past several months on a documentary film about pregnancy among teenagers. I've talked to the girls themselves and to experts on the problem, so I've learned more about it than maybe the average person knows." As he spoke, Mr. Kaufmann, whom Ross had met briefly before, seemed interested in what he had to say, but Mrs. Kaufmann was tight-lipped and reserved.

Feeling less and less confident of his ability to persuade them of anything, Ross forced himself to continue. "One thing that helps tremendously is having an objective, knowledgeable person to talk to. A psychologist, counselor, someone from Planned Parenthood or a group like that . . ."

"Those people will simply tell Stacey to have an abortion," Mrs. Kaufmann broke in abruptly. "That's out of the question."

"Not necessarily. From what I understand, it may be too late for that anyway. What they will do is help Stacey see what options she has in this situation and give her advice on how to deal with whatever option she chooses."

"Stacey has no options," Mrs. Kaufmann said angrily. "She isn't capable of making decisions about this situation. She's still a child—"

"Who will soon be a mother," Ross interrupted firmly. "I'm sorry, Mrs. Kaufmann, but the truth is that in one sense, at least, Stacey is no longer a child. And despite your efforts, she's the one who's going to have to deal with this situation she's gotten herself into. It's her life and her child, not yours. You can't make these decisions for her. I'm sorry if I've offended you; believe me, I sympathize with you tremendously. I know all too well that it could just as easily have been Betsy in this situation."

"What gives you the right to come here and tell us how to handle our daughter?" Mrs. Kaufmann asked furiously.

"Nothing. Except that I've seen what happens in these cases and you haven't. Neither you nor Stacey has any idea what's ahead of you. I do have a pretty good idea because I've talked to girls like Stacey. And believe me, the only chance both Stacey and her baby have right now to survive this is to get all the help they can find."

Ross stopped, frowning deeply. He'd done what he could; there was nothing left to say.

Suddenly Mr. Kaufmann, who had been silent during the entire bitter exchange, said quietly, "If it was Betsy in this predicament, what would you do?"

"I'd give her all the information I could. And then I'd let her make the final decision. But more than anything else I'd let her know that I love her enough to want what's best for her, instead of simply punishing her."

Mrs. Kaufmann stared stonily at Ross, while Mr. Kaufmann was thoughtful for a long moment. Finally he asked politely, "Could I call you tomorrow to get a list of people to talk to—counselors, perhaps?"

Breathing deeply in relief, Ross said quickly, "Of course. I'll have the information for you first thing in the morning."

Mrs. Kaufmann turned angrily toward her husband and started to speak, but he stopped her with a hard look. "Don't say *anything*," he ordered bluntly.

Ross left then, and went out to his car, where Betsy was waiting anxiously.

"Well?" she asked as he opened the door.

"We'll see. At least they're going to let her get some help now."

Smiling softly, Betsy said happily, "I love you, Daddy."

"I love you, too, honey."

Later that night, after Ross had brought Betsy home and she went to bed, he told Ginny everything

150

that had happened. Shocked and worried, she was concerned about Stacey and disturbed by Betsy's easy acquisition of drugs. "I'll call the school . . ." she began angrily.

"It won't do any good," Ross said patiently. "They know they have a drug problem. Hopefully, at least that one guy has been removed from the situation."

"Oh, Ross, how hard it must have been on Betsy, wanting to help Stacey and not knowing how to. The worst part is that she didn't feel she could turn to either of us."

"I know. But I think she feels differently now. She and I started getting close again today."

"As soon as you two walked in I could see a difference. She trusts you again." She added sadly, "Unfortunately, she doesn't feel that way about me. She can't seem to accept the fact that our marriage is over and we each will go on to different lives now."

"You mean with Demaris?" Ross asked awkwardly, unable to hide his curiosity.

Ginny looked at him carefully, then answered evenly, "Dan and I aren't getting married, if that's what you're getting at."

"It's none of my business . . ."

"You're right."

The relaxed closeness that had existed between them when Ross first brought Betsy home was gone now, replaced by the old tenseness. Finally Ginny asked, "What will happen to Stacey now?"

"I don't know. But at least she'll be put in touch

with people who can help her. Frankly, I think it would be best if she had an abortion, but it may be too late for that."

"I hope it isn't too late." There was something in her tone, a deep feeling that went beyond her concern for Stacey. Ross looked at her, surprised.

"Ginny . . . is that what you wish you had done?" he asked abruptly, finally verbalizing a fear that he'd never wanted to face before.

"No!" she responded, shocked. "My situation was completely different from Stacey's. I was eighteen and you were twenty-five; we weren't children. We loved each other and wanted to marry. It wasn't the best way to start a marriage, and it certainly led to problems down the line, but it wasn't a disaster for either of us. I don't think our marriage failed because of Betsy."

"I don't either," Ross responded, sighing in relief. "I think it failed because I went through the typical male mid-life crisis and handled it like an idiot."

"Don't blame yourself entirely, Ross. Neither of us was happy at the end. Over the years, our love just gradually died. I suppose that happens with most people."

"I suppose," Ross agreed reluctantly. "After all, how many happy, long-lasting marriages do we know?"

"None," Ginny answered, smiling wryly.

"Still, I wonder sometimes . . ." His voice trailed off as he looked away in embarrassment.

"Yes?" Ginny prompted.

"Nothing. I'd better be going. I thought, with everything that happened today, Betsy would be more comfortable at home this weekend. But next weekend I'd like to take her with me while we do some shooting on Catalina. I think she'd enjoy that."

"You must be nearly finished with the movie," Ginny commented with polite interest.

"Yeah, just about. I've got to hurry to get it done in time to show it at that Paris film exhibit."

"I'm sure it will be well-received. It sounds like one of the best things you've ever done."

"Thanks. I hope so. Well, good night, Ginny."

"Good night, Ross."

He left slowly, reluctantly, as if there was something more he wanted to say. Ginny watched him expectantly, but he said nothing.

On her way to her room, Ginny stopped to look in on Betsy, and was surprised to find her still awake.

"You'd better get some sleep now," she urged, standing in the doorway.

"Mom . . ."

"Yes?" When Betsy looked away nervously, unsure how to continue, Ginny came in and sat down next to her bed. "What is it, honey?"

"Dad broke up with Lisa, you know."

"I know."

"I think he might . . . might come back if you'd let him."

"Betsy, that isn't going to happen. Your father and I are divorced. You've got to accept that."

"Are you going to marry Dan? Is that it?"

"No. Dan and I care very much for each other, but we don't have that kind of relationship."

Looking disappointed, Betsy insisted stubbornly, "I bet you'd go back to Dad if it wasn't for Dan. He's ruining everything!"

"Betsy!" Reminding herself that Betsy was going through an exceptionally difficult time, she continued more calmly, "It's unfair to blame Dan for the divorce. Whether I was involved with him or not, your father and I would still remain apart." Then, "It would make things so much easier if you could accept that and not resent Dan so much. He's really a very nice person, you know."

Betsy said nothing, staring stonily past Ginny. Sighing heavily, Ginny rose. "Good night, Betsy."

But Betsy said nothing, and Ginny went to bed feeling a million miles apart from her daughter.

11.

"Ginny, you know that normally I wouldn't pry, but after seeing you on the cover of the *National Enquirer* I think I have the right to ask—what's happening with your relationship with Dan?"

They were sitting in the small, flower-filled garden of Kate's lovely English-style "cottage" in Beverly Hills. Ginny's earlier joke to Martie about the *National Enquirer* didn't seem so funny when they ran a candid photo of herself and Dan leaving a premier. The caption read: "In Love at Last— superstar playboy Dan Demaris has told close friends that he's finally found the girl of his dreams and is seriously considering marriage for the first time. His girl friend, Virginia Carlson, is a noted artist."

"Oh, hell, Kate, I don't know. We were simply having a nice time and then the Hollywood press discovered us. Things haven't been sane since. I came by today partly to give you my new phone number. It's unlisted and I'd appreciate it if you'd consider it top secret information. Reporters were calling me constantly on the old number. And there

155

were some crank calls from jealous women that I don't want to even discuss."

"I'm sorry to hear that. I know how that sort of thing can put tremendous pressure on a relationship."

"Oh, Dan's used to it. He said that's the fourth time the *Enquirer* has reported that he's in love." She added shyly, "But he said it was the first time they were right."

Kate looked up from watching Scottie, who was playing nearby. "It sounds serious."

Ginny watched Scottie for a moment, reluctant to reply. He was such a beautiful little boy, with his mother's dark hair and gentle expression. Dressed in a blue and white striped T-shirt and jeans, he was a miniature dynamo, running around the garden, playing energetic make-believe games.

Finally, Ginny answered, "I think it might be— and that's what worries me. In the beginning it was so nice—just fun and companionship and terrific sex, all with no strings attached. Dan was kind and reassuring when I really needed that, and he did wonders for my ego. But I always knew that it was purely temporary, that sooner or later he would go on to someone else. And although I was a little saddened by the thought of being alone again, I really didn't mind too much."

Watching her friend closely, Kate said matter-of-factly, "It doesn't sound like you're exactly head over heels in love with the guy."

"I'm not. I like him a hell of a lot, but . . ."

"But you're the kind of woman who only falls in love once."

156

"I'm afraid so. Martie thinks I'm crazy for not latching onto him. You're the first person who's understood."

"That's because I'm the same way, I suspect."

"You mean you couldn't imagine falling in love again after breaking up with Kevin?"

"Oh, no, it's not that," Kate responded firmly. "I never really loved Kevin, you see. I married him because I desperately wanted a family, someone to belong to, someone to need me. Even so, it could have worked. I tried hard enough, giving it everything I had. If only he'd been capable of making a commitment, I think we could have had a fairly happy marriage. But it would never have been a marriage built on love. I've thought about this a lot, especially since Martie's been pressuring me to go out with other men. And I think the reason I'm so uninterested in other men is that I'm simply monogamous by nature. I'm beginning to suspect that I gave my heart a long time ago and there's nothing left to give now."

"I know what you mean. Some people give their love like an expensive but not irreplaceable gift. If it doesn't work out, they can always give the same thing to someone else. But others give it only once, because what they offer is their soul, and when it's gone there's nothing left to give anyone else. I gave my heart to Ross long ago, and for better or worse it will always belong to him even though I'm not in love with him anymore. But Kate . . . who did you fall in love with?"

"Oh . . . it's not important now," she shrugged

157

listlessly. Then, "I saw Joan yesterday. She's been trying to call you but you're always out."

"I know. I'm either on the beach painting or running around with Dan. How's Joan doing? Is she happy?"

"You know, I really think she is. I'm embarrassed now to remember how pessimistic we all were about this marriage. I think it's working out fine. She seems—oh, I don't know, relaxed, somehow. They're leaving next week for a vacation in Tahiti, just the two of them, where they're going to start trying to have a baby."

"I'm so happy to hear that. I've thought about her a lot and planned to call her a dozen times, but it always seemed like something came up."

"I know the Hollywood social scene can keep you busy, especially on top of a booming career. I noticed that the L.A. *Times* art critic gave your new one-woman show a rave review."

"Of course. Now that I'm making lots of money, the art establishment has decided to accept me. But I remember too well how those kinds of people rejected me in the beginning to ever be flattered by their attention now."

Kate looked at her thoughtfully. "You know, Gin, you're different now, harder in a way. I don't mean that as an insult at all. You needed to develop a little healthy selfishness and a stronger sense of your own identity. Finally you've done that."

"All it took was the end of my marriage."

"Is there any possibility that you and Ross might get back together?"

"No. Our love died a slow, lingering death. Nothing can bring it back again."

Changing the subject, Kate said brightly, "Why don't we go inside and have some peach pie. I made it fresh this morning with peaches from my own tree."

"You've certainly become a little homemaker. I never would have expected it from someone who looked so glamorous on all those *Vogue* covers."

"That was a mirage resulting from good bone structure and tons of makeup."

"And you really don't miss it? The glamor, the money, the fame.——"

"The parties at Park Avenue penthouses and Beverly Hills mansions, the weekend trips to Paris and Rome, the clothes that cost more than most people earn in a year," Kate finished, laughing. "No. I don't miss any of it. I have Scottie, and he's more real to me than any of that was. Having him simply proved what I always suspected—I'm a 'nester,' I love having babies and creating a happy home." Then, looking around at the empty garden, "And speaking of the little devil, where on earth has he got to?"

"He was here just a minute ago," Ginny answered, looking around also. "Maybe he's in the house."

"No, the door's closed and he always leaves it open when he goes in and out, despite constant reminders from me—oh, no . . . the pool!"

Kate leapt up and started running toward an open gate leading to the neighbor's backyard.

Ginny remembered Kate saying that Scottie was fascinated with the neighbor's pool, which was strictly off-limits to him because he couldn't swim. Telling herself that they were being ridiculously paranoid, that Scottie was undoubtedly all right, she ran after Kate. But her heart was beating fast and she prayed as she ran.

Ginny caught a glimpse of a small blue and white form lying at the bottom of the pool before Kate dived in. Thoughts raced wildly through Ginny's distraught mind—that Scottie had only been out of sight briefly and couldn't have been in the pool for long, that he looked so tiny and helpless down there, that Kate looked awkward and strange swimming fully clothed, kicking with high-heeled shoes . . .

But all thinking stopped when Kate pulled Scottie's body, weighted down with wet clothes, up to the surface. Ginny grabbed him, pulling with all her might to get him out of the water. As she laid him down next to the edge of the pool, Kate who had just pulled herself out, bent over him and began mouth-to-mouth resuscitation. Looking back once to see if the little chest was moving, Ginny raced into Kate's house to phone the paramedics. As she dialed frantically, she kept thinking, "He wasn't moving . . . oh, God, he wasn't moving at all . . ."

The paramedics took the three of them to a nearby hospital. In the brief ride over, one of them continued mouth-to-mouth breathing, despite the fact that Scottie wasn't responding at all. By Ginny's count Scottie hadn't breathed for at least five minutes now, maybe more. Looking at Kate, who seemed in

160

a daze, she put her arm around her, saying nothing.

At the hospital, Scottie was wheeled immediately into the emergency room. A tall, young doctor with red-gold hair and a firm air of competence who followed the stretcher into the room seemed vaguely familiar to Ginny. Turning to reassure Kate, Ginny found her staring open-mouthed at the doctor.

In a shocked whisper, Kate said, "David . . ."

They waited outside the emergency room for several long minutes, in a state of utter silence and agony. Kate seemed oblivious of the fact that she was dripping wet, her hair plastered damply around her face. Ginny wished desperately that there was something she could say or do to help relieve Kate's guilt and terror. But there was nothing. Scottie would either live or die, and neither of them could do anything about it.

In those interminable minutes, Ginny came to understand the meaning of the word *eternity*.

Finally the young doctor who had gone in with Scottie came out looking tired and thoughtful. But his deep blue eyes looked squarely at both women, and there was an aura of victory in them, as if he had faced a dreaded foe and won.

"He'll be all right," he reassured Kate, smiling softly.

"Oh, thank God," Kate sobbed, falling against his shoulder.

He held her as if it were the most natural thing in the world, as if she belonged in his arms.

Watching them, Ginny was both relieved and perplexed. Though the doctor looked very familiar, she still couldn't place him.

Pulling herself away, leaving a wet spot on the doctor's white tunic, Kate wiped her eyes and asked tentatively, "Can I see him?"

"We'll be taking him up to a private room shortly. You can see him then. He'll have to stay here for a couple of days, but I don't foresee any complications at all. By Friday he'll be back home, playing happily."

"And by Saturday he'll be enrolled in a swim class," Kate responded grimly.

"That's a good idea. I'm glad to see you're taking that attitude instead of deciding to keep him away from water forever. That just doesn't work. It's much healthier to have a child who knows how to handle things than one who's afraid to try anything."

Suddenly feeling like an intruder in this conversation, Ginny said to Kate, "Well, I'll leave you here and take a cab back to the house to pick up my car. I'll come back and wait in the cafeteria for you. Don't worry about hurrying."

"Oh, Ginny, thanks," Kate mumbled nervously, still badly shaken by the ordeal.

As Ginny walked off, she glanced back once and saw the doctor watching Kate carefully, his expression surprised and interested.

Kate stayed with Scottie as much as the visiting hours allowed. At some point each day, sometimes twice a day, the doctor stopped by to let her know how Scottie was progressing. At first their conversations were brief, limited to a discussion of Scottie's health. Though the doctor was playful and engaging with Scottie, who already worshipped him, he seemed curiously shy and withdrawn with Kate.

Then one day as Kate was leaving after spending the evening with Scottie, she ran into the doctor in the corridor outside Scottie's room.

"That's some little boy," the doctor said admiringly. "You and your husband must be very proud of him."

"My husband and I are divorced. He rarely sees Scottie," Kate explained curtly.

"I see," the doctor responded, not quite masking the relief in his voice. Then, "You probably don't remember me, but we went to high school together."

"I know," Kate said softly. "I remembered you the first day I saw you in the emergency room. I'm surprised you remember me."

"Why wouldn't I? I've seen you in newspapers and magazines from time to time. I know you were a very successful model and traveled a lot, probably meeting quite a few interesting people. After leading an exciting life like that, it's kind of remarkable that you would remember a boy from high school who never had the courage to ask you out."

Stunned, Kate asked, "You mean you wanted to go out with me?"

"Desperately."

"But why on earth didn't you ever ask me?"

"I was sure you couldn't possibly be interested in me. You were so beautiful, I knew that you must have all kinds of boyfriends. Hey, why are you laughing?"

Kate was laughing so hard that tears were streaming down her face, but they were tears of relief now, not sadness.

"Oh, David, I don't believe it. We were both so silly. God, teenagers are incredibly stupid!"

"Wait a minute. You mean you would have actually gone out with me?"

"Of course. I may as well tell you, I had the worst crush on you. On graduation night I cried for hours because I knew I would never see you again."

"But you were always so cool, so reserved."

"That was terminal shyness and an inferiority complex that wouldn't quit. As far as I was concerned I was much too tall and horribly awkward, and I was sure you were simply being nice to me because you were the kindest person in the world."

"Damn!" he exploded, then started laughing, too. Finally when they had both calmed down, he continued, looking at her slyly, "When I think of all the hot summer nights at drive-in movies that I could have shared with you . . ."

Leaning toward her, he asked, "Well, since fate seems to have given us a second chance to get to know each other, will you have dinner with me tonight?"

"I'd love to. But would you mind if we have dinner at my house? I just don't feel like going out."

"I understand. But I don't imagine you really feel like cooking. How about if I just pick up some Chinese food and bring it with me?"

"Sounds great. I'll see you later then."

"Yeah. Bye, Kate."

As she walked off, he watched until she was out

of sight, then walked slowly, thoughtfully into Scottie's room.

"I knew right from the beginning of med school that I wanted to be a pediatrician," David was saying as he and Kate sat near each other on a sofa in her living room. They were sipping wine, feeling full from a surprisingly good dinner and enjoying the unexpectedly relaxed feeling they had with each other.

"What made you decide so quickly?"

"I had a little sister, Tammy. She died before I got to high school. It was leukemia, and as I watched the disease gradually take her, I made up my mind that I wanted to be able to do something about that sort of thing someday. After this year of residency at the hospital I'll go into private practice."

"Dr. David Hanson . . . it has a nice sound."

Grinning, his eyes flashing humor, he replied, "I hope other people feel that way. Getting started in practice can be tough."

"Perhaps, but you're such a good doctor that I'm sure people will be flocking to you right from the start."

"That would be nice. One thing's for sure, I'm too old to try basketball again."

"Did you ever consider turning professional?"

"Not really. I enjoyed playing in college, and the scholarship helped get me through. The offers I got from pro teams were tempting in terms of money, but I knew what I wanted to do. Some of my friends couldn't understand how I could turn down six-figure contracts. But, you see, Kate, I've never felt money was the thing that would really make me happy."

"I understand. You know, I was ambitious enough and lucky enough to know great success, yet I was miserable the whole time."

"But judging from the pictures I saw of you in magazines, your life looked glamorous and exciting."

"It was neither. Modeling wasn't glamorous, it was plain hard work, real drudgery much of the time. Wearing a skimpy bathing suit in the ice-cold ocean in the middle of winter to meet magazine deadlines for spring issues, being on my feet for hours, putting up with groping photographers. And most of the time it was far from exciting since I had to go to bed early to avoid looking tired in front of the camera. In order to stay excrutiatingly thin I existed only on lean meat and salad. I felt bored and useless."

"You met some interesting people, though, I imagine. Your husband, for example. Someone told me he was a producer."

"Kevin is a very fine producer, but a lousy human being. When Scottie was born, Kevin wasn't there. He was attending the Academy Awards. He was nominated and he refused to miss it just because I was in labor. You know, David, I hate to admit it but I was sort of glad when he lost."

"He sounds like a jerk."

"Actually, I was the jerk. I tried to make him something he didn't want to be—a family man. I never should have married him. But money and fame weren't nearly as satisfying as I expected them to be and I wanted someone to love, a man I could make a home for, whose children I could bear. More than anything else, I wanted what I never knew as a child—a traditional, secure, close family life. My parents divorced early, after deciding that one child was one too many. I always envied Ginny her home life—loving parents, security, happiness.

Sighing heavily, Kate continued pensively, "But in trying to find that kind of life for myself I ended up with the wrong kind of man. Kevin, like most men in the movie business, is self-centered, totally committed to his work. He liked having a glamorous wife and didn't especially mind when I wanted to have a child. But he didn't even pretend to be a devoted family man. After years of trying desperately, against all logic, to make Kevin what he wasn't—a loving husband and responsible father—I gave up. The love I felt for him had died long before; only my fierce determination to somehow make it work lasted."

"So now you're raising your son alone."

"It's not so bad. One parent who loves you deeply is better than no parent at all."

"But two parents are even better. Kate, Scottie needs a father."

"Unfortunately, he's going to have to learn how to get along without one." Kate's tone had grown bitter, which was not what she intended. "I'm sorry. That whole subject is rather a sore spot with me. I think I'd rather listen to your romantic history for awhile."

"It's pretty short," David answered, grinning.

"Did you ever marry?"

"Nope. In college I was too busy playing ball and trying to keep my grades up for med school. Then, once I got into med school there was no time for anything but studying. Oh, I dated now and then. Even doctors are human, whether we like to admit it or not." His blue eyes showed real amusement now. "But I kept putting off any serious involvement, telling myself that there would be plenty of time in the future for that. I think the truth was that I kept comparing every girl I met to you, and none of them measured up.".

Laughing to cover her embarrassment, Kate responded, "I can't believe that. The only thing I have over other women is a few extra inches."

But David was looking at her soberly now, no longer joking. "You have a great deal more than that, Kate. You're very special."

The obvious sincerity in his voice pleased and disturbed her. After three years of numbness, feeling nothing but love for her son, suddenly her determination to avoid other feelings was beginning to crumble. Though she was frightened, she didn't resist.

When Scottie had been home for several days, David asked Kate to go out with him. After seeing a movie that neither of them paid very much attention to, they went back to David's apartment for drinks. As Kate sat on his sofa while he mixed the drinks, she felt eager and expectant. There was something electric in the air, a feeling that neither had acknowledged but was nonetheless powerful. Kate sensed that something was going to happen that night, and to her surprise, she wasn't tempted to run away. For the first time in years she was allowing herself to be open to the possibilities.

Sitting down next to her, David handed her a drink and began, with a touch of nervousness in his voice, "How's Scottie doing at home?"

"Fine. He was really glad to get out of the hospital. But he misses you. When I told him he'd get to see you tonight, he was so excited."

"I enjoyed seeing him again, too. I miss his cute little face at the hospital." Then he continued awkwardly, "Well, I'm afraid that wasn't much of a movie."

"No, I've seen better," Kate agreed.

"The acting was pretty bad, I guess." Suddenly setting down his drink, David turned to Kate and continued firmly, "To hell with the movie! I don't want to talk about it, I want to talk about us. Oh, Kate, I know it sounds crazy and stupid and everything else, but I love you. I've always loved you. The minute I saw you in the hospital last week, it was like the past fifteen years had never existed. I don't care about anything that happened during that time, what you've done or where you've been or who you've known. The only thing that matters is that I can see you and touch you again." His hand reached out to her, stroking her cheek. She felt herself quiver at his touch. "After all this time, I've found you again. And this time nothing between heaven and hell is going to take you away."

They kissed, tentatively, awkwardly at first, then

with a passion that seemed to envelop both of them immediately. Kate didn't think it was crazy or stupid. She simply felt that it was *right*, that it was meant to be. Rising, she let David lead her into the bedroom, where she gladly offered him the love she had never been able to give completely before.

12.

"Oh, Kate, he looks terrific!"

Ginny was happily watching Scottie play in his room. Immensely relieved to be home again, he still hadn't quite calmed down.

"Mommy, Mommy, where's my truck?" he asked anxiously when he couldn't find the big red firetruck, an unexpected gift from Kevin. Scottie treasured the truck, refusing to go to sleep unless it was sitting on the end of his bed where he could see it.

"It's probably under your bed where you usually leave it," Kate answered, smiling. Then, turning to Ginny, "I really appreciate your stopping by. I don't think I thanked you properly at the hospital."

"Kate, you know it isn't necessary to thank me. Hey, why don't the three of us go out to dinner and a movie? There must be a Disney picture or something playing somewhere. Betsy's with Ross tonight and Dan's out of town on a promotion trip for his new movie, so I'm alone and available."

"Oh, Gin, I'm sorry, but . . ." Kate hesitated. She hadn't told anyone about David, and now, suddenly, she felt very embarrassed about the whole thing. How could she tell Ginny that she was involved with her high school idol?

Watching Kate, Ginny wondered why she looked so funny. Then, intuitively, she guessed the truth. "Wait a minute! Have you got a date?"

With anyone else the question would have been a casual one. But with Kate it was fraught with significance.

When Kate nodded sheepishly, Ginny continued, "Don't tell me—it's that cute doctor from the hospital, the one I could swear I've seen before."

Grinning, Kate explained, "You have seen him before. He's David Hanson, from high school, remember?"

"Of course! How stupid I've been. I didn't actually have any classes with him, but I saw him play basketball often enough."

Scottie was happily playing with his fire truck now, so Kate led Ginny into the living room to talk privately.

"We're going sailing together this afternoon. He'll be here any minute now. Actually, we've been seeing a lot of each other since Scottie's accident."

"Kate—is this serious?"

Sighing deeply, Kate answered, "I don't know. David's incredibly nice, but . . ."

"But what? He's nice, handsome, a doctor, and taller than you. What could be the problem?"

Ginny was grinning, but Kate looked unhappy.

"It's Scottie. I'm afraid it would be unfair to him."

"What on earth do you mean? If David is nice, if he likes Scottie . . ."

"Oh, he likes him. You should have seen how terrific he was with him in the hospital, so gentle and reassuring. Scottie is crazy about him, too. He calls him Dr. Dave."

"Then what's the problem?"

"I just don't think it will work on a permanent basis. Scottie misses his father terribly and would probably resent David trying to take his place. I grew up with a stepfather, and I know how difficult and complicated that whole situation is. And David might end up resenting Scottie."

"Somehow he doesn't strike me as the kind of guy who's so petty he would resent any child of yours," Ginny said calmly. Then, "Kate, there's something I've got to say. You may disagree, you may even get pretty mad at me, but it's something that's been on my mind for quite awhile. You're starting to develop an unhealthy relationship with Scottie. Because Kevin has behaved so abominably, you've got this us-against-the-world philosophy. You've taken it to the point of not wanting Scottie to fulfill his natural desire to grow independent from you, and you're reluctant to let anyone else into your private little world."

"Ginny!"

"Kate, you're too good a friend for me to continue silently watching you ruin your life and possibly Scottie's. You've got a real chance at happiness here, both for yourself and for your son. Sure, there are problems, nothing is ever easy in any family relationship. But this could work. Give it a chance . . . give *David* a chance."

"I don't want or need your advice," Kate responded stonily. "If you think so highly of combining families, why don't you marry Dan?"

The question didn't really require an answer. Ginny knew that Kate was merely trying to get back at her because she felt wounded and insulted.

"I'm sorry if I've hurt you," Ginny finished quietly. "But I hope . . . I hope you'll at least think about what I've said."

Aware that she had alienated Kate, she left, wondering sadly if there was anything left of their friendship now.

As she lay on the sailboat that afternoon, lazily watching David teach Scottie how to handle the boat, Kate couldn't help remembering Ginny's hard but honest words. She tried to put them out of her mind, but it was useless. They kept coming back to haunt her, especially the disturbing accusation that she was not doing what was best either for Scottie or herself.

And then there was David. He seemed seriously interested in her. But Kate was unsure and frightened, not of her feelings for him but of what would happen to Scottie. Because of Kevin's abandonment of his son, Kate thought of herself as the only person in the world who could protect Scottie. He was so helpless, so vulnerable . . . she simply couldn't let any harm come to him. Without hesitation she would willingly die defending him. Yet now she found herself in a position where she might bring unhappiness into his life by forcing an unwanted stepfather on him.

As if all that wasn't enough, she was also concerned about David—could he really love Scottie or would he resent him? Would Scottie be a barrier between her and David?

As these disturbing thoughts raced back and forth endlessly in her mind, Kate suddenly noticed that Scottie was dangerously close to the edge of the boat. Rising quickly, she ran to him, pulling him back to the center of the boat.

"You mustn't get so close to the edge," she chided him firmly. "You might fall over."

His small face, which had been lit with excitement, abruptly grew fearful. He vividly remembered how terrified he had been when he fell into the pool and couldn't get to the surface. Now, looking at the ocean surrounding them, he once more grew frightened of the water. Shrinking against his mother, he said anxiously, "Maybe we better go back, Mommy."

Before Kate could answer, David spoke sharply. "He's wearing a life jacket, Kate, and I'm watching him carefully. I wouldn't let him fall in. But even if he did somehow get in the water, the jacket would keep him up until I could get him. He wouldn't be in the water more than a minute or two." Then, to Scottie, "Why don't you help me with this, son."

But Scottie hesitated, afraid now to go near the edge of the boat again. David waited for a moment, then abruptly turned the boat back toward the harbor. He didn't say another word until they were home and Kate had fed Scottie and put him to bed.

"We've got to talk about this, Kate," he began firmly as she walked into the living room after kissing Scottie good night. "What you did out there today just reinforced his fear of the water."

"I was simply protecting him, he might have fallen in—"

"Which would have been all right. He was in no danger." Then, firmly, "You don't trust me with him, do you?"

"Oh, David, it isn't that. This is so unimportant, why don't we just forget about it."

"It's important, Kate. Important to all of us. I understand your concern for Scottie after he nearly drowned, but I'm afraid this goes beyond that. You hover over him as if he were made of porcelain and might break any minute. That's not good for the boy."

"I know what's best for my son, David."

"When we get married he'll be my son, too, Kate. I'm crazy about the little guy and I want to adopt him."

Kate was stunned.

"Married?"

"If you'll have me. And the sooner, the better. We've wasted too many years already. Let's don't waste anymore." Then, uncertainly, "Unless . . . you don't love me . . ."

"David, I've loved you for fifteen years. I loved you all the time I thought I would never see you again. And I loved you even more when fate brought you into my life so unexpectedly. But Scottie . . ."

"Kate, normally, I wouldn't dream of taking a child away from his natural father, but Scottie's father has made it painfully clear that he doesn't want him. *I* do. Kate, I want us to be a family."

"Oh, David, I just don't know if it will work."

"The only reason it won't work is your reluctance to share Scottie with anyone else. Kate, I love you,

176

and I'm growing to love Scottie. I want both of you." His blue eyes grew serious and his voice turned hard. "But you've got to understand something. Despite my love for you, I won't sit quietly by and watch you make tragic mistakes in the way you're raising him. I would rather lose you than do that."

Kate's heart sank as she realized that he meant what he said. "I was afraid this would happen," she responded slowly, looking away. "I suspected that either we would hurt Scottie or he would come between us."

"Don't use Scottie as an excuse," David cut in impatiently. "I know all of the problems, I'm a doctor, remember? I know there will be times when both Scottie and I will resent each other. Someday he'll have to deal with the fact that his father has rejected him, and that won't be an easy thing to handle. There will be disagreements between you and I about how to raise him. But we can deal with all of that successfully if we love and trust each other enough. Kate, you've got to let down that wall you've built around yourself and the boy, you've *got* to let me in. If you can't do that, if you can't let me be a real father to him, then we're just not going to make it."

Rising, David picked up the jacket he had discarded earlier. "You've got a lot to think about, so I'll leave. Call me if . . . if you decide you can trust me."

And then he was gone. For a long moment Kate stood rigidly, trying furiously to put out of her mind every word David had said. But she couldn't stop thinking about it because she knew that she was losing him. The miracle of finding him again, after all those years of thinking he would never be more than a dream, was degenerating into bitter heartache.

The days passed painfully slowly. The nights were empty and endless. Kate threw herself into caring for Scottie with a vengeance, cooking his favorite foods, taking him to his favorite places. Occasionally he asked wistfully when they were going to see Dr. Dave again. Kate always responded noncommittally, avoiding any definite answer. She stole quietly into his room each night after he was sound asleep and watched him lying in his bed, a tiny figure in rumpled pajamas, his brown hair tousled, one arm hanging loosely over the edge of the bed. One night when he woke crying from a nightmare, she comforted him, and as he fell asleep in her arms, she whispered softly, "I'll love you forever."

One evening Kate was watching Scottie play in his room just before bedtime. He was pushing the fire truck around and around, pretending he was a fireman rushing to a fire. Suddenly the plastic axle broke and the truck skidded to a sloppy stop, turning over on its side. Scottie's face fell. Scooping up the damaged truck and the broken axle he took it to his mother.

"Mommy, look, it broke!"

"I see, honey. Well, maybe I can fix it."

"You can't fix it," Scottie replied firmly, "you're a girl."

"Can't girls fix trucks?"

"Of course not." Then, his expression brightening, "Maybe Daddy can fix it."

"Scottie, your father isn't here, so I'm afraid he can't fix it."

His face fell once more, before he thought of something else. "Then let's take it to Dr. Dave. He fixed me, I'll bet he can fix my truck."

Kate felt her heart stop. Scottie had made the transition so quickly from wanting his father to wanting David.

"Scottie . . . do you like David?" she asked hesitantly.

"Yeah, he's neat."

"Do you like him as much as your father?"

"I don't know." Then, "Maybe."

Maybe. It was the last thing in the world Kate would have expected him to say. It had never occurred to her that even though Scottie missed his father, he might be willing to let someone else take over the role. In a flash of understanding, she realized that Scottie simply needed a father, and whether it was Kevin or David didn't much matter to him.

"Scottie, would you like to see David again?"

"Yeah," he looked at her happily. "Could we go sailing again?"

"Perhaps. Are you still afraid of the water?"

"Sort of. But . . . but Dr. Dave would be there wouldn't he?"

"Yes."

"Then it would be all right."

God, what a fool I've been, Kate thought miserably. Then, with an air of determination, she went to the telephone and dialed David's number. It rang several times, and with a feeling of deep disappointment Kate was about to hang up when abruptly he answered.

"Hello," he said breathlessly, obviously having run to catch the phone.

"David, I've been thinking . . ."

"Yes?" he responded hopefully.

"Would you like to take Scottie sailing this weekend, just the two of you?" There was a stunned silence on the other end of the line as Kate continued nervously, "I thought . . . it would give you two a chance to get to know each other, and it would give Scottie a chance to learn how to sail without me hovering over him the whole time."

When David didn't respond immediately, Kate assumed unhappily that she was too late. Fighting back tears, she steeled herself for rejection.

"I would like that very much, Kate," he said quietly. "And afterwards you and I can have dinner. We have a lot of plans to make."

Kate sighed deeply in relief. It wasn't too late after all.

13.

Before Kate flew with David and Scottie to Lake Tahoe for the wedding, Martie and Ginny took her out to lunch at Ma Maison for an impromptu wedding shower. As they sipped white wine on the patio under a balmy Los Angeles sky, Kate opened her presents, a beautiful, sexy peignoir from Martie and a small portrait of Scottie from Ginny.

"I should put this painting in a vault somewhere," Kate said, smiling broadly. "The way your career has taken off, it's sure to be worth a fortune some day."

"That's only part of your gift," Ginny responded happily. "The rest is more valuable than money. It's a free weekend of babysitting. Any time you and David feel like you need some time to yourselves, just bring Scottie out to the beach, and Betsy and I will take care of him for you."

"I'll take you up on that offer," Kate said meaningfully to Ginny. They smiled warmly at each other, both of them immensely relieved that the tension between them was gone.

"Joan will die when she learns that you fell in love and got married, all while she was gone. She'll

181

never forgive you when she finds out she missed your wedding," Martie commented wryly.

"I know, I wish she was here. I actually considered putting off the wedding—for about half a second." They all laughed. "But now that I've found David, I'm not going to wait one more day to make him mine."

"Well, I feel a little cheated, too," Martie continued. "At least Ginny has met David. I had to dig out our old yearbook to find out what he looks like. I've gotta say he was pretty cute."

"Well, he's even cuter now. But enough of this, I want to hear what's happening with you two."

"Dan and I are going down to Acapulco for a long weekend in a couple of weeks," Ginny responded. "He starts a new movie right after that, so we won't be seeing as much of each other. Which will be for the best in a way because it will give me a chance to get some work done. The gallery has been hounding me for more paintings. Being a social butterfly was fun for awhile, but it's bad for my career and my figure. I've gained ten pounds."

"Well, while you've been busy snatching up what has to be the last available handsome young doctor in the entire world," Martie said to Kate, "I've been nurturing a genius. And thanks to me he's going to be a rich genius very soon."

"Is he that writer you were telling me about, Stuart Mendoza?" Ginny asked.

"Yup. I just finished negotiating a contract that will give him a million-dollar advance for his first novel. And three studios are bidding for the movie rights."

"Wow, he must be a pretty happy genius right now."

"The last time I talked to him he still couldn't believe it," Martie said, grinning. "He really is incredibly sweet. And I meant it when I said he is a genius, not just another Hollywood hack with a commercial idea. It's been a very different kind of experience working with him—sort of refreshing in a way. For once I feel like I'm doing something worthwhile."

"Is this Martie Bass talking about higher values as opposed to big bucks?" Kate asked, laughing.

"Hard to believe, isn't it? But I'll tell you something that's even harder to believe. I think I may be announcing my own marriage in the not-too-distant future."

Kate responded with surprise and happy interest, but Ginny looked troubled.

"Don't tell me your boyfriend's going to leave his wife?"

"I think so. We've been living together for the past few weeks and it's gone extremely well."

Looking at Ginny, who was silent, Martie asked gaily, "Are you too shocked to speak?"

"I'm sorry, Martie, you know I'm happy for you."

"Thanks, Gin. I realize you've never been too crazy about this whole situation but, believe me, it's going to work out."

"I hope so," Ginny responded, trying to sound more confident than she felt.

"Well listen, girls, I've got to get back to the office. I've got a million things to do and I won't be through until late tonight. I'm taking Stuart to a

183

cocktail party his publisher is throwing this evening so he can start mingling with his fellow literary giants."

Her expression worried and thoughtful, Ginny watched Martie confidently stride away.

At the office Martie was swamped with work, as usual. The senior partner in the office was retreating further and further into alcoholism, and his work was being piled on Martie. At the same time that she was trying to build up her own struggling novice clients, she was also devoting a great deal of energy to his more important, established clients, who required a great deal of attention. The situation had been worsening for weeks, the pressure growing more intense, until now Martie routinely took pills each day just to make it through without collapsing.

"You have three calls that have to be returned immediately," her secretary Denise said as she walked in.

"Well, I only have two ears, so one of them, at least, is going to have to wait," Martie responded curtly. Then, sighing, "I'm sorry, it's not your fault. Get them for me one at a time, will you? And cancel that doctor's appointment I have tomorrow, I'm just not going to be able to make it."

Frowning, Denise replied, "You really should try to go. You look exhausted."

"All he'll do is tell me I'm working too hard and charge me twenty-five bucks. Since I already know I'm working too hard, I think I'll just save myself the twenty-five bucks."

"Has it ever occurred to you that you might slow down?"

"If I don't make deals, my clients don't work. And besides, I have a mortgage and a Saks Fifth Avenue charge account to support."

"Even Sue Mengers takes a vacation sometimes," Denise replied, referring to the most successful woman agent in Hollywood.

"When I get to her level I'll take a vacation, too. In the meantime, I'll just keep on hustling my butt. By the way, after you make those calls, get hold of Stuart Mendoza and remind him he's supposed to wear a tux tonight. He has an unfortunate tendency toward casualness."

The afternoon went by in a blur of phone calls and meetings, and as Martie drove to the party that evening, her mind was still racing. But Michael was constantly at the back of her thoughts. Any day now she expected him to call his wife and ask for a divorce. It had now reached the point where she not only expected it, but counted on it. She had completely put any other possibility out of her mind.

As usual, the party bored Stuart. After being briefly introduced to several other writers who seemed completely uninterested in meeting him, he decided he'd had enough.

"I'm leaving," he announced firmly to Martie.

"But you haven't met everyone yet."

"I don't want to meet everyone, and I'm sure they don't want to meet me."

"That's only because they haven't heard of you yet. By next week when this deal is announced, they'll be dying to know you."

"I don't want to bother with people who are only dying to know me because my clever agent made a terrific deal."

"It's a good thing for you that you have a clever agent because you have no head for business!"

Grinning, Stuart responded, "I think we've set a new record tonight. We're not even halfway through the party and already we're fighting." Then, cajolingly, "Come on, let's get out of here."

"Well . . . okay. But only if we take my car. I refuse to ride in yours."

"Actually mine's in the garage anyway. I had to take a cab here, and frankly I was planning on bumming a ride home with you since I can't afford to take a cab back."

Shaking her head, Martie said sarcastically, "I don't believe it. On paper right now you're a millionaire, but you don't have cab fare. Come on."

As Martie pulled up in front of Stuart's place, he asked easily, "Want to come in for a drink or something?"

"What kind of drink could you possibly have in your little garrett?"

"Cold beer. When you told me they're buying the book, I splurged and bought one of those little portable refrigerators."

"This I've got to see. But I can only stay for a minute."

A few minutes later, Martie was sitting comfortably in an ancient chair, sipping beer, while Stuart sprawled across his bed, watching her intently.

"So why do you have to hurry off?" he asked pointedly.

"Because my boyfriend will be waiting for me."

"I see, " he responded, disappointed. "Are you living together?"

"Yes."

"Why aren't you married?"

"What a rude question!"

"Writers are allowed to ask rude personal questions. It's all part of perfecting our knowledge of human nature. So—why aren't you married?"

"Because he's already married," Martie answered abruptly.

"Oh."

"What is *that* supposed to mean?"

"Nothing. Just 'oh.' "

"Anyway," Martie continued defensively, "he's going to be leaving his wife. They've been separated for a long time."

That wasn't exactly the truth, since they were separated geographically, not legally. But for some reason Martie felt it necessary to justify her behavior to Stuart.

"I suppose you think it's immoral or something," she said angrily.

"No. Just stupid."

"Sorry I asked. Why don't we change the subject?"

"Okay, tell me about yourself."

"What do you mean?"

"All I know about you is that you're a terrific deal maker and are living with someone. I'd like to know more—where do you come from, if you like onions, that sort of thing."

"I come from L.A., believe it or not. I grew up in

187

Santa Monica, and my constant goal was to some-day make enough money to shop on Rodeo Drive without having to look at the price tags. And I *hate* onions."

"Were you ever married?"

"Yes."

"That's rather a brief answer to an important sub-ject."

"It was a brief marriage. I thought he wanted an intelligent, fully functioning woman. I was wrong." Then, "And you? Were you ever married?"

"No. I came close once but the girl wanted me to become a publicist because the money was steady. I just couldn't see doing that."

"She must not have realized how talented you are."

"Nobody realized how talented I am until you came along."

"It didn't take a great deal of perception on my part. I deal with garbage so often, it was easy to spot something that didn't smell."

"You know something? Beneath that cold, ruth-less agent's exterior beats the heart—"

"Of a cold, ruthless agent," Martie finished.

"Of a very nice person," Stuart disagreed. His brown eyes watched her intently, as though he were looking deep inside her, into her very soul.

Fidgeting nervously, Martie quickly downed the last of her beer in one long gulp and rose. "I've got to go."

"Not yet. We've got a lot to talk about."

"What we've got to talk about is the immense

sum of money you will shortly receive, and we can do that at my office tomorrow."

He walked with her to her car and as she slid onto the seat, he leaned over and kissed her briefly on the mouth. "Thank you. For everything."

Without saying a word, Martie drove off. Though she tried to dismiss Stuart as a likeable fool, she couldn't forget the way his lips felt against hers.

"Did you hear the news?" Denise asked the next afternoon when Martie came back from yet another business lunch.

"What news?"

"Doyle just made a big deal. He got the Simpson property for Michael Gregory to direct. They say it's going to be the biggest picture of the year. They're going to film the whole thing on location in Africa."

Martie's heart fell to her stomach, but she tried to hide her shock from Denise. No one in the agency knew about her affair with Michael. That was something he had insisted on firmly from the beginning.

"When . . . when are they supposed to start shooting?"

"I think the start date is sometime in June."

June . . . only two months away. Martie knew enough about the Simpson property to realize that they would have a shooting schedule of at least six months, perhaps longer.

"Well . . . I'll have to congratulate Doyle," Martie managed to say, trying to smile. Rushing to her office, she closed the door and immediately called Michael's office at Universal Studios.

189

When he came on the line, she began urgently, "I just heard about the Simpson property—"

"Yes, isn't it fantastic! Doyle called me a few minutes ago. This is the break I've been waiting for, a really big picture. It'll make my reputation in this town, Martie."

She couldn't believe he sounded so happy, as if there were no drawbacks to the situation.

"But, Michael, you'll be going to Africa."

"Yeah, I've always wanted to travel there. I hear it's a fascinating place."

"Won't it be . . . rather lonely being there for such a long time?"

"Not really, they're letting me take my family along even when we go out into the bush to shoot."

Martie had to force herself to ask, "You mean you're taking your wife?"

"Yes." Then, "Listen, I'm supposed to meet with Simpson tonight, so don't wait up for me. It's likely to be a long meeting. And tomorrow I'm flying back to New York to get some things taken care of back there. I'll take all of my clothes and things with me."

"Why do I get the feeling you're trying in some subtle way to tell me it's over?" Martie responded sarcastically.

"Hey, babe . . . I never lied to you. I didn't make any promises. You're a big girl, you knew what you were getting into."

"Yeah, I'm a big girl." *And big girls don't cry*, she thought, fighting back the tears that stung her eyes.

"When the movie's finished and I'm back in town, I'll call you, okay?"

"Sure," she whispered, her voice hoarse. Then, summoning up that defiant pride that was so familiar to her friends, she said, "Michael, love . . ."

"Yeah?"

"Go to hell!"

As she slammed down the phone, she burst into terrible, wracking sobs. Crossing her arms over her desk, she lay down her head and cried bitterly for the empty hopes that she'd built her life around and for all the long, lonely nights to come.

After several minutes, when she had stopped crying and was just sitting listlessly in her chair, looking like a victim of shell shock, Denise tapped on her door and came in.

"Bad news, I'm afraid. Latham wants to see you, and he's furious. He just found out that Hillman's leaving the agency to go with William Morris, and he's blaming you."

Saying nothing, unable to absorb any more pain, Martie rose silently and walked over to Latham's office. He was the senior partner in the firm, as hard-nosed as they come, with a reputation for hanging onto clients unmatched in Hollywood.

When Martie walked in, he began coldly, "Did you hear about Hillman?"

Martie nodded, unable to speak.

"He's only the biggest client we've got, you know. And now he's leaving because, as he says, he's not getting enough personal attention here. Reynolds just turned him over to you last month, and already you've managed to drive him away."

Martie could have explained that Hillman was leaving because he was insulted by her refusal to go to bed with him. But there was no fight left in her now, so she merely stood mutely, taking the abuse that Latham dumped on her.

"This agency can't afford mistakes like that," Latham continued with an awful finality in his voice. "You're fired. Get your things and get out."

Still saying nothing, Martie turned and left, stopping only to pick up her purse in her office. When she walked out the door she didn't bother looking back.

That night, Martie, dressed in her loveliest nightgown, sat in the middle of her bed, a notepad and pencil lying in front of her. She had just finished writing a brief note, explaining how she wanted her personal possessions disposed of. Beside it was a sealed envelope addressed to Ginny. The letter inside said simply, "I'm sorry. Don't grieve for me."

Carefully lining up all of her pills, she counted them to make sure there were more than enough to do the job. She didn't want to miscalculate and wake up in the hospital.

She didn't want to wake up, period.

Ginny was roused from a sound sleep by the insistent ringing of the telephone. When she answered sleepily, she was surprised to hear Maurice's voice.

"Ginny, I'm sorry to bother you so late, but a problem has come up."

"With my pictures?" Ginny asked, confused.

"No, it's rather strange, actually. A young man

192

called me, wanting to get in touch with you. He insisted that it was urgent, that it couldn't wait until tomorrow. I would never give him your number, of course, but finally I did agree to call you and give you his number in case you want to talk to him."

"Who is he?"

"His name is Stuart Mendoza, and he says he is a friend of a friend of yours, a Miss Bass."

Martie's client, Stuart . . . what on earth could he want with me at this time of night? Ginny wondered.

"It's okay, Maurice, I think I know him. What's his number?"

He gave it to her, then added, "The poor man seemed quite distraught. I hope it's nothing serious."

"I hope so, too. Thank you."

Ginny lay back down in bed, yawning deeply, and dialed Stuart's number. He answered immediately, after only one ring, and when he learned who it was, began hurriedly, "I'm sorry to bother you but I've got to get hold of Martie and I don't have her address or phone number. She mentioned once that you were a friend of hers and that your paintings were being shown at the Moreau gallery. I know Mr. Moreau thinks I'm crazy, but I'm tremendously relieved that he finally agreed to call you."

"But can't you get in touch with Martie through the agency tomorrow?" Ginny said reasonably.

Stuart explained abruptly, "That's just it, she was fired today and no one there would give me her personal phone number or address."

"*Fired?* What on earth for?"

"I have no idea. But the more I thought about it,

the more worried I got. I would have expected Martie to call me to tell me about it, but I haven't heard from her."

Ginny was impressed by the concern in his voice. It flashed through her mind that he was more than simply a client of Martie's. He obviously cared about her a great deal.

She gave him Martie's phone number and address, then added, "Will you call me as soon as you've talked to her? Just . . . just to let me know everything's okay."

"Sure. Thanks, Ginny."

Try as she would, Ginny couldn't go back to sleep. Finally she dialed Martie's number just to reassure herself, though she was sure she was being ridiculous. When there was no answer, she grew worried. Since Michael had started living with her, Martie had been spending all of her nights at home. There was no place else she would be at this time of night.

Driven by fear that she couldn't quite face, Ginny threw on some clothes and wrote a hasty note to Betsy, explaining where she was going, in case Betsy should wake up. Then she drove quickly to Martie's house.

The ambulance was pulling away as she drove up. Stuart was just getting in his car when Ginny ran over to him.

"Stuart?"

"Yes. Ginny?"

"What's happened? Where's Martie?"

"In the ambulance. I was just going to follow

them. I'm afraid she took an overdose of some kind of pills."

"Oh, my god!"

"Get in, I'll take you to the hospital."

As they rode over together, neither of them spoke. Both of them were overwhelmed with fear for the person they each cared so much about.

Martie was dreaming. It was a nice dream and she didn't want it to end. But there were voices coming from somewhere far away, calling her, insisting she wake up. The voices irritated her—didn't they realize she didn't want to wake up? Ignoring them, she let the dream envelop her . . .

14.

"It won't do any good to pretend you don't want any. Go ahead, take one. The ones in the middle are caramel."

Ginny was speaking matter-of-factly to Martie, who was sitting up in the hospital bed, looking angry and trying very hard to ignore the large box of chocolates that Ginny had just brought.

Martie glared at her, saying nothing.

Knowing Martie so well, Ginny decided that she would simply have to be totally honest. "You hurt me very much, you know." Martie looked up at her, surprised. *At least I got a response from her*, Ginny thought, relieved. She continued, "I would have expected you to call me if things were that bad. I thought we were better friends than that."

"You don't understand," Martie responded finally, her tone resentful.

"What don't I understand? Fear of failure, rejection, loneliness, the feeling that everything worthwhile in your life is gone and that there's nothing to look forward to?" Her voice hardened. "I understand. It hasn't been that long since I went through all of that, you know. I let you help me. Why didn't you let me help you?"

"I didn't want to be helped," Martie explained reluctantly. "I just wanted . . ."

"To die," Ginny finished for her. "Fortunately, Stuart cared enough about you not to let that happen."

"He had no right to interfere! Who asked him, anyway? If you two had let me alone I'd be dead now and . . ."

"And there would be no pain." Ginny sighed heavily. "Oh, Martie, I understand how badly it hurts. If I hadn't had Betsy to think of . . ." Her voice trailed off. Then, "I thought about it, you know, more than once. Fortunately for me I had someone to live for."

"Well, I don't!" Martie responded bluntly. "Michael is going to Africa with his patient wife."

"Michael is an ass! You're better off without him, and somewhere in that stubborn little mind of yours, you know that. He's also not the only person you had to live for. You have very good friends, and I'm not just talking about Joan and Kate and me."

"If you're referring to Stuart, forget it. He had no business butting into my life."

"Did I hear someone sweetly mention my name?" Stuart was standing in the doorway, holding a bouquet of fresh yellow and white daisies.

Ginny rose, picking up her purse. "Hi, Stuart. I'll leave you to cheer up the patient." Then, to Martie, "But I'll be back tonight. And I'm going to keep coming until sooner or later you get tired of being angry."

197

When she was gone, Stuart put down the flowers on a table, then sat down next to the bed.

"You look very nice today," he began kindly.

"I haven't washed my hair in three days and I have no makeup on," Martie replied.

"I love the natural look," he answered good-naturedly. "If you would make some attempt to get well, they would let you go home and wash that red mop and put on all the makeup you want."

His brown eyes were amused, but his face looked tired and drawn, reflecting his concern.

"Why didn't you just let me die?" Martie asked simply, her hazel eyes staring up at him helplessly.

"After spending ten years trying to find an agent, I didn't intend to lose my first one that quickly," he answered. Then, seriously, "Did you really love him that much?"

Martie started to say yes, then stopped. It wasn't true—she knew it wasn't true—and despite everything, she still felt compelled to be honest. That part of her hadn't changed.

"No," she answered in a voice so low that Stuart could barely hear it. "I just . . . I just felt so alone."

Stuart took her pale hand in his darker one, softly caressing her fingers. "You're not alone, Martie."

As she looked up at him, the tears that she had refused to give in to for three days suddenly filled her eyes, and she cried in his arms like a baby.

Ginny insisted that Martie come straight to her house from the hospital to stay for awhile before going home. She cooked delicious, irresistible meals for her to build up her strength, and kept her entertained with conversation and games.

Betsy was shocked and disbelieving when Ginny explained to her what Martie had done. She watched Martie curiously, feeling somehow too embarrassed to talk to her at any length. Finally one day while Ginny was visiting Dan on the set of his new movie, Martie asked Betsy if they could talk about something rather important.

"Sure," Betsy said uncomfortably, sitting down in a chair across the room.

"You don't have to sit so far away," Martie began, smiling. "Suicide isn't contagious, you know."

Reluctantly, Betsy moved closer.

"I can see that all of this bothers you a lot. I think we should talk about it," Martie continued evenly.

"I don't know what you mean," Betsy insisted coolly.

"Hey, don't try to kid me, kid. I've known you too long. I've kept secrets for you that would make your mother furious if she knew the truth." Then, softly, "Come on, Betsy, we've always been able to talk to each other."

For a long, tense moment Betsy said nothing. Finally, lowering her eyes, she said in a low voice, "Why did you do it?"

"Because I was frightened and lonely," Martie answered honestly. "My boyfriend left me and I thought I had nothing left to live for. I'm just beginning to realize how wrong I was." She continued slowly, "Being a woman isn't easy, Betsy. Pursuing a career, trying to maintain a close, mutually supportive relationship with a man—all of that is very complicated. When it doesn't work and you lose both the man you love and your job, it's a hard thing to handle."

Betsy looked thoughtful, her blue eyes clouded with confusion and worry. Martie could see that she was struggling to understand something that she didn't want to face. Finally, looking directly at Martie, she asked, "Mom's been going through the same thing, hasn't she?"

"Yes. It's been even harder on her because she felt guilty about letting you down. You know, from the moment you were born your mother's primary concern has been protecting you. She knew the divorce would hurt you, and that bothered her a lot."

Listening to Martie, Betsy looked pensive. She had a great deal to think about.

"Mom?"

"Yes," Ginny answered absentmindedly, putting the finishing touches on a painting in the sunroom.

"Am I interrupting you?"

"No, it's okay." Laying down the brush, she turned to Betsy. "Actually, I've been meaning to talk to you. How's Stacey?"

"Much better. She's gone to stay in a home for unwed teenage mothers. When the baby comes, she's putting it up for adoption and then coming home."

"That must have been an extremely painful decision for Stacey to make. I admire her a great deal for having the courage to do that."

"Yeah, I do, too. I don't know how well she'll be able to handle it, but she does realize it's the best thing for the baby. There are so many people who want children and can care for them. Her baby deserves to be raised by people who really want it and won't resent it."

"I hope that the knowledge that she's doing the right thing will help Stacey recover from this experience. She still has a life to lead."

Betsy was silent for a moment, then continued slowly, "I was talking to Martie the other day."

"I know. She told me. I understand how disturbing this whole experience has been for you, but for Martie's sake we've all got to put our feelings aside and concentrate on trying to help her. She needs all the love we have to give right now."

"Yeah. At first I was mad at her. I felt like she let me down because I always looked up to her as someone who really had it all together, and then she . . . she did what she did. But I'm not mad at her now. I didn't have the right to expect so much from her."

Feeling a surge of maternal pride, Ginny responded, "I'm glad you understand that."

"There's something else . . ." Betsy continued awkwardly, hooking her thumbs in her jean pockets and looking past her mother out to the ocean. "After seeing how lonely and unhappy Martie was because she didn't have anyone, I'm glad that . . ." she hesitated, then forced herself to go on, "that you have Dan. I don't ever want you to feel like Martie did, because . . . because I love you."

Ginny simply stood there for a moment, overwhelmed with conflicting emotions—tremendous relief that she need no longer feel guilty about Dan, sadness that Betsy was going through so much and growing up so suddenly, but more than anything else, *love* . . . she felt she would burst with love for her daughter. Trying not to cry, she said softly, "Thank you, Betsy. I love you, too."

Then suddenly both mother and daughter were crying and smiling and hugging each other tightly.

Later, when they had both recovered, they sat in the sunroom, talking more honestly, more intimately than they ever had before.

Betsy smiled. "Martie said that being a woman isn't easy."

"It isn't. We have to worry about a lot of things that simply don't apply with men—like, if we're successful in a career, does that take away from our femininity? One of the things I like best about Dan is that he isn't bothered by that question. He is genuinely happy about my success and isn't threatened by it. That's very important to me now because it took me so long to develop that part of me."

"Mom, do you love Dan?"

"I'm extremely fond of him."

"But what's the difference?"

Ginny leaned back in the chair, pulling her knees up and wrapping her arms around them comfortably. She thought for a long while before finally responding, "It's hard to say because love is different things to different people. Martie convinced herself that she was in love with her boyfriend, but I don't think she was, at least not according to my definition of love. I believe that real love involves a depth of commitment that just isn't there with mere infatuation. That person touches you more deeply, is more necessary to you, than anyone else and can't be easily replaced by someone else. It isn't a temporary thing that disappears when problems arise. It's forever. Even though the relationship that develops from it may end."

"Then you still love Daddy?"

"Yes. And I always will. But the romantic part of it, the infatuation, the passion, is gone. And that's why we're no longer together."

"But what's passion? I've asked a couple of people and no one can tell me. Not even Stacey, and she's not a virgin, obviously." Then, grinning at her mother knowingly, Betsy said, "In case you've wondered, I'm still a virgin."

Smiling back at her, Ginny responded, "The question had crossed my mind. But not for the reasons you might think. I don't want you to remain a virgin because sex is bad. When you handle it in a mature, responsible, caring way it's the most beautiful thing in the world. But it's infinitely complicated and much too important to play with sex the way you play with clothes and music. I'm not surprised that Stacey couldn't tell you about passion. I doubt that she knows what it is. She may have had sex but that doesn't necessarily mean that she experienced passion and fulfillment." Then, bluntly, "I'm afraid you may resent this, but I've got to say that sex isn't for children. Stacey is a child—her irresponsibility proved that, if there was ever any question. And you're still a child, though you're very close to being a woman now."

"How do you know when you're ready?"

"You'll know. When it feels right, when you have no reservations."

"You mean, you're not going to tell me to wait until I'm married or I'm twenty-one, or something?" Betsy asked, surprised.

"No. That would be rather useless, wouldn't it? This is something so personal that you've got to make the decision. All I can do is hope that you'll do what is truly best for you, that you will be strong enough not to allow yourself to be abused by anyone. But I'm not really worried, you know. I think someday soon you're going to be a terrific woman because you're pretty terrific now."

Rising, Betsy came up to Ginny and hugged her warmly.

15.

"Home at last," Stuart said, smiling, as he dropped Martie's suitcase on the floor of her living room. As Martie looked around carefully at the house she hadn't seen in three weeks, he continued, "I've been watering the plants, which is practically a full-time job. You've got your own mini-jungle here."

Martie grinned. "It's not that bad. But . . . thanks, Stuart."

"It's okay. Look, if you don't have any other plans, I thought we might go out to dinner tonight, maybe a movie, too."

Shaking her head slowly, Martie responded, "No, I've got to be alone for awhile. I need to start getting used to that." Seeing Stuart's worried look, she assured him, "Don't worry, I'm not going to do anything 'foolish,' as they say. I've come to the conclusion that Michael isn't worth it."

"I'm glad you've finally realized that. Okay, I'll leave you alone. But I'll be home if you change your mind and want some company."

As he started to leave, Martie stopped him. "Stuart . . ."

"Yes?"

"Thanks for . . . for everything." Her hazel eyes looked at him warmly, and her voice was so touchingly vulnerable that for a moment he wanted badly to go to her and take her in his arms. But he held back, knowing that it would be unfair to her to rush her right now.

However as he drove off, he told himself that one day soon when she was stronger he was going to have a very serious talk with her. And not about book deals.

Martie slowly walked through her house, running a finger through the dust on the furniture, straightening some crooked pictures. The dirty dishes that she remembered leaving in the kitchen were clean now, and she smiled as she realized who must have done them.

But as she came to her bedroom, her mood sobered and she had to force herself to go in. Stuart hadn't cleaned in here, whether because he simply didn't think about it or out of a sense of respect for her privacy. Her clothes, the ones she had worn to the office that last day, were still lying in a crumpled heap on a chair, and the bed was rumpled. Only the plastic container that had held the pills was gone now—probably taken by the police, she realized with a grimace.

For a moment she felt her throat tighten and tears come to her eyes as she remembered the depth of her depression that night and the awful finality of the act that was only barely thwarted in time. Another few minutes, the doctor said, and she would have succeeded. Listening to him, she'd wished she *had* succeeded. But now her tough, resilient personality was taking over again, and she was beginning to be very glad indeed that she had failed. Gradually that constant, dull ache for Michael was being replaced by her usual go-to-hell recklessness and stubborn determination. Thinking back now on the loss of her job and of Michael, she whispered to the empty room, "You bastards took your best shot at me and it almost worked. But I survived. And you'll never get me down that low again."

Quickly, impatiently, she began cleaning her house.

Later that night she was sitting at the desk in her small den, figuring out exactly how grim her financial situation was. When the phone rang, she jumped slightly, startled by the abrupt noise cutting through the silence.

"Hello," she finally answered, feeling foolish for being so nervous.

"Martie, it's Stuart."

Somehow the familiar voice was very reassuring. But before she could tell him so, he continued quickly, "Don't think I'm checking up on you or anything, I just wanted to say good night."

Smiling, she responded, "Don't worry, I'm not mad. I'm glad you called. It takes my mind off what I'm doing."

"What's that?"

"Going through my bills. If I don't get another job soon, the old house is going to have to go on the market."

"I didn't want to ask you before, but I'd like to know now. What happened at the agency?"

"Oh, Latham wanted a scapegoat for something and I was handy. It happens all the time in Hollywood. Aside from the fact that I'll miss being your agent, it was probably for the best. The pressure was really getting to me." Then, dryly, "Obviously."

"What will you do now?" Stuart asked, concerned.

"Look for something slightly less hectic. Don't worry—failing upward is a common occurrence in show business. I probably won't have too much trouble signing on with another agency."

"Is that what you really want to do with your life—work for one Latham after another?"

"I don't have much choice."

"I'm sorry, I know I had no right to say that. Listen, why don't you put off your job-hunting and spend the day with me tomorrow?"

"What did you have in mind?"

"Something boringly old-fashioned and un-Hollywood—a tour of the zoo, a picnic at Griffith Park, browse through some book stores, then dinner at a cheap but romantic little Italian restaurant that serves the best fettucini in L.A."

Laughing, Martie answered, "Sounds terrific. I'm really into boredom right now."

"I'll pick you up at ten."

"Okay. Good night, Stuart."

"Good night, Martie."

That night she slept better than she had in a long time.

The day went by in a happy blur—laughing with Stuart at the monkeys in the zoo, stuffing herself with French bread and cheese and wine in the park, buying paperback murder mysteries at used book stores, and finally eating fettucini that was every bit as delicious as Stuart had said. Sitting at the quiet corner table in the dark restaurant, Martie and Stuart talked about everything under the sun, never seeming to run out of things to say to each other. They didn't leave until the restaurant was empty and the waiter was eyeing them impatiently.

As Stuart walked with Martie into her house he watched her carefully, his expression, which had been so light-hearted all day, suddenly serious.

"Oh, Stuart, I had a wonderful time. I'm happier than I expected to be right now." Smiling at him, she continued gratefully, "I owe you so much. Not just my life, but my eagerness to get on with life now. You've been the best friend I've ever had."

To her surprise, he responded forcefully, "I don't want to be your friend, Martie. I never did. I didn't say anything while you were involved with that other guy, and I wasn't going to say anything yet. I was going to wait, but I just can't." Then, softly, "I'm sorry, but I happen to love you to the point of utter distraction." Taking her in his arms, he held her against him, and finished huskily, "And I'm afraid if you don't make love to me immediately I'm going to die of terminal lust."

"Stuart . . ." Martie breathed, stunned. Then, tentatively, she kissed him. It was brief and hesitant but unexpectedly nice. Martie felt herself stir in a deep, profound way that she hadn't anticipated. Kissing him again, this time she held nothing back.

His arms enveloped her protectively as his lips took possession of her . . .

When Martie woke up the next morning, Stuart was lying on his side, his head propped on one hand, watching her. Yawning, she asked sleepily, "What do you think you're looking at?"

"The woman I love," he answered simply. Then, teasingly, "You don't have to say you love me, but I would appreciate an indication of fondness, at least . . ."

"I love you," Martie responded, surprised at how easy the words came. Then, "I didn't expect it, I didn't go looking for it, but here I am in love. And it's not like anything I've felt before."

"Good. Now don't say another word. I like to quit while I'm ahead. Don't worry, I'll make all the arrangements, the blood tests, the minister—you don't mind a church wedding, do you? My parents would kill me if I deprived them of that spectacle."

"Stuart—are you asking me to marry you?"

"Actually, I guess I skipped that part. But I thought it was sort of obvious from everything that's happened."

"Oh, Stuart." Martie rose, slipping into a robe. After staring out the window for a long moment, she turned and said sadly, "It would never work. You want a wife who will be committed to you, who will spend her time having kids and decorating your two-story colonial. Despite everything, I still need a career. I need my own accomplishments—without that I have no identity. And I'm thirty-three years old, it's too late for me to have a lot of kids."

Rising, Stuart went to her. Looking at her determinedly, his brown eyes grim, he insisted, "The life you were leading, your *career*, made you so unhappy that you wanted to die. Martie, I want to take care of you forever. Is that so bad?"

"No. Right now that seems incredibly wonderful. But I have to be honest with myself, Stuart. I would become miserable after awhile just being your wife, watching you get more and more successful while all I had to show for my time was a clean house."

"I think deep inside you want children. You were meant to be a mother."

"All right, I would like to have a child. But don't you see, after awhile I would start to be so resentful and unhappy that I would make that child miserable. I don't want that to happen."

"So that's it? I'm not looking for an affair, Martie. I want you to be mine forever, to build a life with. I'm not playing games."

"Neither am I, Stuart." Martie felt herself dying inside but she knew that what she was saying was true. She loved Stuart too much to lie to him.

He looked at her angrily, then hurriedly dressed and left. When he was gone the house seemed unbearably empty.

"Oh, Ginny, am I being a fool?" Martie asked, sighing. "For the first time in my life I know what real love is, positive, healthy, happy love. And I'm letting it slip through my fingers."

"For the first time in your life you're looking at the long-range consequences before committing yourself to someone," Ginny responded frankly. "Whatever happens, that's got to be good."

"That's true," Kate agreed, then added, "But couldn't you compromise somehow, have your career *and* Stuart?"

The three women were sitting on the redwood deck outside Ginny's house, sipping wine and watching the sun setting over the ocean.

"Oh, I don't know," Martie answered thoughtfully. "You see, even if I get a job at an agency that's smaller and less pressured than the old place, it's still going to take a lot out of me. I'm not sure there would be enough left for Stuart. He's awfully old-fashioned and he needs a certain kind of attention from a wife that I probably wouldn't be able to give."

"Well, don't give up yet," Kate responded encouragingly. "I can testify from recent experience that marriage to a man you really love and respect, who is truly committed to you, can make up for a lot of problems. Speaking of which, I've got to be going. David and Scottie will be back from sailing and will be demanding dinner."

When Kate had gone, Martie commented enviously, "She seems so happy now."

"Yes, but it wasn't easy. She and David nearly broke up at one point, but it's all worked out wonderfully well. You know, I've never seen her so . . . so fulfilled. She's finally found what she's looked for her whole life."

"She and Joan both . . . living happily ever after. Six months ago, who would have thought it?

212

Now if you and I could just get our acts together . . ."

"Forget about me, I'm not looking for that story-
book ending anymore," Ginny insisted firmly.
"However, you and Stuart—"

The doorbell rang before she could finish her
thought. A moment later she returned to the deck,
trying hard to conceal her excitement. Following
right behind her was Stuart.

"Stuart!" Martie sat up, spilling her wine.

"I'll leave you two alone," Ginny said easily.
Then, grinning broadly, "If you need a referee, I'll
be in the kitchen."

Sitting down in front of Martie, Stuart began
teasingly, "See, you *do* need me. You can't even
hold a wine glass alone without spilling it."

"What are you doing here?"

"Looking for you, of course. Don't be dense. You
and I have some negotiating to do."

"What?"

"Negotiating. I thought you were familiar with
the term. It's what people do when they basically
want the same thing but can't quite agree on the
small print. In our case, I want you and you want
me, but there are some areas of disagreement. Minor things—"

"Like lifestyle, children, et cetera," Martie interrupted.

"As I was saying," Stuart continued doggedly,
"minor things compared with the fact that my life
will be empty and boring without you. While it may
undermine my bargaining position, I have to say

. . ." He paused, his expression softening as his brown eyes stared into hers. "I love you. You mean more to me than any of the things I used to think I wanted."

Blinking back the tears, Martie responded feelingly, "Oh, Stuart, my life is crazy and meaningless without you. I love you, too. But . . ."

"But we seem to fight a lot." Then, soberly, "I don't really think our battles have to do so much with your career as with the fear we both share of rejection and loss. You're afraid I'll abandon you the way other men in your life have done. And I'm afraid I'll lose you to another man because I don't entirely trust you to make a commitment to me. But, Martie, we can't miss out on what we want out of life just because we're afraid of being hurt. We've got to admit we need each other and hope it will work out."

"Oh, Stuart, I need you so much it scares me."

"I know. I need you, too." Then, brightly, "So the only problem is your career. Well, I have a suggestion regarding that. Why not start your own agency with me as your first client? Who knows, maybe I'll get so big you won't even have time for other clients."

"What about Latham-Reynolds-Newbrough?"

"My contract with them is up in one year. I simply won't do anything else until then. It'll take me about that long to finish my next book anyway."

Martie looked thoughtful for a moment. "It might work," she admitted slowly. Then, more excited, "It *would* be nice not having to take orders from someone else, doing things *my* way for a change." Her voice grew more animated, "I wouldn't even need an office at first, I could work out of our house."

"That was exactly what I had in mind," Stuart responded happily. "We'd be able to spend a lot of time together. With the money I've got coming in we could hire a full-time housekeeper so you could concentrate on developing your agency and having babies."

Martie looked at him slyly. "About those babies . ."

"Let's go for a walk down the beach," Stuart suggested amiably.

As they set off, hand in hand, he continued, "Now, what I had in mind was five . . ."

"One," Martie responded.

"All right, four."

"Two. And that's my final offer."

"I'll tell you what. Why don't we just leave that clause in the contract open."

Smiling broadly, Martie agreed, "You're right. It could be kind of fun negotiating it."

And she leaned her head comfortably against his shoulder.

16.

Ginny lay by the pool, looking at the breathtaking sweep of Acapulco Bay. Mountains and promontories surrounded the tall luxury hotels that crowded the bay, while perfect white beaches formed a crescent around the vivid blue water. It was an artist's dream, the dazzling sunlight, richly colorful flowers and birds, and the water itself, bluer than Ginny had ever seen the ocean at Malibu. At first she had tried to get some work done, responding as much to the gorgeous scenery as Maurice's relentless requests for more pictures. But there was little time to work. Dan was determined that she have a good time, a relaxing vacation to relieve the pressure of the last few weeks when Ginny had worried so much about Betsy and Martie.

They were staying at the exclusive Hotel Las Brisas. Overlooking the bay, it featured rooms that were like separate villas built into a terraced hillside, each with its own private pool.

At night, the light of all Acapulco twinkling across the bay made this the most romantic place Ginny had ever seen.

Dan knew Acapulco well, and he showed it all to Ginny.

They walked around the zocalo, the town square, looking in the quaint shops and admiring the cathedral, whose big blue spires made it seem more like a Russian Orthodox church. They drank the surprisingly potent coco preparado, coconut milkshakes with gin, as they watched the famous high divers jump from a tiny ledge hundreds of feet into the thrashing surf of La Quebrada. The gorge was lit with floodlights, and after each successful dive the divers climbed up the rocks, dripping and smiling, gathering in gifts from the onlookers.

Dan even persuaded a reluctant Ginny to try the thrilling ride through the air in a parachute pulled by a motorboat. Ginny was terrified as the parachute pulled her higher into the air until she was above the roofs of the hotels. Then, forcing herself to relax, she gradually began to enjoy the ride, especially the magnificent view.

But Ginny's favorite experience was the jungle cruise. The boat slid gently, silently into the jungle, penetrating the wilder, undeveloped area of Acapulco. Ginny couldn't decide which was more dramatically colorful, the tropical birds or the sunset.

Amidst all the decadent luxury and natural beauty, there was only one disquieting element. Though most of the time Dan was his usual charming self, at times he was preoccupied and moody. He seemed to be wrestling with an inner problem that he refused to confide to Ginny.

One afternoon while Ginny was lying by the pool,

she suddenly became aware that he was watching her from inside the villa. But when she smiled and shouted to him to join her, he shook his head and disappeared into their bedroom.

That night they were on a moonlight cruise of the bay, the two of them alone save for the crew of the yacht that Dan had hired. Romantic music from a stereo drifted over the calm water as a discreet servant mixed their drinks. Standing next to the rail, Ginny looked out at the lights flashing in the distance.

"You look very pensive," Dan said quietly.

"It's all so beautiful and peaceful—almost like being in a fantasy come true. Nothing seems real here, especially problems. They seem very far away somehow."

"I know what you mean. That's why I come here so often. I can forget everything for a while. And there are so many famous people here that nobody pays much attention to me." He finished dryly, "Even Dan Demaris pales in comparison to Jackie Onassis."

"I almost wish I could stay here forever," Ginny admitted slowly.

A subtle change came over Dan's expression. His tone was more than mildly curious as he asked, "Is it just the celebrated beauty of Acapulco or the company you're keeping?"

Ginny smiled affectionately. "It's definitely both. You've been *marvelous,* Dan. I've never had such a wonderful time."

"Neither have I. You're a delightful companion, patient, interesting, and sensitive. You're quiet at the right times and thrilled at the right times. I've *never* enjoyed being with anyone so much."

He was obviously sincere, and for a moment Ginny felt embarrassed and awkward, not knowing how to respond. Dan was normally happy-go-lucky, full of laughter with a lighthearted attitude toward life. Ginny had never heard him seriously discuss any subject, and sometimes wondered if he held firm views on politics or religion or morality. His easygoing nature and open-mindedness made him a delightful companion. But at times Ginny missed the stimulating discussions and heated arguments she used to have with Ross.

Ginny continued, "Unfortunately we both have jobs to get back to. You've got that new movie and I've got to placate Maurice with at least a few new works."

"Ah, yes, the movie. And after that, another one, then another. I'm booked solid for the next two years with one project after another."

"Why do you work so hard? You don't need the money."

Smiling, he answered, "No, I don't need the money. My accountant spends all his time figuring out how to spend my money so the government won't get it. The reason I work so hard is ruthlessly simple. I'm forty-four now. In another ten years, maybe even five, I won't be able to get a job in Hollywood. I'm not talented enough to develop into a character actor, so I've got to take the jobs while they're being offered. Because pretty soon they won't be offered anymore."

"What will you do then?"

"Produce or direct, maybe. I've learned quite a lot, actually, in twenty years." Then, looking at her intently, "Maybe I'll even settle down finally."

There was that look again, so unexpected, of thoughtfulness and curiosity, instead of the usual playful, amused glance. Ginny didn't understand what was going on in Dan's mind. *Perhaps,* she thought, *he's just preoccupied with his career.*

When she glanced up at him she found him staring at her intently. There was something in the look that vaguely bothered her. Trying to lighten the mood, she wrapped her silk shawl more tightly around her shoulders and said brightly, "My goodness, it's turning downright cold. Maybe we'd better head back to the hotel."

Dan smiled perceptively. "You're running away, Ginny."

"I don't know what you mean."

"You may not know for sure, but you suspect something is up. And you're right." He sighed deeply, as if finally coming to a decision about something. "Our relationship's always been special. I think we've both felt that. And since we've been down here, away from everyone else and other distractions, it's become even more clear. Do you realize we've spent four days together, rarely out of each other's sight, barely talking to anyone else, and yet we're not bored with each other?"

Ginny grinned. "You're the least boring person I know."

"Thanks. I know I've been a little moody at times but that's because I had something very important on my mind. I admit I've been struggling with a question that was hard to resolve. But I've finally decided to stop fighting my feelings." Putting his arms around her, drawing her close, he finished tenderly, "I love you, Ginny. I've never said that to anyone before. I want to marry you."

Ginny was stunned. This was literally the last thing in the world she was expecting, despite Dan's earlier teasing remark about love and marriage. She had been so positive that he was dead set against marriage and would never change.

"But, Dan, I know how you feel about marriage," Ginny argued fervently. "You've never wanted it before, you couldn't imagine being monogamous . . ."

"If I asked you to simply live with me, would you?" he interrupted firmly.

"No," Ginny admitted softly, looking away. "I just couldn't do that."

"I know. It's not your style. I thought about suggesting that—in fact, I hassled with it in my own mind for days. But I finally decided that was simply a way of avoiding the real issue. That's why I'm asking you to marry me. Because it's the only way I can have you. And having you with me, knowing that you'll be there at the center of my crazy life, matters more than anything else in the world to me."

He was pleading now, his tone cajoling and persuasive.

"Oh, Dan, I'm not ready for this! I wasn't expecting it." Ginny's mind was in turmoil, her emotions at war in a battle she wasn't prepared for.

"I don't think either of us expected this would happen. But it *has* happened." His brown eyes were warm, loving. That look, so bold and yet so tender, enchanted Ginny. "You know, the Hollywood press for years has speculated about when I would finally decide to propose to someone. It never seemed to occur to them that the person I proposed to might not leap at the chance to marry me."

"Dan, you know how deeply I care for you. It's just . . . well, only a few months ago I was still married to Ross, convinced that my marriage would last forever. The ink's barely dry on my final decree."

"What you're saying is that I'm rushing you."

"Yes, I'm afraid so."

"Ginny, I understand how you feel. But there's one thing I'm convinced of—time isn't going to make any difference with us. You'll still be affected by your divorce whether it's a month from now or a year. Right now we know each other as well as it's possible for two people to know each other without actually living together. Time simply doesn't matter. You either want to marry me or you don't."

"Are you so positive, then, that *you* want to marry *me*?"

Cocking his head to one side, Dan looked at her quizzically. "Are you asking for an ironclad reassurance?"

"No—just a persuasive reassurance," Ginny answered, smiling.

"I do have some reservations—not about you but about marriage. You'd know I was lying if I pretended otherwise. But, believe me, I've thought it over very carefully. I'm not an impulsive person when it comes to things that matter. The fact that

222

I've waited this long to propose to anyone should prove that."

Ginny couldn't help being flattered, though she tried not to be. One of the most eligible bachelors in Hollywood was paying her the ultimate compliment. And he was being almost irresistibly charming about it.

"Well, I must say, you picked the right place for this. Acapulco Bay in the moonlight, romantic music in the background, a luxurious yacht slicing through the water . . ."

"I have learned something about the importance of background in a scene. The question is—is it working?"

Ginny hesitated. Why did she suddenly find herself thinking of Ross? she wondered unhappily.

Before she could speak, Dan continued patiently, "Why don't you think about it for awhile. I don't have to know tonight, although I would appreciate it if you didn't prolong the agony too long. What I had in mind, you see, was a quick wedding in L.A., then a quiet honeymoon on a private island in the Caribbean. I don't have to start my new film for three weeks. We could have a wonderful time until then."

"It sounds marvelous," Ginny admitted. Then, teasingly, "I guess we couldn't have the honeymoon without the wedding?"

Dan looked at her soberly. "I'm afraid not. I think our relationship has gone as far as it can under the current arrangement. I know you, Ginny—you have too much pride to happily continue being

Dan Demaris's girl friend. I think it's already begun to bother you."

He was right. The jealous women, the prying press, had become more than just a minor irritation—they were a major distraction affecting her work.

"You were meant to be someone's wife," he continued, echoing Martie's sentiment. "You have what it takes to make that kind of commitment. I can't honestly say I'm positive that I do. But I'm willing—no, eager—to find out."

"What about other women?" Ginny asked bluntly. "You said once that you couldn't imagine restricting yourself to one woman."

"Right now I don't want anyone else. I don't expect that to change. But if it does, I have too much respect for you to make a fool of you. I'll simply be honest with you and let you go, if that's what you want."

It wasn't as romantic and reassuring as his previous words—but it was honest. Ginny felt she could trust him, despite his background as a determined philanderer.

"There's just one more thing I'd like to know, Dan."

"Of course."

"Why me? Why did you fall in love with *me*? There are so many other women—younger, prettier, more famous . . ."

"I told you once before, you're not exactly over the hill," he insisted.

"I'm almost thirty-four," she responded reluctantly.

"Which makes you ten years younger than I am. I love the way you look—that gorgeous hair, those green eyes that are utterly beguiling . . . you look absolutely adorable. But it isn't just that. It's more than the really nice way you look or the sexual intimacy we share. There's something about you—a peacefulness, a serenity, as if you're in tune with what really matters in life. You're the still center in a furiously spinning world."

The words, so familiar, jolted Ginny so that she felt an almost physical shock of *deja vu*. They were so nearly what Ross had said to her when he asked her to marry him . . .

"And now," Dan continued softly, "unless there's something else you want to know, I think we'll head back to the hotel where I will do my best to persuade you that you actually do want me as much as I want you . . ."

They returned to L.A. two days later. Dan didn't mention marriage again, but Ginny was well aware that he wouldn't wait very long before pressuring her to make a decision. He wasn't used to being kept waiting.

Ginny told no one, including Martie, of Dan's proposal. For a little while, at least, she didn't want to think about it. She hoped that somehow her subconscious would work it all out so that when he asked her again, she would instinctively know what to say.

17.

"We found the *perfect* place in Santa Monica," Martie was saying happily. "Two stories, four bedrooms, with a den downstairs for me to work out of and a sitting room off the master bedroom for Stuart to work in."

"*Four* bedrooms?" Ginny teased.

"Well . . . we're still not sure how many kids we're going to end up having," Martie admitted shyly. "I'm just going to start popping them out and see how it goes. When it reaches the point where I start feeling torn between them and my agency, I'll stop. But, you know, I'm not really worried about that right now. Stuart's being completely supportive. We're using part of his advance on the book to bankroll the agency, and he told me to hire whoever I need to help me, housekeepers, secretaries, whoever."

"You're very lucky he feels that way," Joan commented. "You know, Stan used to get really mad when I would hire any kind of help. He felt a woman should be able to run a house and care for children without relying on anyone else."

Martie, Ginny, Kate, and Joan were sitting in

Martie's living room, having an impromptu wedding shower for her. The floor was littered with wrapping paper and presents, including a small engraved wooden sign from Ginny that read simply, *The Martie Bass Mendoza Agency*.

"More coffee?" Martie asked Joan.

"No, thanks. I've got to cut down on caffeine for a few months." She smiled broadly and they all grinned in return.

"Another baby?"

Joan nodded. "It seemed like a good way to cement our marriage."

"It sounds like things are going very well. I'm so happy for you, Joanie," Ginny responded warmly.

"You know, at first I wasn't sure it was going to work. Combining two families was much more difficult than I had expected. At first I tended to dump a lot of residual hostility toward Stan onto Alan. And he expected me to be like his late wife, who was a very exceptional person. Then there was the kids' fighting with each other. Not to mention the fact that *his* kids resented me and *my* kids resented him."

"Any one of those problems is enough to wreck a marriage. All of them together must have been impossible," Kate commented.

"They were impossible. But before I could even say anything Alan sat me down and said he sensed there was something wrong. I was so shocked. Stan never did anything like that. He refused to face up to problems even when they hit him on the head. When I told Alan about some of the things that were beginning to bother me, he suggested we have

227

some counseling sessions with our rabbi. It was incredible how helpful that was. We sorted out a lot of things before they reached the crisis stage. Now we go to a therapy group once a week. It's designed to help reconstituted families deal with their special problems. No matter what else is happening in our lives, we never miss those weekly sessions."

She added confidently, "I feel very optimistic now. Just knowing that Alan is willing to listen to what's bothering me, and to do something about it, means so much."

Martie responded thoughtfully, "I'm beginning to think we've shortchanged men. Or maybe we just picked the wrong ones the first time around. Because now it seems like some of them, at least, are capable of responding to our feelings and needs. After my experience with Ed I never expected to find a man like Stuart, who actually encourages me in my career."

Finishing a slice of cake, Joan said, "Well, it's a new decade. Maybe times *are* changing." Then, turning to Ginny, "From what you've said, Dan certainly is supportive of your career and of your right to have your own identity. That's more than Ross ever did."

"Yeah," Ginny answered absently, feeling uncomfortable somehow with the conversation. *Does finding yourself have to mean leaving behind the person you once loved? Do you have to go on to someone new?* she wondered sadly.

"Perhaps it isn't so much men who are changing, but *us*," Kate said thoughtfully. "I suspect that men

228

are actually simply responding to the fact that women are different now."

"What do you mean?" Ginny asked, intrigued by the thought.

"Well, for example, look at my relationship with David. In high school he reacted to my extreme shyness by being reluctant to make the first move. So it ended up taking fifteen years and a terrible accident to bring us together. Even then, my reluctance to trust him, my tendency to expect the worst of him instead of the best, nearly ruined everything. I finally decided that I had to be in charge of my own life, to be in control of what was happening to me instead of sitting passively. And it worked because all David needed was a chance to prove himself."

Joan smiled. "I certainly agree with that. I've decided that the happiest marriages are those where the woman has a life and a mind of her own and feels free to express herself honestly to her husband."

"Or to disagree with him," Martie added. "Being married to a man who is supportive, who isn't frightened by change, makes it so much easier to handle the problems that inevitably come up. I think in that kind of situation both people can really fulfill themselves in a way that doesn't happen otherwise."

"I don't think any of us realized that when we were first married," Ginny said. "We all married for sexual appeal, but it takes good communication to stay married. I used to think Ross and I had that. It wasn't until he was gone and I was on my own that I realized how little we knew each other, and how dishonest we had been."

"I don't think you can love someone else until you love yourself," Martie responded soberly. "You have to be genuinely happy with who you are and what you're doing before you can transfer that basic good feeling to someone else. I realize now that I couldn't possibly have loved Michael because I hated myself so much for having a relationship with a married man."

She added, brightening, "You're doing so well now, pursuing your career the way you always wanted to and being so successful at it, that you must find it easier to have a relationship with Dan than it was with Ross."

"Oh, it's easier in some ways," Ginny replied evasively.

"There's nothing better than finding yourself *and* finding someone to love," Martie continued. "My career means as much to me as ever, and I intend to forge ahead with it. But while I'm doing that, I want a hand to hold and a shoulder to lean on."

"I agree," Joan said fervently. "I've always felt that if the price of change and progress for women had to be separation from men, then it was too high. But now I'm beginning to believe that it doesn't have to be that way."

Looking at Joan, who was radiant and confident, Ginny couldn't help feeling uncomfortable. Joan, Martie, Kate . . . they all had someone. *But I have someone, too*, Ginny reminded herself forcefully.

Abruptly, without thinking, Ginny came to a decision.

"Dan asked me to marry him," she announced suddenly.

The reaction was stunned surprise, then elation.

Martie recovered first, "Oh, Gin, that's terrific! I must admit, I never would have expected it. I thought he was an absolutely *confirmed* bachelor. You must have completely captivated him."

"I don't know about that, but he proposed while we were down in Acapulco. Perhaps the atmosphere got to him."

"Well, whatever it was, I'm incredibly happy for you and more than a little bit jealous," Joan said, grinning. "Wait till I tell everyone that I know the woman who finally captured Dan Demaris. I know a dozen women who will be green with envy."

"*Thousands* of women are going to be green with envy," Martie corrected her merrily.

Only Kate seemed subdued by the news. Looking at Ginny curiously for a long moment, she finally added her own congratulations. But Ginny knew that Kate sensed a certain reservation in her tone. Kate knew too well that Ginny couldn't possibly have given her heart to Dan because it still belonged to Ross.

"When's the wedding going to be? And are we invited?" Martie asked impatiently. "Because if we're not, we'll probably *kill* you."

"The wedding will be very soon. I'll let you know exactly when. And, of course you're all invited. But I really want it to be a very private ceremony, with-

231

out the press crashing in, so could you please keep it confidential until we're off for our honeymoon?"

"Sure, I understand. The press would have a field day, if they found out about this!" Martie responded knowingly. "But, Ginny, it's going to be hard to keep it a secret."

"I know. I thought we might have the ceremony at my house instead of a church. And I'll tell the caterer that it's just another party."

"If you want, I'll order the wedding cake in my name," Martie offered. Then, laughing, "But the baker is really going to think I'm nuts when I immediately order a second one."

"If there's anything I can do to help, Ginny, just let me know," Kate said softly. "Would you like me to ask David to handle the blood tests? He can keep a secret."

"Thanks," Ginny responded, not quite able to meet Kate's glance.

On her way home, Ginny stopped at Dan's. He looked at her anxiously, aware that she had probably made a decision but unsure what it might be.

"Well?" he asked, trying unsuccessfully not to sound nervous.

"Yes," Ginny said simply.

Breathing a sigh of relief, he took her in his arms. But while Ginny tried to tell herself that she was doing the right thing, she couldn't get Ross out of her mind . . .

18.

"Betsy?"

"Yeah, Mom?"

Ginny sat down next to Betsy on the sand. It was a scorching hot day, perfect for tanning, and the beach was crowded with scantily clad people. In the shallow water near the sand, where the waves broke gently, children played merrily, screaming and laughing and splashing, their parents watching with mild interest. Older children and teenagers ventured further out where the waves curled powerfully.

"What is it?" Betsy finally asked, when Ginny said nothing further.

"You're getting kind of red, you know, maybe you'd better go in soon."

"I will." Then, "Is that all?"

Ginny hesitated. Damn, this was hard. Harder than she had expected, considering how well Betsy and Dan got along now.

"Honey, I . . . well, the fact is, Dan and I have decided to get married."

Looking at Betsy anxiously, Ginny was surprised at her lack of response. "It's okay," Betsy said quietly. "I've sort of been expecting it. You haven't

233

been going out with anyone else, and the way he looks at you I can see he's crazy about you."

"Then you're not upset?" Ginny asked, tremendously relieved.

"Not too much. I mean, you know I'll always wish you and Daddy could get back together. But Dan is pretty nice. And if it's what you want . . ."

Betsy's voice trailed off as she watched Ginny carefully. Her penetrating blue eyes, so like Ross's, shook Ginny for a moment. Finally, Ginny responded evenly, "I think it's what I want. I care about Dan and . . . I don't want to be alone."

"I understand. What's going to happen now?"

Ginny explained that the wedding was set for the following week, that she would be gone for two weeks on her honeymoon, and that she was sure Ross would like Betsy to stay with him during that time. Betsy seemed to accept it all surprisingly well.

All that remained was telling Ross.

He came by the next night to take Betsy to a movie. When he brought her home, Ginny asked him to wait for a few minutes to discuss something that had come up.

"Would you like some coffee?" she offered.

"Sure."

He sat at the small table in the kitchen while Ginny made the coffee. Since dealing with Betsy's drug problem, he and Ginny had been closer, more comfortable with each other. Often now when he picked up Betsy, he stayed for awhile, talking to Ginny about his movie and mutual friends.

"Is it Betsy?" he asked now. "Any more problems?"

"Oh, no," Ginny reassured him quickly. "I really think she's over that."

"I heard from Stacey, by the way. She had her baby and gave it up for adoption. She'll be home any day now."

"How is she?"

"She sounded very quiet and serious. That's a hard thing to handle at any age, but it's especially hard for someone who's still a kid. But she seemed very . . . accepting, I guess, is the right word. She didn't seem to be having any second thoughts about how she handled it. She said she just wanted to thank me for talking to her parents, but actually I suspect she wanted to make sure it would be all right with us if she continued her friendship with Betsy."

"Of course it's all right."

"I told her you'd feel that way," Ross responded easily. Then, "What was it you wanted to talk to me about? Do you need some money?"

"No," Ginny answered quickly. Then, defensively, "My painting's going rather well, actually."

"So Betsy tells me." Looking slightly uncomfortable, Ross continued, "Ginny, I'm sorry I didn't have more faith in you. It wasn't that I doubted your talent. I just . . . I just wasn't sure you were tough enough."

"I am now," she responded coolly. Then, "I may as well get to the point. Ross, I'm going to get married again."

He was speechless for a long moment, and Ginny was vaguely irritated that the subject would surprise him so.

Finally, he asked, "To Demaris?"

She nodded. "The wedding's set for next week. We're going away for two weeks. I was hoping you could keep Betsy."

"Of course." His voice was tight, his expression suddenly guarded.

Feeling a need to defend herself, Ginny continued, "I've thought this over very carefully, Ross. I think it will work. I wouldn't go into it otherwise. I know that Betsy resented Dan terribly at first, but they get along very well now, so that won't be a problem. We'll be living in his house, so I'm selling this one. I think it's only fair that you and I split the money."

"No, thanks."

"Oh, come on, don't be proud. I know you've poured everything you've got into this film, you can probably use the money. At the prices beach houses are going for nowadays it should amount to quite a lot."

Smiling humorlessly, Ross answered, "It's odd, somehow, you offering me money. While we were married, it was always the other way around."

"Which got to be rather demeaning after awhile," Ginny said bluntly.

Looking at her carefully, he asked, "Did it really bother you so much? I wanted to take care of you, you know."

"I know. It never seemed to occur to you that I could take care of myself sometimes. Actually, it never occurred to me either until I had to do it."

"You've changed, Ginny," Ross observed. And though Ginny found it absurd that it had taken him

236

so long to realize that, somehow she didn't feel like laughing.

His blue eyes looked wounded in a way Ginny had never seen before. He was such a strong man, both emotionally and physically, that Ginny had come to assume nothing could really hurt him. In all their years together she had only seen him cry once, when his oldest friend was killed in Vietnam. He wept uncontrollably then, while Ginny tried desperately to soothe him. Now, seeing him look so unexpectedly hurt, Ginny felt her heart melt.

"Oh, Ross . . ." she sighed deeply.

"It's okay," he responded heavily. Then, standing, "I think I'll pass on the coffee."

As he was walking out the door, he turned and finished huskily, "I hope you'll be happy, Ginny. I mean that."

And he was gone.

19.

Ginny stood silently in her bedroom, looking at her reflection in the full-length mirror. Despite her tendency to be extremely self-critical, today she thought she looked pretty good. More than pretty good. Almost beautiful. Her rich chestnut hair was pulled back in a sleek chignon with a few wispy tendrils curling softly around her face. Her makeup had been applied expertly by a makeup artist who was a friend of Dan. Her gown was made of cream-colored silk that hugged the soft curves of her body, falling in gentle folds to the floor. The overall effect, from the tiny white Lillies of the Valley in her hair, to the two satin pumps, was simple, understated, classy. Ginny looked the way a bride should look, absolutely perfect in every detail. And she felt, she told herself firmly, exactly the way a bride should feel, happy and excited.

If there was any anxiety it was due solely to the hordes of photographers and reporters outside the house, she reassured herself. Despite her elaborate precautions, news of the wedding had leaked out when Dan took out the license. An armed guard hired at the last minute kept the press at bay, but Ginny could hear them outside, talking, occasionally shouting, pressuring each arriving guest for information about the wedding.

I guess it was inevitable it would turn into a circus, Ginny admitted grimly. Dan Demaris's marriage would be front-page news.

A moment after knocking softly at the door, Martie entered. "Ginny, it's a madhouse out there," she announced breathlessly, smoothing her ruffled hair. "Those reporters are piranhas, they attack everyone who comes in, trying to get some inside news."

"I know. God, Martie, it's awful! We should have just run off to Las Vegas or something."

"Hey, don't take it so hard," Martie reassured her, noticing the tense look on her friend's face. "At least they're outside. They can't get past that guard, you know. And believe me, inside everything is going great. Everybody's drinking like a fish and having a great time." Then, smiling warmly, "You look absolutely beautiful."

Ginny blushed. "Thanks. I don't want Dan to be disappointed."

"He won't be. By the way, he's here, you know, hiding out in Betsy's room. He wanted to come and see you, but I told him it simply isn't done."

"How did he look?"

"Do you mean physically or emotionally? Physically, he looks gorgeous, as usual. He's wearing a great-looking gray tux. Emotionally, he looks much calmer than I would have expected. I really think he intends to go through with this, kiddo," Martie teased. Then, her expression suddenly growing concerned, she continued, "Hey, you look a little strange. Is there something bothering you?"

"Oh, it's just the usual jitters plus those stupid reporters," Ginny replied irritably.

"Are you sure?"

"Of course. Listen, don't worry, I'll be fine."

"Sure. I don't know what I was thinking of. Any girl in her right mind would love to marry Dan."

Any girl in her right mind, Ginny repeated to herself, pensively.

Looking at her watch, Martie continued, "Well, only five minutes to go. I'd better get back out there and tell everyone to be seated." Hurrying to Ginny, she hugged her quickly, then left.

Ginny was alone in her beautiful wedding dress with tears welling up in the corners of her infinitely sad green eyes.

And then all hell broke loose.

There was some sort of commotion outside. People were shouting, then suddenly there was a collective gasp. A moment later, Ross burst into the bedroom trailed by the irate guard who was rubbing his chin carefully as if he had just been hit.

"Hey, you can't go in there!" he shouted furiously.

Ignoring him, Ross slammed the bedroom door in his face.

For a moment he and Ginny stood staring wordlessly at each other.

"God, you're beautiful," he said incongruously.

Recovering her senses, Ginny responded angrily, "What do you think you're doing?"

"What I should have done the minute I heard about this stupid wedding," he answered firmly. "Stopping it."

"Oh?"

The voice was sardonic, but there was an undertone of determination. Both Ginny and Ross turned at once to find Dan standing in the doorway.

"The guard told me a crazy man broke in here," he continued calmly. "Obviously he was right." Closing the door behind him, he finished reasonably, "I don't believe you were invited, Carlson."

Ignoring Dan, Ross turned back to Ginny. "I know the divorce was all my fault. I deserve whatever you want to say to me or do to me. I hurt you and I guess I'll spend the rest of my life kicking myself for being so stupid. But one mistake doesn't have to destroy everything we had together, Ginny. We belong with each other. You can't tell me honestly that you love this guy."

Popping her head through the door, Martie asked anxiously, "What's happening in here, anyway?" Then, seeing both Ross and Dan standing there, she continued, "I think I'd better tell everyone there's been a slight delay," and disappeared.

Turning back to Ginny, Ross demanded, "Look me right in the eyes and tell me you love him."

"Well, I certainly don't love *you*," she answered furiously. "It's over, Ross, it was over long before Lisa came into our lives. The romance, the magic, whatever you want to call it, was gone."

241

"Very good," Dan commented.

"We can get it back," Ross insisted stubbornly. "Oh, Ginny, it was too good to just let it die like this."

"Ross, you don't understand. I'm not the same girl you married fifteen years ago. I'm not passive, dependent Ginny who basked in your reflected glory. I have my own glory now and I like it. I can take care of myself, financially and emotionally. I'm marrying Dan because I want him, not because I can't function without him."

"But you don't love him!" Ross persisted. "Ginny, I'm not asking you to go back to the past. I know that can't be done. I'm not asking you to give up anything you've worked so hard for. But you're making a decision right now that will affect the rest of your life. You're throwing away all those years we spent together, all of the experiences we shared."

Ginny's eyes filled with tears as she remembered those special times that could never happen again with anyone else.

"It's over, Carlson," Dan interrupted firmly. "You're too late. You threw her away once and she's not coming back to you now that you've changed your mind."

"I don't need you to tell me what I threw away," Ross responded angrily. "Ginny means a hell of a lot more to me than she could ever mean to you! You're not capable of any kind of real commitment. You want Ginny now because you've grown bored with the usual women in your life. But you'll grow bored with her, too, eventually, because you're like

242

all actors—you're a child who never grew up, who doesn't understand mature emotions."

"I wasn't the one who childishly turned to another woman, practically a child herself, from what I hear. I haven't hurt Ginny. You have."

Dan's words, cold and true, cut through Ginny's heart like a knife. He hadn't hurt her as Ross had. He could never do that because she could never care about him as she had cared about Ross. As the two men in her life fought over her, she felt strangely removed from it, almost as if she didn't really care what either of them thought.

Turning back to Ginny, Ross pleaded, his usual arrogance thrown aside, "Give me another chance. Give us another chance."

He stood there anxiously, his expression tense but determined, looking irresistibly handsome and compelling. Ginny felt herself drawn to him as strongly as she had been fifteen years earlier as she remembered what they had once meant to each other.

Walking up to her, Dan said soberly, "What you had with him is gone. Once that happens you can never get it back again." Then, taking her hands in his, "We have the magic, Ginny. We have that romantic, passionate love."

Shaking her head sadly, Ginny whispered tearfully, "No, Dan, we have passion but not love. I gave my heart to Ross, and despite everything it still belongs to him."

"Come with me to Paris, Ginny," Ross said suddenly, breaking the fragile silence. "I'm due to leave today for that film exhibit. The plane leaves in forty-five minutes, we can just make it."

"But Ross . . ."

"Don't think, just do it!" Ross begged.

"It won't work," Dan repeated sternly.

Turning to face him, Ginny nodded. "You're probably right. But I've got to give it one last chance. You don't understand what it means when you give fifteen years of your life to someone . . . first love and young dreams and creating a child together. Defending each other in the bad times and sharing the joy of the good times. Dan, I can't turn my back on those things. It's worth too much to let it go without a fight." As she looked deep into his eyes, she finished with profound regret, "I'm so sorry."

"I can't say good luck," he responded frankly, "but I'll still be here when you get back."

Ginny kissed him quickly on the cheek. "Thank you for being here when I needed you. Please forgive me for hurting you."

She took Ross's hand and they fled through the living room, pausing only long enough to kiss a surprised but delighted Betsy and to ask Martie to take care of her for awhile. The wedding guests stared at them stupidly. Only Kate smiled knowingly. Then they ran through the throng of confused reporters and photographers.

Forty minutes later, Ross and Ginny, still in her wedding dress, fell into their seats on an Air France 747 bound for Paris. Sitting quietly next to each other, neither had any idea how to begin talking to the other.

Ross was nervous, embarrassed. Ginny was frightened. She had just thrown away an opportunity for happiness, to take a last desperate chance at the most beautiful, most elusive dream of all—that one perfect love that lasts a lifetime.

In Paris, she knew, she and Ross would either see their love die forever—or see it rise like the phoenix from the ashes of pain and heartbreak.

20.

The desk clerk at the exclusive Plaza Athenee Hotel had seen some interesting things during his employment there; the rich, the famous, the infamous. But he had never seen anything like this. Not only was the woman still wearing her wedding dress, which looked as if she had slept in it, but she was insisting on separate rooms for herself and her husband. He must be her husband, the clerk assured himself, for they share the same last name.

"One moment, madame, I must just check to see if there is an extra room. We only had a reservation for Monsieur Carlson."

Ginny waited patiently, but stubbornly, while Ross watched her silently, intense disappointment on his tired face. He had assumed they would share the same room. Clearly he would have to go a bit slower with Ginny than he had expected.

Momentarily the clerk looked up and asked, with a slight hesitation, "Would you take a suite with a sitting room and two connecting bedrooms?"

Ross looked at Ginny, who nodded. "Yes, that will be fine," he responded coolly.

Ginny added matter-of-factly, "Could you have

someone bring up a selection of dresses, size five, and shoes, size six, as soon as possible?"

"Of course," the clerk replied with Gallic imperturbility. This, at least, he understood. The woman couldn't remain in her wedding dress forever. As Ginny and Ross, accompanied by a bellboy carrying Ross's luggage, headed for their suite the clerk watched them, shaking his head sadly. If madame was insisting on separate bedrooms already, monsieur would find this a cold, comfortless marriage.

"Ah, les Américaines," he sighed knowingly, convinced, as all his countrymen are, that only the French truly understand love.

After taking a quick, uninterested look at his bedroom, Ross joined Ginny in the sumptuous, beautifully furnished sitting room. She was standing by the window, looking out at the city that she had wanted so badly to see for such a long time. The brilliant Paris summer sunlight drenched her in its special golden glow, making her rich chestnut hair look even glossier and her green eyes shine like emeralds. She looked excited and a little anxious, but Ross thought hopefully, happy.

"Unfortunately I have to go to the film exhibit office to make some final arrangements. I'll be gone all day. Wednesday is the showing of my film and Thursday the final judging. Would you . . . would you come with me?" he finished hesitantly.

"Of course," Ginny smiled sympathetically.

"Why don't we have a late supper tonight? I'll make reservations at someplace expensive and decadent."

"Good."

He hesitated awkwardly for a moment, then said, "Okay, well, I'll see you later then."

When he was gone, Ginny lay down on the velvet sofa and sighed deeply. *What on earth am I doing here?* She asked herself for the hundredth time. *What can we possibly hope to accomplish by this silly, impulsive act?* Suddenly Dan's words, delivered with utter certainty, came back to haunt her— "What you had with him is gone. Once that happens you can never get it back again."

A tear rolled down her cheek. Brushing it away irritably, Ginny insisted to herself that she was just exhausted from the long flight. Though she had slept on the plane, it was hardly a restful, refreshing sleep.

Before she could sink lower into worry and regret, there was a soft knock at the door and a moment later a young woman entered with a long rack of dresses and several boxes of shoes. For half an hour Ginny lost herself in deciding what to wear on her first day in Paris.

When she was finally out of her wedding gown and into a lovely, cool sundress made of royal blue silk dotted with tiny white flowers, her courage and determination returned. After replacing her satin pumps with bare little leather sandals, she decided to call Maurice. The call went through quickly. When she told him where she was, he was astounded.

"Paris? But what are you doing there?"

"Well, it's a long story," Ginny began, laughing.

"Is Dan there with you?"

"No. We didn't get married. Ross persuaded me

248

to run off to Paris with him. He has to be here for a film exhibit, and . . . and, well, we've decided to give things another try."

There was a momentary silence on the other end of the line, and for a second Ginny was afraid the connection had been broken. Then abruptly Maurice said, "You've just proven you're a true artist. You've done something wild and impractical and glorious. By the way, Ginny, if you do nothing else in Paris, you *must* visit the gallery of my old friend Elise Jobert. She is utterly marvelous and you will love her as much as I do. It's on the Champs-Élysées."

"Okay, Maurice; in fact, I'll go right now. I have some free time."

"Ginny?"

"Yes?"

"Good luck, child. I hope you find what you are looking for in Paris."

"Thank you, Maurice. I hope I do, too."

Leaving the hotel, Ginny stepped into a taxi. When the driver asked in heavily accented English, "Where to?" Ginny hesitated. The whole city was around her. She could go anywhere, do anything. She had money, her own money, to spend. Abruptly, a memory came back to her, a professor in college who had talked excitedly of Montmartre. For years the center of the Parisian art world, many famous painters had lived there.

"Montmartre," she told the driver confidently.

He nodded and they were off.

As the taxi headed toward Montmartre, Ginny

stared wide-eyed at the city she was rapidly falling in love with. In a doorway of an apartment house, a sharp-eyed Parisian concierge, or caretaker, relaxed, watching the traffic go by, without losing his look of sharp-eyed inquisitiveness. Driving through the Place de l'Opéra, the busiest square in Paris, she saw big department stores, restaurants, threatres, and music halls. Looking across the Seine, she caught a glimpse of the Cathedral of Notre Dame, its facade bathed in a golden sheen.

And then they were in Montmartre.

Leaving the taxi, Ginny stepped into the Paris she had always fantasized about, the physical and spiritual home of artists. As she walked slowly along the narrow, cobble-stoned street of Rue Saules, where some of the most famous Parisian painters once lived, Ginny passed bakeries, cafes, green trees, and benches full of people. Though the wide boulevards of Paris were only a short distance away, here in Montmartre were the delightful twisting lanes and small courts of a village. Steep stone steps led to open terraces where people basked in the sun.

Walking through the Place du Tertre, Ginny found artists sitting in the square on stools, painting, selling their work to tourists and passersby. Carefully perusing these paintings by unknown artists, Ginny felt a sense of comradeship with them. She was one of them, she understood what they were striving toward. She empathized with their struggle to get something just right, with that undisguisable look of anxiety as they wondered if anyone would appreciate their work enough to buy.

Happy, unexpectedly, Ginny felt completely at

home. Paris was not a disappointment, as she had feared, but a revelation, a confirmation of herself as an artist, and, she secretly hoped, as a woman. She was at one with this lovely, peaceful, civilized city.

The only question now was whether she and Ross could find that same intimacy with each other.

Later, strolling down the Champs Élysées, looking for Elise Jobert's art gallery, Ginny happened by a *guignol*, a puppet show, a tradition of the Right Bank of Paris playing to successive generations of children. Acknowledging the cheers of an enthusiastic young audience, the puppeteer popped up with one of his stars. As Ginny watched the delighted faces of the children staring gleefully at the colorful puppets, she knew she had to paint them. It would be fun to spend the day here tomorrow, painting this adorable scene. And Maurice, Ginny realized dryly, would be happy she was getting some work done on the trip. She couldn't seem to keep up nowadays with the insatiable demand for her work. But she couldn't complain about the pressure of success; she was simply overwhelmingly relieved that people liked her work.

By the time Ginny found Madame Jobert's art gallery, it was early evening and nearly closing time. *I'll just go in for a moment to say hello and give her Maurice's regards*, she decided hurriedly. Inside, a well-dressed young clerk approached her, asking in French if he could help her.

"Do you speak English?" Ginny asked, not trusting her rusty high school French. When he nodded, she asked to see Madame Jobert.

"One moment please, madame."

He left, returning a moment later with a tall, dark-haired woman who looked to be about Maurice's age. With classic bone structure and artfully applied makeup, she was the sort of woman who is forever beautiful. When she was young, Ginny knew, she must have been stunning. Even now, when she was well into middle age, there was something special about her that set her apart, even from other fashionable Parisians with their unerring good taste.

"May I help you?" she asked in flawless English.

Explaining who she was, Ginny barely had a chance to mention Maurice's name before the woman broke into a huge smile and exclaimed, "Ah, Maurice's little discovery. He calls you his 'petite Ginny,' you know, in his letters to me. What a very pleasant surprise. But I will have to chastise Maurice for not letting me know you were coming."

"It was rather sudden," Ginny explained awkwardly. "Actually, I didn't know myself that I was coming until yesterday."

"You must let me offer you tea. If you are like most newcomers to Paris, you have probably been walking about the city all day and are thirsty and exhausted."

"I'm afraid I'm a very typical tourist," Ginny admitted, smiling. "That's exactly what I've been doing."

Leading Ginny into a salon at the rear of the gallery, Madame Jobert rang for a maid. When the girl arrived, she asked her to bring tea and pastries. Then she settled into a beautiful antique satin sofa, motioning for Ginny to sit down opposite her in a comfortable wing chair.

"Maurice has sent me photographs of some of your paintings so I am familiar with your work. You are quite good, of course, but then I expect you know that by now."

"Thank you, Madame Jobert," Ginny responded, feeling embarrassed, as usual, by praise.

"You must call me Elise." Her tone was autocratic, as if she was accustomed to being obeyed, and yet Ginny felt very comfortable with her.

The maid returned, depositing a silver tray with a lovely porcelain tea service and a small plate of pastries on a nearby table. As Elise poured two cups of tea, she continued brightly, "Are you here for work or pleasure? Though any Parisian will tell you that working in Paris is a pleasure."

"I hadn't planned on working, actually, but I've already seen some things that I just have to paint. I'm going to buy some supplies tomorrow."

"Ah, yes, it is inevitable. May I suggest that you visit the Tuileries gardens? Children sail boats on the ponds there. From what I know of your work, I think you will find that great fun to paint."

"Thank you, that sounds marvelous. I'm beginning to suspect that I will return home with a great many paintings, which will make Maurice happy."

"Of course, he is a great businessman, that one. That is why he opened a gallery in California, you know, instead of remaining in Paris. He was convinced he could make more money there, since his visits to Los Angeles had persuaded him there were no decent galleries in the entire town."

"Have you and Maurice known each other long?" Ginny asked, too curious to resist asking about their relationship.

"All our lives," Elise responded, smiling warmly. "We grew up together in Montparnasse, a very artistic area much like Montmartre. When we were children we each decided that we wanted two things out of life—to be rich and to be surrounded by art. Although neither of us is exactly wealthy, we have achieved the most important part of our goal."

"I owe Maurice everything," Ginny said simply. "He gave me a chance when no one else would."

"That sounds like my old friend," Elise nodded happily. "But now, child, let us talk about you. Are you here alone?"

"No," Ginny responded, unsure how to continue. "I . . . that is, I'm with my ex-husband."

Elise, too French to be surprised by anything involving love or marriage, merely raised one eyebrow slightly. "Oh?"

Fidgeting nervously, Ginny continued stupidly, "You see, we were divorced early this year, but now we're, uh, having second thoughts."

"So you came to Paris to see if you could rekindle that flame that once burned so brightly?" Elise responded knowingly.

"Well, yes," Ginny admitted.

"There is no need for embarrassment, child. What you are attempting to do is quite admirable. A marriage is too important to simply let it go when things become difficult. Although we French have a reputation for rather loose morality, the truth is we take love, and especially marriage, very seriously."

As Elise talked on about how the French viewed marriage, Ginny listened intently, sipping the strong, dark tea that Elise had poured for her. Her hand kept reaching for the irresistible little pastries that were more delicious than any she had tasted.

Finally, Elise finished deprecatingly, "I must apologize for talking at such length. The French are bred to talk, you know. Some people, usually ill-tempered Germans, like to say we actually prefer that to making love."

Smiling, Ginny replied, "I assure you I was not bored. You are very witty and charming, and I'm glad that Maurice suggested I meet you."

Elise offered Ginny a cigarette, which she declined, then lit one for herself. When Ginny wrinkled her nose at the acrid odor, Elise laughingly explained, "The most Parisian of odors, the rich, intoxicating smoke of Gauloises. Maurice has been after me for years to stop, but I say life is too short to spend it worrying about whether something will make it shorter. In this, I am typically French. Our philosophy is to enjoy life to its fullest, whether it is food, love, children, or the creation and contemplation of beauty. There is simply too much potential pleasure all around us to let ourselves be restricted by a set of absolute rules that do not allow for exceptions."

Her dark eyes watching Ginny shrewdly, she continued, "I imagine some people have told you it is foolish to try to recapture the love you once knew with your husband."

"Yes," Ginny admitted reluctantly, remembering Dan's harsh words.

"Do not listen to those people. Not everyone can obtain their heart's desire. But for some special ones, those who have the capacity to love truly, all it requires is a little bit of courage at the right time."

She was smiling affectionately at Ginny now. As Ginny looked back at her, she thought what a wonderful, unusual person she was—graceful, witty, charming. Talking with her, Ginny felt her confidence returning. Perhaps she and Ross could make it work after all.

That night they drove in a taxi down the Champs-Élysées, brightly lit now with street lamps and the lights of innumerable cars, streaming beneath the golden glow of the floodlit Arc de Triomphe. In the darkness the ghostly gray Eiffel Tower rose above the Paris rooftops, looking, from a distance, like a work of lacy filigree.

"You know, this is the first time all day I've had a chance to see much of Paris," Ross remarked, trying to make conversation. "Did you do much sight-seeing today?"

"Yes." Then, animatedly, Ginny began to tell Ross about Elise. "I can see why Maurice likes her so much," she finished.

"Maurice?" Ross looked puzzled for a moment. Then, remembering, "Oh, yes, the guy who shows your pictures at his gallery."

Ginny was a little hurt that Ross cared so little about her work that he could barely remember the name of the person who had made her success possible. Once more, she felt, he was slighting her work.

"They're showing some interesting films tomorrow," Ross continued easily. "I thought we might go early and catch them all."

"I won't have time," Ginny responded bluntly. "But if you'll let me know what time they're showing yours, I'll go then."

"Why won't you have time?" Ross asked irritably.

"Because I'll be working. I found some things today that I very much want to paint."

"But this is supposed to be . . . well, a vacation," Ross insisted awkwardly, not exactly sure what this was supposed to be. "Can't it wait?"

"Till when? You were busy today with your work and you obviously plan to be busy tomorrow viewing those films. It's all right, I understand it's part of your work. But you have to understand that my work is just as important to me."

"I see," he responded curtly.

Leaning back against the cold leather of the taxi seat, Ginny sighed heavily. Things were not going well at all. For a moment she was tempted to tell Ross that she had earned more in the last six months than he earned all the previous year. But she knew that was childish and she resisted the impulse. Still, she felt the old resentment coming back.

The restaurant, La Tour d'Argent on the Quai de la Tournelle, had a spectacular view of Notre Dame. It was quite possibly the most famous restaurant in the world, and Ross had chosen it deliberately. He felt like a teenager again, desperate to impress his date. As he looked around the elegant, beautiful restaurant, the tables graced with fresh flowers, precisely folded napkins and gleaming silver and crystal, he thought he had chosen well.

Sparkling crystal chandeliers lit the room, full of glamorous, beautiful people.

Though Ginny enjoyed the sumptuous dinner, she found herself thinking wistfully of the Bistro Allard, where she had eaten lunch earlier in the day. It was a plain restaurant featuring simple, home-style cooking, with sawdust on the floor. She had actually enjoyed that meal as much as this one, and it cost quite a bit less.

Through dinner, both Ginny and Ross said little. Afterward, back at the hotel, Ginny tried to explain to Ross how she felt.

"Ross, it was inevitable that as I moved out into the world and became more assertive, more self-confident, I would find it impossible to relate in the old way. Now with each of us having a career that we find exciting and fulfilling, perhaps we can have a more total relationship than we had before. We can share our interests."

"You don't seem very interested in my film. And you know how important it is to me."

"You don't seem interested at all in my work. And, believe me, it's just as important to me as yours is to you."

Then, with painful honesty, she continued, "I told you we couldn't go back to the past. I'll never again be the person I once was. That person was just too unhappy, despite the beautiful house and the expensive clothes. I know who I am now. I'm letting myself go as far as I can go, without holding anything back. I may be frightened sometimes, or lonely sometimes, but I'm not unhappy anymore. If your ego can't handle that, then we might as well give up now and avoid inflicting more pain on each other."

Ross looked at her silently, his brilliant blue eyes both angry and hurt. Then, reaching out to her, he asked tentatively, "Will you share my bed tonight?"

Ginny hesitated. She knew what it cost his pride to ask that. But she also knew that if she made love to him now, feeling as she did, it would be a travesty of passion. When she went to him, it must be willingly, because she wanted him, not out of a sense of duty. That sense of duty had impelled her for years to make love to him when she secretly felt resentful and angry. And that had finally killed the passion they knew in the beginning.

Her voice barely reaching above a whisper, she said softly, "No, I can't."

Saying nothing, he turned and went into his bedroom, closing the door behind him.

Lying in bed, Ginny tried to make some sense of her feelings. Why had she felt so uninhibited, so sexually free with Dan, and yet still felt so tense with Ross? With Dan, everything was a fantasy, from the way he made love to her, to the place where they made love. With him, she felt free to explore every facet of her sexuality, to be sensuous and giving. But with Ross she was withdrawn, constantly on her guard as if always expecting to be hurt . . . *That's it,* she thought with the eagerness of sudden understanding. *I never felt Dan could hurt me because I didn't really love him. But Ross . . . because I loved him once so much and he hurt me so deeply, I'm afraid now to really let him touch me for fear he might hurt me again.*

But it was a vicious circle, she knew. If she continued to hold back, to not let Ross touch that vital part of her, then she would never feel pain . . . but she would never feel love either.

That night, Ginny, who had been so happy earlier in the day, cried herself to sleep.

She spent three days watching the children at the puppet show, painting them carefully, then doing quick drawings of the children sailing their boats on the ponds at the Tuileries. At night when she looked over what she had accomplished during the day, she felt happy. She was doing her best work and she knew it. Her feelings about Ross were put out of her mind as she concentrated intently on her painting.

Because Ross spent most of his time at the film festival, they saw little of each other. That helped them avoid arguments, but it brought them no closer to the reconciliation they had come to Paris to achieve. On Wednesday night, Ginny accompanied Ross to the showing of his film, and felt her old intense pride in him return when his movie was given a loud ovation.

"Oh, Ross, it's excellent," she told him honestly.

"For once I can't say there's anything I would have done differently," he admitted, smiling. Then, looking at her intently, he finished, "Your praise means more to me than anyone else's. If you hadn't liked it, it wouldn't matter what anyone else said."

She believed him. He had always trusted her judgment and turned to her for confirmation of his achievements. But though that pleased her, it also bothered her because that was exactly what she needed from him. She needed to know that he thought her accomplishments were worthwhile, too. For a moment she nearly told him this. But she didn't want to spoil his moment of success with another argument. And so she said nothing.

The next day Ross's film won the grand prize, and from the way people were talking about it, Ginny knew it would probably be a great commercial and critical success. Ross had finally achieved what he had strived so long for. But when Ginny congratulated him, he responded unexpectedly, "The prize isn't really what I came to Paris for." Then, "Now that this whole business is over, we can spend more time together."

Ginny knew what he was getting at. The distractions were out of the way. Now they must get down to the business of finding out once and for all if there was really any love left between them. For several days Ginny had run from him, avoiding learning the truth. But she couldn't run any longer.

Like any typical tourist couple, they went sightseeing around Paris. And only a very observant onlooker would notice that they seemed slightly strained with each other, just a little too polite and formal to truly be husband and wife.

They strolled along a tangled maze of medieval lanes in one of the oldest parts of Paris. Ginny loved the lively jumble of shops, bars and theatres along the Left Bank, while Ross was fascinated with the intriguing smells from the exotic restaurants.

"It's like the Venice area of L.A.," Ginny commented happily, for a moment enjoying herself too much to remember that she and Ross still had a problem to solve.

"Yeah, only better. We'll have to come back here for dinner. I'll bet these places are pretty good."

He looked at her excitedly and she smiled back at him. But her smile faded when she realized that what she and Ross were feeling now, this shared excitement, the sheer fun of being together in an interesting place, was once how they constantly felt with each other. Now it stood out as a rare close time in the midst of unhappiness and isolation.

I mustn't think of the past, Ginny reminded herself forcefully. *At this moment, what we have is good. That's all that matters.*

Tentatively, she took Ross's hand. He looked at her quickly, surprised, then casually put his arm around her. They walked that way, together, through the happy, bustling crowd.

Ginny had been too busy so far to actually go walking along the Seine. Now, she thought, would be the perfect time for that, while she and Ross were beginning to grow closer. When she suggested it, he agreed enthusiastically, and a few minutes later a taxi deposited them on the colorful quay of Montebello. A street always full of life, it was the headquarters of the *bouquinistes*, the sellers of old and new prints and books.

Ginny and Ross made their way through the crowded street, stopping often to look at the rare and curious things on display. Suddenly Ginny spotted a drawing by Matisse and fell in love with it immediately.

"Oh, Ross, look, isn't ███████████ul?"

"Yes, but it must cost ████ ██e," he responded pragmatically.

"Oh, I don't care, I *love* it!█

Ginny's face fell when she lea█ned that the price was three thousand dollars. *Well*, she told herself, *what good does it do me to make a lot of money if I can't spend it impulsively sometimes.*

"I'll take it," she told the seller happily, knowing she would never regret this extravagance.

Stunned, Ross looked at her worriedly. "Ginny, that's a lot of money . . ." he began.

"I know," she answered, pulling out all of her traveler's checks, glad that she had obtained a generous amount earlier from a bank. As she counted out the correct amount to the seller, quickly signing each check, she was unaware that Ross was watching her curiously. When the seller handed her the carefully wrapped print, congratulating her on her good taste, Ginny turned, smiling, to Ross. But the expression on his face abruptly cut off the excitement.

He said softly, "Until this minute, I had no idea how well you must be doing."

It was painfully obvious that his ego had received a severe blow.

As they walked away, Ginny, clutching her package protectively, responded slowly, "I assumed you knew that I was making money with my paintings."

"I knew you were making money. I didn't know you were making that much money."

There was nothing she could say to this. She refused to do what she had done for so long—pretend that he was the one with the marketable talent while

she was fit for no_____ than to meet his needs.
They had just r_____ ne point that Ginny had
known subconsc_____ ust come sooner or later.
She was proud_____ hard-won success. If Ross
couldn't accept _____ then there was no hope left for
them.

Silent and thoughtful, they returned to the hotel
to dress for a party that Elise had invited them to
that evening.

Later, when they left, Ginny looked stunning in a
lovely, expensive black satin cocktail dress by Yves
St. Laurent. But there wasn't the excitement of anticipation on her face; instead she looked like someone who has just seen her last fragile hope crushed.

21.

The party was a celebration of the first day of a one-man show by a new artist who was just beginning to know acceptance and success. There were champagne and hors d'oeuvres in the gallery, to be followed by supper for a few select guests in the salon. Most of the guests were artists or people seriously interested in art, and Ginny felt at ease immediately. These were people she could talk to, relate to on an equal footing, unlike Ross's friends who usually ignored her because she wasn't a power in Hollywood. For once it was Ross's turn to be relegated to the position of unimportant companion, and though Ginny made a sincere effort to involve him in her conversations with people, he didn't seem very interested. As with Ginny's purchase of the expensive print earlier, his ego was offended at no longer being unquestionably number one in their relationship.

At dinner, Ginny was pleased to find herself seated next to Elise. Though Ross sat across the table from her, he had little to say to her.

"Your husband is extremely attractive," Elise said softly to Ginny.

"My ex-husband," Ginny reminded her pointedly.

"Ah, I sense that all is not well with the reunited lovers," Elise responded wryly.

"Ross suffers from a severe case of egotism. It's difficult for him to accept the fact that the woman who was merely his little wife for so long now has her own success."

Elise looked at her carefully. "You say that as if it were solely his problem. There is no reason why two people who love each other cannot sincerely wish the best for each other. Are you certain you have not perhaps been purposefully trying to outshine him? I believe the British call it one-upmanship."

Ginny started to protest that she was completely innocent and Ross completely guilty, when she realized how stupid she sounded. Whatever had happened in their relationship, she couldn't pretend, even to herself, that Ross was solely at fault. Guiltily, she remembered that there had been other, much cheaper prints that she had liked on the Rue Montebello, but perversely she had felt driven to buy the most expensive one. If Ross had not been there, and there had been no question of impressing him, would she still have bought the Matisse? She couldn't answer her frank question.

As Ross made polite conversation with the people on either side of him, he looked at Ginny wonderingly from time to time, as if he were seeing her in a new light.

"You know, I have been observing Ross," Elise commented to Ginny toward the end of dinner. "I think he cares very deeply for you. And I know that

266

you care as deeply for him, otherwise you would not be so angry with him."

Ginny smiled. "I won't deny that. But it isn't that simple, you know. Even if he can accept me, and respect me, for what I've become, I'm afraid I'll always be a little angry because of the past."

"Forget the past. Put it where it belongs—in the grave," Elise insisted firmly. "Only children carry grudges. You and Ross came here to find a new beginning with each other. Let that happen. Don't look for excuses to destroy the special feeling you have for each other. I'll tell you honestly, Chèrie, we are none of us perfect. Perhaps Ross has made mistakes. I am sure you must have done so, too. I suspect you are dwelling on those mistakes now because you are afraid of being hurt again."

Ginny said nothing. But she knew that Elise was right.

Ginny couldn't sleep that night. She tossed and turned in the huge, lonely bed, until finally, when dawn was breaking over Paris, she rose and slipped on a robe. *At least*, she thought tiredly, *I can do a little work before breakfast.*

She had left her latest unfinished painting leaning against the sofa in the sitting room. When she entered the sitting room, she was surprised to find Ross there, silently looking at her painting.

"What are you doing up so early?" she asked curiously.

"I couldn't sleep either," he answered, looking at her disheveled hair and tired eyes.

Sitting down next to him, Ginny looked at the

painting that Ross had been contemplating. It was the children in the Tuileries gardens, and even though Ginny was sternly critical of her own work, she thought she had captured the right feeling in this picture.

"I've always thought you were talented," Ross continued softly. "But I never took your talent seriously. I thought it was just something you played at. It never occurred to me that you might feel about your work the same way I feel about mine. Today, when I realized that people must be paying you well for what you do, it really jolted me. Money defines the difference between an amateur and a professional, in any field."

"I want to apologize about that print," Ginny responded sincerely. "I was trying to show you up."

"You don't have anything to apologize for. I understand now that's what you were trying to explain to me the other night. You should be able to be proud of what you do and not have to downgrade yourself just to protect my fragile ego. Tonight, when I saw you in your own element, surrounded by intelligent, important people who respect your knowledge and ability, I was jealous at first. I actually found myself thinking that your desire to fulfill yourself was responsible for the end of our marriage. I finally realized how stupid and childish I was being when someone mentioned to me that I must be proud to have such a talented wife." Shaking his head impatiently, Ross finished, "I was an idiot. I *am* proud of you, Ginny." Then, motioning toward her painting, "To think that you could paint something as wonderful as *that*."

Rising, he looked down at her, mumbled "Good night," and went back to his room.

Ginny continued to sit there for a long time before going back to bed.

As all tourists must do, Ginny and Ross went to the Eiffel Tower and spent a pleasant hour admiring its elaborate construction and the unparalleled view from its highest platform. Then, feeling that they had met their obligations, they decided to wander casually around the city, with no plan or goal to restrict them.

Though there was a peaceful feeling of rapprochement between them now, as with two warring nations that have called a truce, there was still something precious and crucial missing. Ginny knew what it was. She had only to look around her to see it in evidence everywhere.

In no other city in the world, she thought, could love be so proudly, so openly expressed. Lovers kissed on park benches and held each other as they lay on the grass of the Bois de Boulogne. They walked arm in arm along the Seine, stopping to embrace on the bridges that spanned the river. It was everywhere—that uninhibited, ecstatic giving over of themselves to the most profound feeling of all.

The more Ginny and Ross saw, the quieter they became.

At the Ponts des Arts, where the Seine branches right and left from the tip of the Ile de la Cité, a weeping willow arcs its limbs over the cobbled walkway into the river. They stopped there, and Ross looked at Ginny wonderingly for a long moment, his expression calm, accepting, yet profoundly disappointed.

"We haven't made it, have we?" he asked, not really expecting a response. Then, looking at lovers who strolled happily past them, he finished softly, "Whatever it is they have—joy, passion, *love*— we've lost forever."

Ginny forced herself to meet his look, saying nothing. Inside she felt as if a hard, cold weight lay at the pit of her stomach, as if all emotion had been drained from her body. She was utterly empty, bereft of the warm, soothing, soft feelings of life— hope, love, intimacy, *I've lost him, and this time it's forever*, she realized with almost unbearable regret. *I made the choice to hold back, instead of opening myself up to him, because I didn't have the courage to risk the pain anymore. Ross is too proud to ever again make the first move. There will be no more chances, no more impetuous, headlong flights to Paris.*

Sadly, curiously she thought, *love dies finally not in a furious, cataclysmic blaze of bitterness and hatred, but softly, quietly, with only a fleeting wonder at the terrible loss.*

That afternoon, while Ross wrapped up some final business regarding the film exhibit, Ginny went to see Elise.

"I came to say good-bye," she began hesitantly, as they sat down in the salon.

"Are you leaving Paris so soon?" Elise asked, surprised.

"Yes. There's nothing really left to keep us here," Ginny explained succinctly.

"I see." The way Elise looked at her, with barely concealed pity and disappointment, Ginny knew that she understood perfectly.

"Is it the ego problem that you cannot overcome?" Elise asked frankly.

"No. Surprisingly enough, that seems to have disappeared."

"I am not surprised. I felt that you and Ross are too intelligent, basically too well meaning to fail at establishing a true partnership in your marriage." Then, perceptively, "Is the problem intimacy?"

Ginny smiled at Elise's graceful and entirely accurate way of expressing it. "Yes. We're just . . . so distant from each other."

"Ah, bed," Elise commented more frankly. "It is the arena where we play out our fear of true intimacy, so that we never completely reveal ourselves to each other. It is such a complicated place. It can be where two children console each other over the terrors of the world, or where a man and woman physically act out a battle to gain superiority over each other. What it should be, however, is neither of those things. It should be the altar where two people worship each other, joining in a union of both flesh and spirit. Making love should be an expression of our joy in each other and in life itself."

"There is no joy between Ross and me, and there hasn't been for some time."

"Was there once?"

"Oh, yes, a long time ago."

"Then you can recapture it, if you truly want to do so. It isn't that difficult, you know."

"How do two people stay in love through the years, through the problems that are always there?" Ginny asked, her tone defeated and hopeless.

"By remembering why they fell in love with each other in the first place. See Ross the way you saw him years ago. Recapture that original excitement. And then realize how much more attractive he is now to you, because of all that you have shared and all that you have learned, both together and separately." She smiled. "I tell you, Ginny, romantic love, especially the love between two people who value each other enough not to seek out others, is the most exciting adventure of all. Embrace it, do not run from it! You may be hurt, as you have been in the past. But I think you realize that it will be worth whatever pain is involved."

"But I don't even know how to begin!" Ginny argued, confused and frightened.

"Talk to each other. Open yourselves to each other. There is no aphrodisiac as powerful as communication. Tell Ross what you are feeling, even the things that embarrass you or frighten you. And then see what happens."

"I don't know if I can do that," Ginny admitted reluctantly.

"You must, child. Your happiness depends on it." Elise's dark eyes were sober with a hard-won wisdom, and Ginny knew that she was right.

If only it isn't too late, she thought.

22.

That night, over a quiet dinner during which both of them seemed to be preoccupied with their own thoughts, Ross told Ginny he was flying back to Los Angeles, the next morning.

"It will be good to see Betsy again," he said, as if trying to salvage something from the dispirited topic.

"Yes," Ginny agreed briefly.

After that they were both once more silent.

Back in their suite, Ginny decided to take a leisurely bath, hoping it would help her to relax. She felt more tense than she could ever remember feeling. As she leaned against the back of the tub, luxuriating in the warm water and perfumed bath salts, she let her mind drift back to the early days with Ross . . . endless happy hours spent in bed . . . one deliciously erotic afternoon spent on the cool grass of a secluded mountain meadow. They were so in love, their bodies so in tune.

Remembering all of that pleasure and happiness, Ginny knew that Elise was right—she couldn't let it end this way, so coldly proper. Slipping into a green silk negligee, she left her bedroom and walked over to Ross's door. She knocked softly and heard a surprised "Come in."

He was lying in bed, naked. The sheet came up only to his waist, revealing the broad chest matted with golden hair and the powerful shoulders. Ginny felt her heart beat just a little bit faster, and that flicker of a passion that she had assumed was long since dead, gave her the courage to go on.

"What is it?" Ross asked, confused.

"We need to talk."

A shadow of disappointment passed over his face, and Ginny sensed that he had hoped she was there for a different reason.

"We *have* talked."

"Not really," Ginny disagreed firmly. "In some ways we've communicated more honestly with each other over the past couple of days, but there is still so much that's been left unsaid. If it's truly over between us, I can accept that, but I don't want to spend the rest of my life wishing I had told you certain things. I want to get it all out, however ugly or painful it may be."

"Okay," Ross agreed with surprising quickness.

Abruptly, it occurred to Ginny that he, too, must have some feelings he would like to express.

"Well," she began, "for one thing I don't like pepperoni pizza." Her voice was as tremulous and serious as if she were discussing something of monumental importance.

"What?" Whatever Ross had been expecting, it clearly wasn't this. "You've been cheerfully eating pepperoni pizza for fifteen years."

"Yes, ever since you started ordering it for us. I prefer plain cheese pizza with nothing on it."

"I don't understand why you're so upset about something so unimportant," Ross responded irritably.

"Because you never bothered to ask me what I wanted," Ginny explained fervently. "It was the same thing with the house. You didn't even let me see it before you bought it!"

"I wanted to surprise you," Ross answered defensively. "I did it for you. Besides, I thought you loved living at the beach."

"I do. But don't you see, not being able to share in the decision of buying the house took some of the joy out of living there. It was that way with so many things. You forged ahead, convinced that you knew what was best for me, never bothering to consult me. But you can't guess at what another person wants. You have to ask them."

"If I did that, if I went ahead on my own and made decisions, it was because you held everything inside. Your mind, your heart, were secrets that I felt I would never be allowed to share." He finished tiredly, turning away, "Christ, you hardly even ever told me you loved me. I had to simply hope you did."

Though Ginny didn't want to face this, she knew it was true. Perversely, she had always held back from telling Ross how much he meant to her. She couldn't even remember the last time she told him she loved him.

Somehow, she had never thought it bothered him terribly.

For the first time in years she began to focus on

Ross, and on those important feelings that she had never had the time, or perhaps the will, to express. In the turmoil of their life together, the really crucial things had gotten pushed aside.

"I was never sure you wanted to hear it," Ginny finally admitted reluctantly.

"Why wouldn't I?" Ross asked angrily. "I needed to hear it." He finished softly, in a voice so low that she could barely hear him, "Sometimes I needed that very badly."

After a long silence charged with emotion, he continued more lightly, "I'm sorry about the pizza."

"It's okay." Ginny smiled at him shyly. "I guess neither of us realized how much we neglected to tell each other over the years, and how many wrong assumptions we made about each other."

Ross asked hesitantly, "Why . . . why didn't you tell me you loved me?" He looked almost like a frightened little boy at that moment, and with a tug at her heart, Ginny realized what it had cost his pride to ask that.

"I didn't think you loved me. You married me because I was pregnant, after all."

"I loved you," Ross answered simply, looking at her directly. "The longer we were married, the more I loved you." Then he added unexpectedly, "I was worried about the same thing, you know."

"What do you mean?" Ginny asked, surprised.

"That you didn't love me, that you married me only because I got you pregnant. I thought that you didn't tell me you loved me because you were too honest to lie about it."

"Oh," Ginny breathed softly, suddenly faced with something that had simply never occurred to her.

"All those years we were each secretly convinced that the other was only being dutiful . . . all the love we could have shared, held back out of fear of rejection. Like two little kids, each waiting for the other to commit himself first before we would go out on a limb . . ." Ginny's voice trailed off.

Looking at Ross, at the profoundly sad eyes that revealed such pain, Ginny felt a tremendous desire to reach out and touch him. But something held her back. *Strange*, she thought, *that an act as simple as touching someone, offering reassurance, should be so difficult.*

Overcoming a vague, nameless fear, she extended her hand to touch Ross's cheek softly. Surprise, then tremendous relief, flooded his face.

"Your hands are miracles, you know," he said huskily. "They transform everything they touch."

As his blue eyes held her green ones transfixed, it seemed as if time itself stopped. And at that moment all things seemed once more possible between them.

But there were still unresolved problems. Though each was afraid that a word, a wrong gesture, a rekindled doubt could destroy this fragile, tentative reconciliation, they knew they must face everything now if they were truly to be free.

Really listening to each other for the first time, they discussed Betsy, time, money, friends, death . . . in each area they discovered that they hadn't known how the other truly felt . . .

277

"There were times when I resented Betsy," Ross admitted guiltily. "You seemed to give her so much more love than you could give me."

"I needed an outlet for the feelings inside me," Ginny replied. "I showered all of my love on Betsy because I wasn't afraid of being hurt by her . . ."

"You know, I didn't encourage you to pursue a career because I was afraid you might become so successful that you would no longer need me. I assumed that as long as you needed me financially, you would never leave."

"I thought you didn't believe I had any talent. I was always secretly convinced that you found me boring but dependable, a convenience to have around but not particularly interesting."

As they talked, each facing the worst fears they had about the other, they experienced a tremendous joy and excitement that came from exploring each other's minds and hearts. Even when they admitted the very worst, there was still a sense of reassurance in realizing that deep inside they were so much alike, sharing the same needs and fears. Whether man or woman, both were born and both would die. There were, ultimately, no real differences.

"You're like a familiar house that I've lived in for a long time," Ross finished lovingly, "that I thought I knew intimately. Yet now I'm discovering secret passages that lead to hidden rooms that I never knew existed. And though the journey through those secret passages is frightening sometimes, it's also very exciting."

Looking at him, her heart feeling full and light, Ginny realized that the joy and strength of their marriage had gotten lost in the small angers and arrogant assumptions that inevitably grew into bitterness and misunderstanding. All it took to find each other again was time and honest, loving communication.

Suddenly Ginny knew that she wanted Ross, wanted him badly enough to risk whatever pain might lie in their future.

Slowly, provocatively, she slipped her gown off her shoulders, moving slightly to let it fall to her feet. Stepping out of it gingerly, she slid beneath the sheet, pressing herself gently against Ross.

"What do you think you're doing?" he asked wryly, his voice amused but eager.

"Seducing you," Ginny answered, licking his ear and kissing the curve of his neck.

Throwing one arm across her naked shoulders, he said huskily, "Then I must warn you I have no intention of putting up a fight."

He kissed her with all the pent-up passion of weeks of celibacy, and she returned the force of his kiss, determined, finally, to hold nothing back. As they made love, they talked and laughed, filled with the joy of wanting each other, of *knowing* each other.

Elise is right, Ginny thought happily. *Communication is the best aphrodisiac.*

Every touch was a new discovery and joy. Ross knew by the violent beating of her heart, by the change in her voice, by the trembling of her body, that Ginny truly wanted him. Though he had seen her body often and knew it intimately, now he was touching it as if for the first time, feeling the texture

279

of her skin, the softness of her flesh. Passing his hands all over her body, slowly he explored every curve. His mouth travelled hungrily over her face, her throat, her hair.

Ginny had a sensation of tremendous bodily warmth, as if she had drunk choice wine.

The resentment that had destroyed Ginny's love for Ross was gone; the anger he had felt at her rejection was replaced by an eager curiosity about this woman who was so much more than he had ever suspected.

They knew now there would always be something more to discover in each other, if only they would allow themselves to be open and vulnerable.

Ginny accepted the fact that a love as powerful as theirs held the chance of pain to equal the passion. But she refused to be defeated by that fear. What would happen, would happen. They were together now, and if only they would nurture their love, they could remain together forever . . .